HORRORS & HERESIES
ROBERT M. PRICE

HORRORS & HERESIES

ROBERT M. PRICE

2020
Exham Priory
Selma, North Carolina
United States of America

Published by Exham Priory, an imprint of Mindvendor

Introduction & Stories copyright © 2020 by Robert M. Price.

Cover photo elements courtesy of Pixaby
Cover design by Qarol Price

ISBN: 978-0-9991537-5-8

Dedicated to Marc Michaud,
pioneer, partner and pal.

CONTENTS

- INTRODUCTION -
HORROR *Is* HERESY!

The Greek-derived word "heresy" originally denoted no more than "choice," but it came to mean "faction" or "sect." Why? Because, given the thought-control of Catholic orthodoxy, it became sinful to presume to look at religious questions and make your own educated guess. "No, just leave the driving to us. We'll get you to heaven safely." "Heresy," then, meant free thought and dissent. Okay, but how is *horror* tantamount to heresy? The connection may not be obvious, but it is real nonetheless. Conventional belief tells us that good people should aim higher (e.g., Colossians 3:1-2) and studiously avoid polluting their minds with the degrading poison of horrors, real or fictional. Reading, and worse yet, enjoying, tales of Count Dracula, Jack the Ripper, Darth Vader, villains and monsters of all kinds, is to drag one's soul through the gutter. One's character will inevitably be the worse for it. Right?

Wrong! I agree with Jungian analyst Erich Neumann (*Depth Psychology and a New Ethic*) that such a strategy is counterproductive: it suppresses the Shadow side we all have, making the error of Henry Jekyll who thought he could once and for all exorcise man's base nature. That's the surest way to bring about the opposite. Instead, one must "give the devil his due" in a harmless manner, e.g., by exposing oneself to the Dark Side in fictive and fantastic forms. Wayne Booth, on the other hand (in his *The Company We Keep*) seems to me quite correct when he warns readers (or by extension, movie viewers) not to *revel* in the depicted evil, not to root for the bad guys. Don't put your sympathies on the wrong side. That would indeed be degrading. But the fascination of horror poses no threat to one's character if one's enjoyment is an appreciation of the element of *the sublime*, which is ultimately a sense of the numinous, of the *Mysterium Tremendum*. Again, that may not always be obvious, say, in the case of 80s Slasher flicks, but I think it is there when we vicariously feel the threat to, and thus the transient contingency of, our very being. We need to be made mindful of that. Just ask Kierkegaard. And we must face our, and thus *the*, Dark Side. "If only you knew the *power* of the Dark Side!"

9

But for the shivering slave mentality of *das Mann*, that is too dangerous for their tenuous consciences, so for them it is *heresy*. As for us, fellow horror fans, we are heretics. And proud of it.

***

I have been fascinated by religion since I was ten years old, comic books before that. I became a devotee of H.P. Lovecraft and Robert E. Howard a couple of years later. I have never gotten over any of it. Even when I stopped believing in any religion, I remained vitally interested in it, more than ever, in fact. The stories in the present collection partake of my interest in both fantasy and religion. The Lovecraftian theme of ancient manuscripts containing powerful secrets reflects my decades-long fixation on the Bible and related literature, e.g., the Dead Sea Scrolls, the Nag Hammadi Library, and the non-canonical Pseudepigrapha. Some of these stories are based on the imagined contents of fictive texts including *The Testament of Joseph of Arimathea* (in Vincent Sneed, ed., *The Dead Walk!* from 2004), *The Confessions of the Mad Monk Clithanus* (in "The Parchment Chase"), *Al-Azif* (of course) in "The Surah of the Making of Mankind" (*NecronomiCon Providence 2015 Souvenir Book*), and a suppressed chapter of the Book of Revelation (in "The Seven Thunders"). "The Son of Jehovah versus the Cyclops" (a wink to those old Italian Sword-and-Sandal flicks) presupposes some lost gospel. It appears for the first time in print in this book.

Lovecraft once called Poe "my god of fiction," and I must say the same about HPL himself. But I am no monotheist; I serve a wider pantheon containing Robert E. Howard and many others I love Howard as much as Lovecraft and have always been a fan of Sword-&-Sorcery fiction. I've written pastiches of Lin Carter's Thongor, Howard's Conan, and Richard L. Tierney's Simon of Gitta. Here I have ventured a Howardian take on King Jehu from 2 Kings in the Bible. My friend and collaborator Ed Suominen (together we wrote *Evolving out of Eden: Christian Responses to Evolution*) announced that he intended to write a story depicting Jehu as the villain he was, as seen by modern eyes. I countered with an alternative plot outline, but this just wasn't the kind of thing Ed had in mind. So I decided to write up mine, a heroic fantasy with Jehu as a biblical King Kull. I gladly thank Howard expert Marc A. Cerasini for a great line for Jehu. You'll have no trouble spotting it: just look for the best sentence in the story! This is its first publication.

There's more than an influence from REH in "The Castle of the Heretics," whose protagonist is none other than Cormac Fitzgeoffrey, perhaps Howard's fiercest and most fanatical warrior-hero. He is featured in "Hawks of Outremer" and "The Blood of Belshazzar," as well as "The Slave-Princess," a Howard synopsis written up by Richard L. Tierney. I had long thought that the Catholic siege of the Cathari (Medieval Manichee) fortress atop Montsegur would be the perfect setting for a Cormac tale, but it took me a few decades to buckle down to it. It originally appeared in *The Hyborian Gazette*, No.3, 2017.

A trio of tales evidence my religious skepticism, but in what I like to think are novel ways. "The Fear of the Lord" suggests that, if the Christian worldview were verified, it wouldn't necessarily be good news. If you could prove it was all *real*, that wouldn't automatically make it *right*. You will readily recognize that the story runs parallel to Lovecraft's "The Call of Cthulhu" and that the protagonist is a thinly-veiled Christopher Hitchens. The tale initially appeared in John Manning's 2013 anthology *What Scares the Boogeyman?* I wrote "Myth Became Fact" (a phrase lifted from an essay by C.S. Lewis) and sent it to Tom Flynn, editor of the Secular Humanist periodical *Free Inquiry*, where my articles and reviews occasionally appear. I thought he might enjoy it, but I knew *Free Inquiry* seldom used fiction, so I was pleasantly surprised when he asked if he could run it! It appeared in the Volume 38, No. 4 June / July 2018 issue. Now I had also sent it to my old pal S.T. Joshi, long-time editor of *Lovecraft Studies* and current editor of the venerable *American Rationalist*. To my gratified surprise, he wanted to run it, too! Too late for that, I told him, so I wrote another in roughly the same vein, "The Atheist Exorcist." He used it in the July/August issue (which, by the way, was the last issue!). But as for "Myth Became Fact," it was a fleshing out of a premise I'd had echoing in my mind for some 40 years but never knew what to do with! One day I gave it a bit more thought, and you can see the result here.

"The Caliphate of Cthulhu" is a sequel to my "The Horror in the Genizah" (included in my earlier collection *Blasphemies and Revelations*), though I believe it works as a stand-alone tale in its own right. It takes off from the connection made by Lovecraft between Abdul Alhazred and his milieu of Arabian and Islamic magic. But my version is more explicit and certainly even more politically incorrect (which I consider a virtue!). It premiered in *Lovecraft's Disciples* # 25, 2017.

"The Grey Rite of Azathoth" borrows its title from one of those throw-away Mythos name-drops in Lovecraft's letters to his pals. Too good to pass up, I say. I have included the story here because of an easily overlooked religious bit in *The Case of Charles Dexter Ward* implying that Joseph Curwen had raised up Jesus from his "essential salts." Surely more could have been made of that! This one appeared in *Dark Rites of Cthulhu*, edited by Brian Sammons, in 2014.

"An Old and Secret Cult" presupposes that the in-breaking of the Old Ones has occurred, or that at least their religion has spread abroad across the earth. Even a triumphant faith cannot escape certain perennial problems that keep popping up as history repeats itself. The story debuted in the anthology *Through a Mythos Darkly*, edited by Glynn Owen Barrass and Brian M. Sammons in 2017.

"The Nativity of the Avatar" poses as a kind of Mythos gospel of a Messianic advent, not of the Christian Logos but of Nyarlathotep. Coming home from the MythosCon in 2011, my wife and I found ourselves stranded in the airport all night, so I used the time to outline two or three stories, and this is one of them. It appeared in *Horror for the Holidays*, edited by Scott David Aniolowski in 2011.

I hope two more parodies will entertain you. "Fosdick Was Dead," as the subtitle suggests, is yet another mutation of Charles Dickens's *A Christmas Carol*. I wrote it when I served as pastor of the First Baptist Church of Montclair, NJ, the first pastorate, decades before, of the famous Dr. Harry Emerson Fosdick. You may rightly suspect that certain features of this story are semi-autobiographical. It was published in *The Wittenburg Door*, November/December,

1994. Then there is "The Parchment Chase," a take-off on a favorite TV series of mine, *The Paper Chase*. No, you don't need to have watched the show to understand my version, but if you have, I think you'll enjoy it even more. A shorter version of this story appeared as "Medieval Metaphysics" in Lois Gresh's *Dark Fusions: Where Monsters Lurk!* (2013).

"This Is the Dawning" shows the Lovecraftian Occult invading the much tamer and milder but actual occultism of modern times. Think of it as "Cthulhu versus Kuthumi." It first appeared in the pages of *Cyaegha* No. 15, Spring 2016

Apollonius of Tyana, an itinerant neo-Pythagorean sage who lived (if he really *did* live!)[1] in the same time period as Jesus. His gospel-like adventures are related in a strikingly gospel-like narrative, *The Life of Apollonius of Tyana*, composed by Flavius Philostratus in the third century. Apollonius is so like Jesus that controversy has continued for centuries over the possible relation between the two, some insisting that Philostratus was copying from the Christian gospels (like Captain Marvel being cloned from Superman), or whether certain gospel episodes are retellings of this or that Apollonius tale. Some more recent scholars have even speculated that the two were the same man, remembered under two names. My "The Seven Thunders" is set amid this crossfire. It appeared first in Brian M. Sammons's collection ***Tales of Cthulhu Invictus: Nine Stories of Battling the Cthulhu Mythos in Ancient Rome***, in **2015.**

Robert M. Price

Hierophant of the Horde

Epiphany 2020

---

[1] See my article, "Was There a Historical Apollonius of Tyana?" in *Journal of Higher Criticism* Vol. 13, no. 1.

AN OLD AND SECRET CULT

Young Mr. Abernathy looked sheepish and looked both ways as he approached his Ecclesiastical History instructor as class was breaking up. Professor Exeter dropped his stack of rumpled and long-used lecture notes into his briefcase as he focused on his inquirer.

"Yes, Mr. Abernathy? What can I do for you? Can I perhaps clarify some point? Sometimes I take too much for granted, I know." The old man's avuncular manner went some way to putting the seminarian at ease.

"Clarification. Yes, I suppose so, Professor. It's this passage right here." The average-height, brown-haired, unassuming young man had used his finger as a bookmark in his copy of scripture, and now he flipped the well-thumbed text open to the page and repurposed that digit to indicate one particular verse. "Isn't the Apostle saying that the apocalypse is coming *soon*? I mean, we always hear that it means it's going to happen soon *for us*, but he doesn't really *say* that, does he? Isn't he really saying his *own* generation should get ready for it?"

Dr. Exeter sighed silently. It was not the first time a student had seen the problem and raised the same question confidentially. It was not a topic of polite conversation in the halls and dormitory of Miskatonic University's School of Divinity. Talk like that could get a fellow branded as a heretic, a doubter, and that could have career-killing ramifications, to say the least. Still, keen minds could not keep silent forever.

"Ah! It takes a sharp eye and a sharp mind to notice a ripple in what others see as a glassy pond! I'm proud of you, Mr. Abernathy. But hardly surprised. Still, certain matters are best dealt with discretely. We don't want to upset the 'weaker brethren,' do we?"

15

A nervous laugh from the aspiring young clergyman. "Oh no! Certainly not, Professor! I guess I'm just afraid I'm *one* of them!"

Dr. Exeter let out a hearty laugh and clapped the lad on the shoulder. "Nonsense, my boy! I'll be in my office in the Library all afternoon. Come by at your convenience, and we'll talk it over. Oh, and by the way, I was quite impressed with your paper in the Medieval Metaphysics Seminar." The young student perked up a bit at that reassurance and departed. Professor Exeter took off his wire-rims to wipe them clean, returned his handkerchief to his vest pocket, and rubbed his wrinkled forehead. He hoped there would not be a problem this time. The boy seemed so promising.

***

Chapel services were no longer compulsory, but most of the seminary students still attended anyway, most out of sincere devotion, while others were afraid of being looked upon as lukewarm in their faith if they skipped it. Allen Abernathy slipped into a pew hastily, causing everyone else in the row to squeeze together. The fellow next to him passed him a hymnal, and he paged quickly over to the hymn whose number was posted on the boards on either side of the platform area. He just opened to it when the liturgist, Professor Hansen, who taught Pastoral Counseling, took his place standing between the reading desk and the pulpit, a higher structure mounted by a brief flight of stairs. Dr. Hansen began to intone.

"In his house at R'lyeh dead Cthulhu waits dreaming."

Allen always dreaded to be asked to do any of the scriptural readings because, despite the fact that both scripture and liturgy were now read in English translation, some of the proper names were still pretty tongue-torturing. Soon Dr. Hansen turned the proceedings over to Reverend Paul Malherbe, a local pastor and part-time Homiletics instructor, who embarked on a carefully timed sermonette on how, like Great Cthulhu, we, too, must have big dreams if we are to accomplish great things for him. It might have been stirring had it been at all fresh. No luck on that score. Allen's attention began to drift and he didn't bother trying to get it back on target.

The longer he studied scripture and theology, the more struck he became with the hollowness of the standard rhetoric. Scripture spoke in profound tones of cosmic thunder building afar off, of the imminent overthrow of the corrupt order, of the upheavals of a new age dawning, when the Old Ones would return to wrench the world from the fumbling hands of human beings. The faithful adherents of Great Cthulhu and his cousins should reap the rewards of their services, repaid for the persecutions they had suffered at the hands of the squatters, the late-coming humans who vainly claimed the earth for their own.

Oh, in the beginning, when the Rasul al-Cthulhu, the Mahdi of Yog-Sothoth, the Apostle Alhazred had secured the allegiance of desert tribesmen who joined him in a whirlwind that swept out of the Arabian Desert and drove all before it, there was a red tide of slaughter. Cities fell before their resistless assaults as the zealots for the new faith (really a very old one) reclaimed first this empire, then that kingdom, to prepare the way for the Old Ones' return in glory. In an astonishingly short time the Byzantines, the Persians, the Mongols, and all the rest had fallen before the servitors of Almighty Cthulhu, King of Gods, God of Kings. Infidels who would not confess the faith of R'lyeh were offered up in sacrifice, and the sulferous glow of them lit up night skies around the world for many years. Those who valued their lives converted, or pretended to convert.

The centuries passed without the great consummation appearing. Cthulhu's worshippers had to walk by faith, not by sight. The reveling in red ruin ceased. Once it was plain the world was not going anywhere any time soon, the satraps of the world-empire proscribed the chaos and promulgated new laws, not essentially different from those of the old world they had replaced. Institutions were found needful again. An economy had to be rebuilt because people had to be fed.

But the zeal of the faithful did not flag. The love of violence inculcated by Alhazredism merely manifested itself differently. Holy wars erupted between different sects into which the parent religion had divided. Most of the African continent had chosen Ghatanothoa as their lord and god after a group of tribal shamans announced revelatory vision experiences amid the stone ruins of Zimbabwe. For the other gods of the pantheon they had no use, reducing them to disobedient subordinates of Great Ghatanothoa and slaughtering priests and worshippers of Tsathoggua, Cthulhu, and Nyarlathotep alike. Heresy and massacre repeated themselves all over the globe. Western Europe declared for Yog-Sothoth, the Key and Guardian of the Gate, while East Europeans and Eurasians worshipped Lloigor and Zhar in carven grottos deep beneath the surface. Within that sect, visionaries, backed by scheming theologians, caused further strife when some announced that Lloigor and Zhar were in reality twin hypostases of the same deity, whom they called Ithaqua, while others set the two deities against one another in a mythology of dualism. Still others divided the Old Ones' ranks into opposed clans of "elementals," pitting Nyarlathotep of the Black Pyramid against Hastur of the star-winds, Nyogtha of earthen caverns against volcanic Cthugha and Aphoom-Zha. Of *course* the gods fought one another; little else could they do since, in the absence of real apocalyptic miracles, they were no more, really, than factional totems, effigies and incarnations of their bloodthirsty legions' hatred.

Greater was the number of those who perished in the sectarian wars than those initially sacrificed to the newly-regnant Old Ones. But wars on such a scale eventually cease like fire that has consumed all its fuel. Things had been calm on the whole for generations now. Much had been rebuilt, much had been restored. The *de facto* coexistence gradually became *de jure* as treaties were signed, trade relations drawn up. A slow process of secularization began to dawn, inevitably, given that religion must be relegated to a secondary concern when survival and peace have perforce become priorities.

Allen had long thought about these things, wondering if somehow the past did not discredit the present. His religion, as he knew it, as he saw it practiced, seemed by comparison to be a game of childish play-acting. How could this lame pantomime possibly be heir to the earth-shaking early days? Were those days mere myth? Oh, Allen had been raised in these latter days; his values had been formed by them. He had no desire to see the world, his world, torn asunder, shattered like the egg of a newborn Shantak. But he had as little desire to conclude that his faith was a mockery, a sugar-coated domestication of an ancient barbarism.

So Allen Abernathy reflected as he sat in the chapel, until his bench-mates shook his shoulder and told him, chuckling, "Snap out of it, Allen!" Embarrassed, he rose and sidled out into the aisle. He saw Professor Exeter among the crowd, heading back, Allen knew, to his office. He would follow him to take him up on his invitation. There was much to discuss.

***

Both the teacher and the student shrugged off their coats. Dr. Exeter doffed his big, furry hat, revealing his bald dome of a head, stuffed as it was with knowledge and wisdom. He indicated the chair in front of his desk even as he plopped his own posterior down on the well-worn leather padding on his side.

"So! Mr. Abernathy, tell me what's on that fine mind of yours!"

Allen shifted in the chair to get comfortable, then began. "I really appreciate your taking the time to talk with me, Professor. Here's what's bothering me. The verse I asked you about, in the *Necronomicon*, where the Apostle sounds like he's predicting the end of the age in the immediate future. It's not just that by itself. That passage sort of sums up a lot of other problems."

He went on to summarize the sense of contrast between the early, violent era of religious conquest and the present, more staid and mundane state of things. "It's not like I wish there was still bloodshed and religious wars. Just the opposite, in fact. I don't want to live in a world like that. I don't think I'd want to see it return if the Old Ones reappeared. Did I say 'if? I meant 'when.' But I *have* always counted on the Second Coming, like everybody else. But wasn't it supposed to happen a long time ago? In the Apostle's day?"

With that, he held his tongue, fearing to be lecturing the expert.

"Well, you have to remember that the stars have to be right. They have to reach a very precise configuration before anything can happen."

"Yes, sir, but that happened a long time ago! I mean, those star charts in the *Necronomicon*. They're pretty specific. The stars locked in place properly centuries ago, closer to Abdul Alhazred's time than to ours. What *happened?*"

"Good question, Allen, and one to which I've given much thought. Here's a possibility to consider. You know, of course, that these things are cyclical. The stars have wheeled their way into and out of that configuration many times, and they will again. Perhaps scripture intended a *later* alignment, maybe not even the next one coming up. Have you ever thought of that?"

"No, Dr. Exeter, I can't say I have. But wouldn't that only make the problem *worse?* I mean, if that's true, doesn't it push the Second Coming even further, *much* further, off into the future? It's like saying it's *never* going to happen! *We'd* never see it, anyway. I just can't square that with the sense of expectation the *Necronomicon* implies."

"Mmmm... yes, I see what you mean. Well, there's also the theory that Great Cthulhu is tarrying until we show ourselves worthy of him. Perhaps our faith and discipleship are too lax..."

"But astronomy is astronomy, Professor. The Coming is supposed to be determined by the position of the stars. How can anything we do or *don't* do affect *that?*" He sped up, cutting off some new comment from the older man. "And besides, what could we be doing differently? I mean, look at the Hastur's Witnesses and how they've had egg on their faces all those times they set dates for the return of Hastur? How is the case any different with our *whole religion?* Didn't the whole thing pretty much debunk *itself* when Alhazred's prediction failed?" Ouch! Now he had said it.

Though the professor's demeanor did not visibly change, his attitude did. This boy was too smart for his own good. He wasn't just doubting. It was clear, even if not yet to Abernathy himself, that he had lost his faith. He wasn't a troubled soul looking for reassurances. He was engaged in refuting a religion in which he no longer believed.

"You've given me a lot to think about, Mr. Abernathy! Let me think on it. In the meantime, I'd advise you to do some serious praying. That's what I'm going to do."

But that wasn't all. As soon as his student picked up his things and left the office, Professor Exeter made a phone call he'd hoped he wouldn't have to make.

***

Two weeks went by uneventfully. Allen bore the burden of his uncertainty as he had for many months. It sapped his one-time zeal, but he kept focused on his studies. He had few friends on campus anyway, having spent so much time in the library and in his dorm room, nose in the books. He'd had to learn Arabic and Latin for his courses in scriptural exegesis, for all the good it did him. You had to scrutinize the texts in meticulous detail to discover the problems that both a casual and a devotional reading failed to reveal.

At the end of that fortnight he was heading back to campus after a dinner at the local Arkham House of Pizza when it happened: a trio of guys wearing enveloping parkas plus ski masks jumped him as he was passing the mouth of an alley. No knives or guns, as he was soon relieved to realize, but they were none too gentle, either, as they yanked him down the length of the shadowed, junk-filled shaft. There was a waiting car at the other end, and they bundled him into it. Allen was not so much afraid as astonished. What on earth would anyone want with a non-entity like him? He was doubly a nerd, cerebral *and* religious.

To his further surprise, the car turned in to the campus, and his masked abductors wordlessly hustled him through an unlocked door into the basement of a building he had not seen before. It looked like it must be a utility shack of some kind. His burly hosts pulled off their hoods to reveal unfamiliar faces, two with the dreadlock-goatee beards sported by many of the divinity students. But, beyond that, he didn't recognize them. One of them spoke to the others, and their captive heard the words "this infidel." At once he knew what had happened. In that moment he was filled with both rage and sadness at his betrayal at the hands of a respected mentor. But he had only a moment for these emotions to register before the next thing happened.

The car must have been followed because somebody obviously knew they'd be here. Two more men burst in, cudgels and baseball bats flailing. Allen instinctively raised his arms to protect his head when he realized the two newcomers were not after him. The first three dropped, and hidden weapons (they had them after all!) clattered to the cement floor.

"Uh, who the hell are *you* guys? Not that I'm ungrateful! And who were *those* guys?"

"No time for that right now, Abernathy! As for us, we're cultists. As for them, they're from the local ministerial association. They were planning a little counseling session. Tough love—you know."

Great! Out of the frying pan...

***

Allen and his rescuers checked into a room at the King's Grant motel up Route 128. He sat in the desk chair while the others sat, one each, on the twin beds. Their body language was non-threatening, and Allen felt his tensed muscles relaxing. They didn't look imposing. For all he knew, both might be Miskatonic students like him. Despite the small size of the Miskatonic student body, he didn't recall seeing either man before. Both happened to be tall, one black, named Bill, the other white, who called himself Mort. Both were clad in sweats.

"Okay, you win—what's going on here?"

"We hear things. We know things. We know about your 'crisis of faith,' Allen."

"So?"

"Things like that can be dangerous around here. You should know that by now."

"I did know enough not to confide in anyone. Except Dr. Exeter. I thought he must have plenty of experience counseling ministerial students who were afraid of losing their faith."

Bill laughed with irony. "Oh, he does. *Plenty* of experience. And over the years he's given plenty of advice, just not to troubled students. He advises the University authorities, and they send their hired flunkies to separate the sheep from the goats. You're one of the goats, and I don't mean the Shub-Niggurath kind."

Eyes widening, Allen stuttered, "You, ah, don't mean he wanted me *killed?*"

Handing Allen a can of Coke, Bill retorted, "What *else?*"

"Thanks. Well, what do I expect from *you* guys? And what did you mean about your being 'cultists'?"

At this, the pair looked at one another as if to say, "Here goes!"

Mort spoke first. "We belong to an old religion not approved by the Old One worshippers."

"What, you mean you belong to the Hastur faith or the Tsathoggua church, or something like that?"

Bill gave a bitter bark of a laugh. "*Hell,* no. A religion usually thought to have gone extinct centuries ago. It was all but wiped out, but it went underground. Had to. It survives mainly by getting passed down through families who have to pretend to worship those monsters."

Mort added, "I wouldn't bet bigwigs like Exeter really even *believe* in that stuff. It's just that their power, their positions, depend on it."

Taken aback, Allen realized he'd never even considered the possibility.

"What we believe in is a god who came down from the stars ages ago to enlighten men. He had to suffer, and it's our privilege to follow in his footsteps. But things are about to change—big time! He promised to return soon, and to turn the tables on the persecutors, the idolaters, the devil-worshippers. So we keep an eye out for people like you. People dissatisfied with the Cthulhu nonsense and open to something else. Would you want to know more?"

"Um, do you guys have a name?"

"We're the Nazoreans. Don't know exactly what it's supposed to mean. Just inherited the name."

"Never heard of you."

Mort fell to expectant silence, but Bill took the opportunity to reassure Allen, "Look, if you don't buy it, you can just walk out of here. We'll give you a ride to anyplace within a reasonable distance. But I don't know where you'd go. They're after you now."

Why think anymore about it? They could at least provide temporary shelter, and their faith, what little he'd heard about it, sure didn't sound any more outlandish than the one he'd embraced until now. Hell, he was even planning on going into the Cthulhuvian ministry!

***

After a few weeks went by, a student raised her hand in class to ask Professor Exeter what had happened to Allen Abernathy. He wasn't the sort to just drop out. Exeter had expected this to come up sooner or later. "I miss him, too, Ms. Gilman. It's my understanding that he is participating in a special seminar at our sister school, Brichester, across the pond. I'm not his academic advisor, so I don't know the details."

Nor was that all he didn't know. He actually had no idea of Allen's whereabouts. He was well aware of his student eluding the hunting dogs he had sicked on him. But he wasn't worth further trouble. The important thing was that he had been knocked off course for the ministry, where his doubts would surely have infected others whether he intended it or not. Exeter was content to think no more about it. He had other matters on his mind, like the paper he was preparing to present at the upcoming ecumenical dialogue event in Sauk City with Ghatanothoan and Hasturian theologians in attendance.

***

It wasn't long before Allen agreed to be baptized into the Nazorean faith. Or rather, rebaptized; he had some years before received Cthulhuvian baptism. The rite had symbolized Great Cthulhu sinking beneath the waves of the Pacific and his expected rising to break the surface in the Last Days. Any theological meaning to the Nazorean immersion had been forgotten. All anyone knew was that it marked one's entry into the fellowship.

That was good enough for Allen. He had found himself a new home in the Nazorean underground community. Their beliefs tended toward vagueness, all real detail having been eroded by centuries of oral transmission. Each generation of believers knew less than the one before it, except insofar as their predecessors had embellished the old stories to fill the gaps. No authoritative texts had survived the incessant persecutions. With his love for theology, Allen found this at once fascinating and frustrating.

He did what he could to carry his share of the load supporting their rural farm settlement. He dared not be seen in public working at some mundane job, since he thought he was still being actively sought. He was afraid his intellectual skills and theological training were going to waste, atrophying. But one day things changed.

When evening prayers were done, Mort approached him with a smile on his face.

"Brother Abernathy, I have some exciting news. I think you know we have a colony of Nazoreans over in Palestine and Syria. They sometimes assist in archaeological digs. But they also work on their own, selling any finds on the black market. Well, they've now found something we never dreamed existed. It is a partial manuscript of the Nazorean scriptures."

Allen's ears were open and his eyes wide.

"You don't mean the 'shunned and abhorred *New Testament*'?"

"Part of it, anyway. They're sending us a copy of the papyri. We can't wait to read it! But we *can't*. It's written in ancient Greek! Who knew?"

Bill had come up to join them. He said, "That's why we're coming to you. Am I right that you studied ancient languages at Miskatonic? We were hoping you might be able to translate it for us."

"Hmm. Greek, you say? Well, I spent most of my efforts on Latin and Arabic so I could study *De Vermis Mysteriis* and the *Al-Azif*. But I did some work on Byzantine Greek so I could cross-check the Arabic text with the Greek *Necronomicon* translated by Theodorus Philetas. It's not quite the same, but I think I could manage it.

When do you expect the copies to get here?"

***

A new chapter in Allen's life had opened, and he was thrilled. Most people gain their religious beliefs either by heredity or by osmosis. He had repudiated his parents' faith and replaced it with that of the Nazoreans. It was not a matter of evidence. When was it ever? He grew to love the group of people who had welcomed him. To embrace them was perforce to embrace their beliefs. Why not? And now he had found the venue he never thought he'd have, where he could teach as he had been taught, though the content was altogether different. But here he was, surrounded by eager, albeit informal, students, sitting in a semi-circle on the floor, drinking up his teaching of scripture like parched flowers enjoying the rain. All was well. Their scripture, their savior, whom he (and they) now knew to call "Jesus," had many good things to say. The ideas and stories Allen was expounding were captivating, challenging, enriching. The glowing treasure contained in the new scripture instilled in him a deep and sincere faith in Jesus the Nazorean.

All was well until the day a bright student, Bill's wife, raised her hand.

"This passage really puzzles me, Brother Allen. Maybe you can clear it up for me. '*Some of you standing here will not experience death till the kingdom of God comes with power.*' Doesn't that sound like he's promising his Second Coming would happen in that same generation? But that was, like, two thousand years ago, right?"

FOSDICK WAS DEAD
A CHRISTIANITY CAROL

Fosdick was dead, dead as a door-nail. This must be distinctly understood at the start.

It was getting on toward Christmas in Montclair, surely one of the merriest of towns in North Jersey, but I took little note of it, ensconced as I was, and late the hour, in my book-lined study, the only lit space in a lowering pile of Romanesque Revival brick. The rest of the building had long since been rented out to other congregations, and now I found myself alone at the computer, while other, saner pastors were cozily home where they, and I, belonged. But as it chanced, I was at work on my dissertation and had not spared the clock a glance in many an hour.

At length, a singular noise began to intrude upon my concentration, nosing its way like a church mouse from my subconscious to my conscious awareness. In fact, it might have been a church mouse, despite our bi-weekly efforts to exterminate them. Or, more likely, perhaps it was thieves. In any case, I soon dismissed the thought. Should it be robbers, better not to run afoul of them. Tomorrow was my monthly reconnaissance of the Bloomfield Avenue fences, or as they euphemized themselves, antique shops, and if they stole anything tonight, I would no doubt recognize it in the morning.

Moments later, though, the noise sought me out in person. At first I heard but a clearing of a throat apparently not cleared for many a year. Looking up from my computer screen, I saw only a cloud of chill breath ascending from behind one of the twisted piles of books rising from the floor like stalagmites. "Who's there?" I said, with a quaver in my voice.

"Don't you know me? My picture's on your wall over there...

Oh, no wonder: you've got books piled in front of that, too!" With this, a tall and stout figure stepped, or, really, seemed to drift, into clear sight. I recognized him then as an illustrious former pastor of my church, Harry Emerson Fosdick. At least I thought so. It had been quite some time since that picture had been visible.

"Dr. Fosdick," I said, dumbfounded yet never at a loss for words, "you're, uh, not here to get your old job back, are you?" I sincerely hoped not, since in Fosdick's heyday, some eight decades ago, the church had counted a full thousand members. Under my tenure it boasted some fifty or sixty. Given the choice, I rather suspected the deacons would choose Fosdick, dead or alive.

"Nothing like that, young man," he assured me with the jovial sparkle you can see even in his photographs (if they're not buried underneath a pile of books, that is). "I've just come with a few pointers for you. After all, you are my latest successor. Let's call it a sermon of sorts, a three-pointer."

"I don't get you, Dr. Fosdick."

"You will, young man, believe me, you will. You see, tonight you will be visited by three spirits. Each will show you something you might not learn from these books of yours. Expect the first when the clock strikes one." And with that he was gone. Honest!

To tell you the truth, in a few minutes I had pretty much forgotten all about this strange visit. I'd had even stranger ones from a few of the local eccentrics this week already. Back to the dissertation.

I sat typing away, oblivious of the passage of time, until the door bell startled me out of my reverie. Seconds later, it rang again. "All right, already!" I snapped to no one who could hear me. Finishing a sentence, I got up to carefully thread my way through the book-cypresses, wondering who the heck it could be at such an hour? Surely not a Human Needs client, thinking the pantry opened at 1 a.m. instead of 1 p.m.

But I got no further than the office door before bumping into my visitor. And I mean "into"~I had walked *through* him before I knew it. So help me, he was as insubstantial as one of my sermons, really just a mass of cobwebs with a face. I knew at that point that Fosdick hadn't been kidding.

28

"Excuse me," I said inanely, stepping back to get a better look, if possible, at the spectre before me. On second glance, the figure was most reminiscent of a carven saint from the stonework of some cathedral, only a statue that hadn't been dusted for some years--even generations. "Uh, who, may I ask, are you?"

He answered in a whisper, "I am the Ghost of Christianity Past. In life I was known as the Apostle Lebbaeus. I'm not surprised you don't recognize me. I occur in only a few manuscripts."

"That explains it," I said. "And what do you want with me on a cold December night?"

"We must be off," the neglected Apostle replied. "You have much to learn before the night is through."

I began to groan in the way I do when my secretary has failed to screen out a church calendar salesman's call. "Listen, thanks, but really, I've got a lot of work to do here, and..."

"Nonsense!" he said. "We're set for a trip into the past. Here, take hold of my robe. Don't mind the cobwebs."

I was hoping at least for the thrill of a ride through the night air, seeing the cozily lit streets of Montclair laid out before me like a page from a Victorian storybook. But in fact we reached our destination immediately. And where was that?

The place was familiar enough. It was a nearby church I had attended many years before, in the heady days when Christianity had first begun to be a living reality to me. I hadn't visited the place in years, and I wasn't too happy being back there now.

"Spirit, will you please tell me what we're doing in this place? I hoped I'd seen the last of it a long time ago." But he made no answer, merely pointing through the plate glass windows separating the sanctuary from the narthex.

I took the hint and stopped talking. It was *deja vue* for real. Transfixed, I watched and listened. There were the eager faces upturned to the pulpit, Bibles open on polyester laps, as the preacher proceeded to show how the prophet Obadiah had long ago urged the Israelites to have a personal relationship with Jesus Christ.

Soon it was over, and, like the old days, I sat through some nine stultifying choruses of the invitational hymn "Just as I Am Without One Plea." I only hoped my guide Lebbaeus wasn't

29

intending to go down to the front. I knew I wouldn't be joining him.

Then came the announcements. Soon the church youth group would be headed up to Rumney, New Hampshire, for a spiritual retreat, where the speaker would be a man who read the Bible entirely through annually and managed to "witness" to several hundred hapless victims each year as well.

At this I noticed a section of two or three pews where all the high school kids were sitting together, and darned if one or two of them didn't look familiar! There was Dean, Cathy, Mort, Kevin, all in the blush of youth... and who had to be next? Yeah, there he was. The kid that looked like Ernie on "My Three Sons." Me.

My first thought was to wait at the door as everybody filed out, take that kid by the collar and try to talk some sense into him, a thing or two about the historical-critical method, for starters. But then I noticed that Lebbaeus had taken *me* by the collar.

"Well," he said, "was it all really that bad?" I guess he knew my mind was spinning with conflicting emotions. True, I was a real nut back then, passing out evangelistic leaflets, witnessing, stuff that struck even me as embarrassing at the time, though I did it, thinking it was the duty of a Christian soldier.

But on the other hand, I couldn't deny all the times of spiritual comeraderie and the "good clean fun" that I had with those other kids in their silly-looking 70's costumes. And I had to admit I owed that church something. Like my interest in the Bible.

I found myself wondering what had happened to some of those others, and I was about to turn to ask my ghostly visitant when to my great surprise I found myself sitting back at my desk! The computer was humming just as I'd left it, and there were no spectral apostles in evidence. I yawned and decided to get back to work. The clock showed only 1:15. Must have dozed off.

A couple of hours passed, and I had reached the end of another chapter. I began to have the odd feeling that I should be expecting someone. My first thought was that I had ordered a pizza (pepperoni, anchovies and extra cheese) from Domino's. But, no, that couldn't be right; even they weren't open this late.

In a moment I was jolted to full attention by another sound, this time not the door bell, but the security alarm! I hate it when that thing goes off! It sounds like a bomb exploding! No doubt one of the renters had armed it, thinking they were *dis*arming it, as they entered. This meant several calls to the police and the alarm company to explain that we were only crying "wolf" again. I guess they were pretty sick of it by now.

This time I made it as far as the front door, only to see another strange figure drift through the solid wood to stand before me.

With the point of a finger toward the vibrating keypad, this new ghost silenced the alarm as if by magic. Come to think of it, I guess that's just what it was.

"And you're...?"

"The Ghost of Christianity Present," came back the reply. "I suppose more of a patron saint, really. You may have heard of me. My name is, or was, Bishop Pike." He was a heavy-set spook, with spectacles, close-cropped hair, and dressed in priestly black.

"An honor to meet you, sir!" I said as I extended my hand, not knowing whether a solid handshake was possible for such a being. It was. I guess Rich Griese had been right in that Sunday School argument about Luke 24 showing Jesus walking through a wall but showing a solid hand to the disciples.

"I get the picture," I said. "Where to?"

The good bishop looked at me with as much of a smile as his ectoplasm could manage. "A bit farther this time, but it won't take a second. Hey, let go of my coat, will you?"

I blinked at a sudden rush of cold air, and when I opened my eyes we were standing on a familiar hilltop, overlooking a street in California, with a gorgeous view of the Bay beyond. I turned around and saw one of the classroom buildings of a famous seminary I had visited two or three times a number of years ago. One time I had the treat of hearing Caesar Chavez speak in the chapel there.

Bishop Pike pointed the way as dawn began to come up. But by the time we had reached the door, the clock showed 11 a.m. Maybe it was all some sort of a dream.

We went down the hall, pausing at door after door to hear what was being taught in theological seminary these days. Once we were nearly knocked to the floor (good thing we were both

31

insubstantial) by a professor leading a group of students as they piled out of one classroom, dressed in fatigues (from the best sporting goods stores, as a label revealed), firing off plastic toy

machine guns. Puzzled, I watched them pass, then turned to the bishop. All he said was "Liberation theology," and I nodded in understanding.

Going on to the next door I was eager to note the words chalked on the board: "The Historical Jesus." Always one of my favorite scholarly topics. A woman's strident voice drifted forth, clothed in a thick German accent, "*Ja, Jesus war eine Lesbian...*"

As we passed the bulletin board, my ecto-piscopal guide spoke, "Remember all those taboos you had in fundamentalism? No movies, no dancing, no card playing?"

"I sure do! You could suffocate in a religion like that! One of the reasons I finally left it! But here you can breathe free! I wouldn't mind teaching in a place like this some day! No restrictions!"

He said nothing but merely pointed to the variety of brightly colored notices posted along the hallway: "Boycott Gallo," "Don't Sleep with J.P. Stevens," "Boycott Nestle," "Boycott Exxon."

At the end of the hall I lifted my eyes and noticed mounted on the wall a teakwood crucifix. The figure suspended there was female and looked for all the world like Winnie Mandela.

When we reached the student lounge, my ghostly guide was gone. Just like that. Which left me stranded. Well, I hadn't been in town for a while, so I decided to see the sights.

I started down Euclid Street to a little pizza place I remembered. But then the darkness descended, the day over already.

And in the deepening twilight I sensed a silent companion keeping rustling pace with my own steps. I stopped when I got to a street lamp and looked up to see if I could identify the ominously looming figure.

The shape beside me was towering and gaunt. He was swathed in the ornately brocaded robes of an archbishop of the church. His height, already impressive, was augmented a foot and a half by the splendid archepiscopal mitre he wore.

But the face framed between headgear and enveloping collar was still lost in shadows. My eyes followed the red, purple and gold embroidery of his sleeve to its end, and I received a shock when I beheld the thin and bony claw that held a bishop's staff.

My breath caught and I fell to my knees, terrified. "Sir," I stammered, "Might you be the Ghost of Christianity Yet to Come?"

A nod was all the reply I got back.

But with that he raised his shepherd's crook, so eerily suggestive of a scythe, and gestured out over the moonlit bay, visible through the palm trees in the distance, as if indicating the expanse of the Pacific. I somehow knew that by this he meant to announce our next and final destination. And in a flash we were there.

Unlike the previous ports of call in my strange night's journey, I had never set foot where we now stood, for all that the place looked dreadfully familiar, as if from old Sunday School books.

The spirit still said nothing, but he held out his staff towards a stark grave marker, unevenly set in the sun-baked ground. I felt in an instant of terror that, were I to look upon that marker and see the letters there inscribed, I should faint at the sight of my own name. I hid my eyes, but the skeletal hand of my host shook me roughly and pushed me to my knees before the grave.

"Look!" I heard, in a half-familiar voice.

I dared open my eyes and traced out the chiseled name...

JESUS OF NAZARETH

I sprang to my feet and gasped, "What joke is this...!" But I was alone.

The voice came again, and this time I recognized it as that of the ghost of Fosdick. "Yes, he is dead, for his religion has perished from the earth. He lies in eternal oblivion with Zeus and Odin and Attis and a thousand others."

"But how? How has this come to pass?" I stammered.

"Have you learned nothing this night? You and your like have taken his seamless garment between you and rent it to shreds till no one could any longer find faith to believe. Fundamentalist and Modernist have warred like Cain and Abel and at length destroyed one another. Christianity lies between them both like a field of blood.

"Let them struggle like the twins of Rebekah's womb, but let that struggle be one of life coming to birth, not one of death. These are the shadows of what may yet be, but need not be. Remember what you have seen this night!"

"Yes! Yes!" I cried as I sought for the origin of the voice that was speaking to me. There was Dr. Fosdick's face~in a picture frame! I was back in my office, and the obscuring stack of books had fallen away.

"I swear, from this day on the spirits of Christianity past, present and future shall strive together within me! I will not shut out the lessons they have taught!"

And so I haven't, much to the puzzlement of my long-suffering congregation, who must shake their heads in befuddlement to hear a Deconstructionist sermon followed by a traditional communion service, or Baptist hymns after a homily from Nietzsche.

MYTH BECAME FACT

Craig Williams was a tireless and highly successful Christian apologist. He was the superstar on the staff of Campus Christian Crusade. His many debates against various atheists and skeptics had fortified the faith of many. He had, for instance, recently kicked Robert Price's unbelieving butt for all to see. YouTube videos of his lectures and debates were many, more being added all the time, and they garnered record numbers of views. Dr. Williams spent precious few weekends at home, so few in fact that he hardly thought of his apartment *as* home, more like a garage with himself as the car. He parked himself there on the rare occasions he was not flying here or there to debate. The wear and tear was nothing to the satisfaction he felt from his work for the Lord Jesus. Not that his work did not present temptations of its own. Who would have guessed that Christian celebrities like himself would attract cute co-ed groupies? But he had politely resisted their advances. The big danger was, of course, that of pride, but he did his best to resist that one, too.

But just now, Craig had a different problem to deal with. He sat, bare-chested, on the tissue-covered examination table, awaiting the doctor's verdict. It always took longer than they said it would, so he spent the time praying. At least at first, but in a few moments he was dozing.

"Mister Williams? Mister Williams? I hate to disturb you..."

The doctor smiled as Craig rejoined him in the waking world.

"Oh, *sorry,* Doc! I didn't mean to..."

"That's quite all right! In fact, I'd like to see you take *more* naps! You need more rest than your work seems to allow. Frankly, you're over-exerting yourself pretty badly, you know."

Putting his shirt back on, Craig did not know what to say. He knew the doctor was right. And he knew that, as a Christian, he had an obligation to take good care of the body God had given him. Still, had not God blessed him with a dynamic ministry? Surely he would take care of him as long as he pursued his assigned mission. But somehow he didn't think his reasoning would impress the doctor much, so he kept it to himself.

It wasn't long before the doctor's advice proved prophetic. It was right in the middle of a vigorous exchange with Stan Parker, President of the Revenge on Religion Foundation, when Craig began to sputter, then collapsed right on stage. His opponent at once rushed to his side, found him unresponsive, and yelled out: "Somebody call an *ambulance* for God's, er, I mean, for *Pete*'s sake!" The invincible defender of the faith had suffered a massive heart attack.

Death came to him as he lay on the operating table, despite the best efforts of doctors and nurses to bring him out of it. Admitting defeat, the medical team shook their heads in sorrow. Some were familiar with his work; others simply regretted the passing of a man so young and vigorous. "I guess God figured it was his time, huh?"

Craig heard all this as from a distance. What did they mean? Who could they be talking about? All at once he thought of a scene from Roger Corman's movie *The Premature Burial* with a paralyzed Ray Milland panicking as the clods of earth piled up on his coffin. As if it were some theological hypothetical, Craig asked himself, "What gives? Am I dead or alive?"

His confusion was only compounded when he felt himself being sucked through some kind of wind tunnel toward a faraway beacon of light. Granted, scripture had little to say of the transition to the afterlife, and it sure didn't describe anything like *this*. He thought of the story of Lazarus and the Rich Man; was he headed for Abraham's Bosom, the antechamber of heaven? He expected he'd find out in short order. Nor was he disappointed (though he soon *would* be).

Craig knew he had left his physical form behind; nevertheless, he felt like he was standing on some firm but unseen surface. In a moment the light he had glimpsed flared up before him. Was this an angel? C.S. Lewis had described them rather like this in *Out of the Silent Planet*. Of course, that wasn't scripture, though many Christians practically treated Lewis's books that way. His thoughts were racing, trying to insulate him from a rising fear he knew was incompatible with faith.

The Light was speaking now, whether to his ears or to his mind he did not know.

"Welcome, Craig Williams."

The voice was deep and soothing, also vibrant and, unless it was his imagination, with a hint of amusement.

"Who are you, Lord? Uh, are you the Lord Jesus... or the Heavenly Father?" Should he have recognized him as one or the other?

"Fear not, Craig Williams," the Being said. "But I must tell you: things are not quite as you have supposed. I belong to none of your religions. I am not like some sports fan rooting for a favorite team, as you all seem to think. But the Hindus have come the closest. The ones, that is, who believe in the creator Brahma. I rejoice to create and multiply worlds as it pleases me. And they are close to the truth about something else, too. The relation between reality and illusion is not precisely what you may think. They are different only in certain respects."

Craig was quite familiar with this doctrine. He made it his business to study up on rival faiths in order better to refute them. But he found himself slipping into serious disorientation. Was he failing his Theology final? And what would happen to him when he got that "F"?

Suddenly he had a sobering realization: he was standing at *the* greatest apologetic opportunity of them all! To persuade "God" himself of the truth of Christianity!

"Behold, I have taken it upon myself to speak to the Almighty!"

He hesitated, waiting for any reaction. There was none, and Craig took this as tacit permission to proceed. He went into default mode, condensing a spiel he had presented hundreds of times. He covered the proofs from prophecy and miracle, the need for God as the basis for morality, the eyewitness testimony of the gospels, and the futility of naturalistic alternatives to the resurrection. There was little sense of time here, and he hoped he was not trying the Being's patience. At length he rested his case. The featureless Entity somehow conveyed the impression of listening with polite interest.

"Your knowledge and your zeal are remarkable! I must disappoint you, however. None of that is true. There was no Jesus. There were no apostles, no miracles, except in ancient dreams. You must forgive me."

Craig felt a gathering storm cloud of dread and panic. He muttered, to himself, "If Christ be not raised, our faith is in vain and our preaching is in vain." He had to think fast.

"But... it *should* be true! Without the gospel, what hope is there? Er, but you can *make* it true, can't you, whoever you are?"

There was silence in heaven for the space of half an hour. Then the voice emerged again from the Light. "In fact, I can. Time is part of the illusion, and I am able to manipulate it. I am intrigued by your suggestion! It *is* in many ways a grand story. Perhaps you are right. Perhaps it *ought* to be true. All right, *let* it be true! Behold!"

Dreams are supposed to elapse in a moment while seeming to the dreamer to last for hours. The dying are said to see their whole lives flash before their mind's eye. In some such way, Craig now witnessed a panorama of gospel scenes, not in real time, but as if remembering things once seen, in rapid succession. He saw shepherds and three kings flanking the Bethlehem manger. The boy Jesus working in Joseph's carpenter shop. His baptism, a dove descending onto his shoulder. A Voice, similar to that of the Light Being, saying first, "Thou art my beloved Son" and, immediately thereafter, "*This is* my beloved Son."

Retreating into the Judean desert, Jesus met the Tempter, who, Craig was surprised to see, tempted Jesus *four* times, suggesting he transform stones into bread, offering him the kingdoms of the world, telling him to jump from the temple rooftop, then repeating the offer of the kingdoms. It made sense now! At Cana he turned the water into grape juice. Jesus rode a donkey into Jerusalem and ejected the money-changers and livestock. He gave the Sermon on the Mount, then, soon after, the similar Sermon on the Plain. Jesus healed one blind man as he entered the town of Jericho and another on his way out. Craig was amazed to see his Lord restoring missing limbs, resurrecting rotting corpses. He heard Jesus say to the crowds, "I am God incarnate. Who else could do such deeds?"

Nicodemus approached by night, and Jesus answered him, "Unless a man is born again and accepts me as his personal savior, he cannot enter the kingdom of heaven." When a scribe asked Jesus about the greatest commandment, he replied, "Thou shalt invite me into thy heart as personal Lord and Savior. Why not pray with me right now?" The Rich Young Ruler addressed Jesus as "Good teacher," and Jesus replied, "Think about what you're saying! Only God is good, no? So what does that make *me*?" The man bowed and exclaimed, "My Lord and my God!" Something about all this struck Craig as wrong but also as entirely right.

Jesus entered Jerusalem *again*, this time precariously balanced on the backs of two donkeys, one smaller than the other. He cleansed the temple again. At the Last Supper he gave the disciples a cup, the bread, and a second cup, saying "This cup of grape juice figuratively symbolizes my blood," etc. He predicted that Peter would deny him at least three times that very night. Before the Sanhedrin, when asked if he was the Christ, he replied, "I Am That I Am!" Peter denied him six times, speaking to a series of several individuals.

On the way to Golgotha, Jesus began carrying his cross, then stumbled under its weight, whereupon a soldier grabbed a bystander by the collar and ordered him to carry the heavy beam the rest of the way. Jesus was crucified at six A.M., then taken down to be crucified again at nine. Despite his suffering, Jesus made a series of seven different statements from the cross.

For the first time Craig got a clear look at Jesus' face—and Jesus looked just like him!

Easter morning rolled around, and the scene was surprisingly confusing, with Jesus appearing and disappearing, two angels morphing into one, then splitting apart again. Mary Magdalene, Peter, and John performed an elaborate dance of sorts, arriving and departing and returning in various combinations.

***

"Look, why don't we give it one more try?" This time the medical team managed to resuscitate him. His heart began to beat again, timidly at first, then more steadily. He was not yet conscious, but there was clearly brain activity. "That was a close one!"

Craig finally woke up later that evening in a hospital bed. Smiling faces of friends and colleagues greeted him. But all he could think of was his Near Death Experience. He asked himself the same question all who had the experience asked: Was it all a dream? He resolved at once not to share the story with anyone until he could determine the reality of the matter.

There was no question now whether to take his doctor's warnings seriously. Craig had his secretary cancel his upcoming appearances and convey his apologies. He was itching to get back in the saddle, but for now he must rest and recuperate. He decided to use the time to study, especially on NDEs. But that didn't last long. Everyone who sojourns on the internet finds himself quickly distracted by the siren song of click-bait. Even so, Craig found himself straying from the path as soon as something shiny grabbed his attention. And the result was some big surprises.

For one thing, the scientific community was in an uproar over the announcement of new genetic research that rendered the theory of evolution obsolete and untenable. Mainstream scientists admitted it was time for a major paradigm shift and suggested Darwinism be given a respectful funeral. The new research had suddenly revived the fortunes of the once-discredited Intelligent Design theory. It was a game-changing event on the level with the dawn of Quantum Physics, and the larger implications had yet to be worked out. But one thing was clear: evolutionism could no longer be wielded like a club over the head of the Christian faith! Craig felt a thrill of long-delayed vindication. It was much like the sense of relief Americans felt with the end of the Cold War. He whispered a brief prayer of thanks. But a moment later it occurred to him to wonder exactly whom he was thanking.

Only days later, even more stunning news awaited him. He saw the report, typically dumbed down, first on Cable News, then went on line to find more detailed coverage. It seemed new manuscript discoveries in the Judean Desert provided solid evidence for Jesus' resurrection! Papyrologists and archaeologists, usually very cautious in issuing such news, were agreed that the cache of early Christian letters dated from the first third of the first century A.D., and that the eye-witness descriptions of Easter encounters contained in them appeared genuine, bearing none of the usual marks of apocryphal forgery. He sank back into his desk chair stricken with wonder. Apologetics such as he practiced would now be much easier, if not actually obsolete. If so, he would be the first to rejoice. It had all been but a means to save souls, and if it should no longer be necessary, all the better!

But the news imparted by a stream of visitors was even more astounding. A few were ex-students of his, apprentice apologists. Others were colleagues at Campus Christian Crusade. Every one of them was bursting with exciting reports of city-wide revivals, once-staid churches now bursting at the seams with newly rededicated backsliders and new converts alike.

"Craig, I swear it's like the days of Charles Finney, Dwight Moody!"

Others shared with him testimonies of strikingly answered prayers for the conversion of hitherto-stubborn relatives and even dramatic spontaneous remissions of deadly diseases! They were starry-eyed, almost as if they had just fallen in love. Clearly, a great movement of the Holy Spirit was underway.

But for Craig Williams, there was a fly, perhaps even a horsefly, mired in the ointment, tainting what should have been unalloyed joy. None of his excited informants was inclined to look a gift horse in the mouth. No one ventured to ask just why this Holy Spirit renaissance had dawned all at once, and at this particular time. Though these developments occurred more or less at the same time as the news concerning evolution and the manuscript discoveries, Craig knew there could be no direct connection. Most lay people, whether Christian or non-Christian, were not engaged with issues like these. They were mainly of concern to "professionals" like himself and his debate opponents, a tiny subgroup of the population.

This became even clearer once Craig's closest Christian friends began to confide in him. They told him of real progress in personal sanctification. Nor did he have to take their word for it; subtle but real changes in demeanor, increased serenity and unselfconscious holiness, spoke for themselves. Neither they nor he said it, but Craig and his friends seemed to share the recognition that the formulaic promises of evangelical rhetoric were finally being fulfilled. What a frustrating sham it had been up till now! These sentiments were typical: "I'm telling you, Craig, for the first time in my Christian life, I am actually hearing the inner voice of Jesus in dialogue with me! I'm actually having a relationship with Jesus Christ!" Craig truly rejoiced in these confessions, though he was noncommittal about his own spirituality.

And he certainly felt disinclined to share his now-solidified explanation for the new spiritual climate, for he had become convinced that his Near Death Experience was, to use his apologist jargon, "veridical." In other words, it had been real. It had been a real encounter, not just in his head. Christianity had *become* true, and in his image! Christianity according to Craig Williams!

Instead of rejoicing, Craig found himself increasingly worried. At first he could not pinpoint the reason for his anxiety. But he knew one thing: he had to abandon apologetics, once pretty much his main reason for living. As he explained to so many who were distressed at his announcement and his immediate resignation from Campus Christian Crusade, he felt his efforts were no longer useful. The war had been, for all intents and purposes, won.

"But Dr. Williams, what about straight evangelistic preaching? You're such a gifted speaker!"

"That's still needful, of course, but I'm afraid it's just not my corner of the vineyard. From now on, I'm planning to hunker down and do something I've been missing for a long time: writing in depth on biblical exegesis and theology." As soon as these comments appeared in *Evangelicalism Today*, publishers including Eerdmans and Inter-Varsity hastened to offer him book contracts. But his efforts soon flagged along with his interest in the once-favored subjects. These things, too, Craig set aside, refunding the sizeable advances he had received.

Several of his friends, marking these dramatic changes, urged him to get counseling. "You sound like you might be clinically depressed. This sudden loss of interest—it's one of the classic signs. There are a number of excellent Christian psychologists I could put you in touch with. Would you like some phone numbers?"

Craig replied noncommittally, implicitly discouraging further contact. In reality he was quarantining himself. "If I had spoken thus, I should have betrayed the generation of thy children." Having suffered the loss, one by one, of every comforting, evasive rationalization, Craig had finally been left alone with the truth he had been hiding from himself.

If Christianity was not true in and of itself but was artificially *made* true, then was it really true at all? Not a simulation? Couldn't the playful deity change his mind and decide to make Buddhism or, for that matter, the Aztec religion of human sacrifice "true"? In establishing his faith, Craig Williams had, ironically, destroyed it.

He began to receive calls, emails, and even personal visits from a whole different quarter: the atheists and skeptics he had once avidly debated. They had surmised he must have become disillusioned with his faith. What a coup it would be if they could enlist him to their cause! Dave Goldman, head of the Westboro Atheist Association, was typical: "Imagine the star apologist publicly recanting! Heh-heh, it'd be like Paul on the road to Damascus, only in reverse!"

"I'm afraid you've got me wrong, Dave. I don't want to switch teams; I just want to quit the damn game and be done with it. But you're kind to think of me."

Besides, though no longer a Christian (as he had to admit), neither was Craig an atheist. He had, after all, encountered *some* sort of deity.

He knew he had no chance of escaping the spotlight if he stayed where he was. So he began the process of legally changing his name, pulling up stakes and moving to another state. He quietly sold his extensive theological library to one of the huge dealers in second-hand religious books. He told no one where, or even that, he was going. Once relocated, he decided to roll up his sleeves and volunteer for local relief work among the homeless and drug-addicted. In this he found a degree of satisfaction. With the obscuring veil of theology lifted, it now seemed plain to him that the fundamental thing was to pitch in and alleviate human suffering.

He spent many months thus engaged, living modestly on the money he had made during his years of speaking and writing. His mood and outlook did not much improve. He felt strangely unmoored from the world, every belief stripped from him, unsure even of the fabric of reality. But he was mostly able to set this confusion aside in his service to others. His co-workers at the shelter were drawn to him, admiring his compassion and dedication, but they could not help noticing his glum demeanor.

"Bill, you seem so, I don't know... introspective, I guess. Is anything wrong? I know it's none of my business, but..."

"I appreciate your concern, Evelyn, but it's nothing I could explain very easily." He forced a smile and walked away.

So it went until the day something dawned on Craig. He had dedicated himself to mitigating human suffering, never thinking that he himself, the one-time champion of Christianity, was single-handedly responsible for unthinkable torment, compared with which the trials of his precious street people were the ecstasies of Paradise. While the Christian belief was still no more than a creation of the human imagination, there had been neither a biblical heaven—nor a hell. *But now there was.* Now the "unsaved" were writhing in unquenchable flames and covered with worms that would never die, and it was *his doing!*

This he could not live with.

The next afternoon, Evelyn and another co-worker, dropping by to give him a ride to the shelter, discovered "Bill's" corpse hanging by a belt from a rafter in his apartment.

***

Standing again before the Being of Light, Craig fairly groveled in self-reproach. The Being knew what was on his mind. But he waited for Craig to say it.

"Can we change it again? Get rid of Hell? Have everybody go to heaven?"

"I'm afraid not, Craig Williams. And I think you know why. It is all interconnected. If there is nothing to be saved *from*, where is the need for a savior?"

"Is there no way to undo what I have done?"

"There is indeed! And you know what that is, don't you, Craig Williams?"

"Make Christianity false again?"

"Correct. Are you sure you want that?"

Eyes shut tight, Craig muttered, "Hell is too high a price to pay for Christianity to be true..."

"It is done. Now you may consider *yourself* the savior, as you have quenched the flames of perdition. Come, sit at my right hand, good and faithful servant."

⁎⁎⁎

Back in the world of the living, things changed quickly. The papyri authenticating the resurrection were debunked by new Carbon 14 dating. And the genetic research turned out to have been based on flawed methodology. There was plenty of embarrassment to go around. Undaunted, new apologists entered the lists, well-trained in the traditional arguments which the mysteriously absent Craig Williams once employed so expertly. Christians entered a collective Dark Night of the Soul, newly bereft of their temporary revitalization. They buckled down and soldiered on.

THE ATHEIST EXORCIST

Jake Stubbins had once been a Christian believer, deep into it. He had "witnessed" to others of his faith in Jesus Christ and how it had changed his life and, of course, how such faith was sure to transform the life of whomever he happened to be speaking to. As he expected, most people were uneasy with this, much as they would feel trying to get rid of a pesky door-to-door salesman. He knew how they felt. He didn't mind if they thought him a bit of a nut. It just showed how much they needed Christ in their lives. He had, after all, felt the same way when he was the object of such evangelistic pitches, until one day someone chanced to approach him at a time of grief and despair. Life had shaken him loose from his typical self-assurance. He was, in those days, reevaluating all the answers he had so proudly cherished. And when he heard the gospel message from an earnest Christian, somehow it sounded new. He was able to recognize it as a lifeline being thrown to rescue him.

Jake had been the most enthusiastic of converts and, to no one's surprise, he eventually decided to enroll at a theological seminary. He was, at age 28, a bit older than most of his classmates, but his instructors assured him that, in their experience, older students were among the best, given their greater life experience. The years of his Master of Divinity degree passed quickly, his fascinating courses (though biblical Greek and Hebrew were pretty tedious) kept him in intellectual ferment, and he made many friends whom he supposed would be life-long colleagues in ministry, however far geography might one day separate them.

The trouble began for Jake at midterm in his Apologetics course, senor year. He knew very well that his attraction to Christian faith had been "existential," that is, emotional, in character. That hadn't bothered him, really, but occasionally someone he sought to win for

46

Christ would point it out and accuse him of arbitrary subjectivism. They wouldn't use those exact words, but that is what Jake knew their skepticism amounted to. And he wanted to reinforce his armor at that point. The apologetics class promised to do just that for him, providing sophisticated defenses of the faith based on historical evidence and philosophical reasoning. He loved it!

But everyone in class fell silent one afternoon when one student raised her hand, asking, "But Professor Holding, we *already* believe. We didn't come to Christ through intellectual arguments. I know *I* didn't. Did any of you? Isn't it a little dishonest to ask people to accept Christ because of all these arguments when, for us, it was simple faith?"

The professor was ready with an answer that surprised everyone: "So you're asking if all this is not really just a mass of after-the-fact rationalizations for something we believe on other grounds? Well, I suppose it *is*. But it *works*, at least *some*times. When it doesn't, we try something else."

As for Jake Stubbins, the class, and indeed all his classes, stopped right there. He left seminary. He returned to the computer programming work he had abandoned. With a little brushing up he was back in the saddle. The work, however, had lost any appeal it had once possessed, but that was all right. Jake's real interest lay elsewhere. In a sense he felt he was still playing the God game, but switching teams. He couldn't leave the faith question up in the air. He now felt the bottom had dropped out. Subjectivity alone *was* inadequate. Indeed, he had never suspected how many intellectual obstacles stood in the way of faith, or how formidable they were, until he began studying how to overcome them! So now he pursued the matter, weighing the Christian answers without rooting for them. If you didn't desperately *want* them to be true, would they sound as good as they did in a seminary classroom? He embarked on a reading program more strenuous than any assigned him at school, reading everything he could get his hands on by William Lane Craig, Francis Schaeffer, Ravi Zacharias, James White and the rest. It was shocking how different all the standard arguments on behalf of Christianity looked when not pumped up by prior belief. As the next five years went by, Jake found that all the chief doctrines he had once sworn by appeared, with the perspective distance provided, to be altogether arbitrary, makeshifts intended to stitch together clashing contradictions, to juggle incompatible notions: "three persons, one essence," "predestination and free will," "fully divine yet fully human," and so on. What a waste of creative intelligence to construct and defend such sacred oxymorons!

He was out. He was done. And yet he could not let it go. Jake was too smart not to realize he was fighting his own demons, his own past. But he felt he had to get his licks in. He had to get back at those plaster saints who had taught him to revere ignorance and special pleading. What hypocrisy! Salvation was by sacrifice, but not that of Jesus on the cross. No, by the sacrifice of the intellect. Those bastards! Jake would do what he could to expose these pious charlatans, and to rescue other naïve seekers from their holy clutches. But how?

First he tried challenging local clergy to public debates, but he got no takers. If they even saw his newspaper ads, they must have figured there was no percentage in it for them. Jake lacked any real credentials, so none of the big name apologists would take him on. It would be like the heavyweight champ agreeing to a bout with some palooka from a neighborhood gym. There had to be *some* way, and a still-simmering Jake swore he'd *find* it.

About this time he discovered the surprisingly extensive network of atheist and humanist organizations. There seemed almost as many of them as there were church denominations, and it looked like they had about as many feuds! Jake had to chuckle at this. But he joined all the groups that had meetings near him. He felt a welcome sense of belonging in the company of the like-minded. It was something he had missed ever since his doubts had divorced him from the fellowship of Christians. Each group had its big-mouth eccentrics, people who were long on brains but short on personality. Well, that was nothing new. He got along well in these circles and was soon serving as a featured speaker at their events. But he was only preaching to the choir, so to speak.

One day, as he glanced through an old issue of *Free Iniquity*, one of the leading humanist journals, it hit him! There was an article on the cult scare of the 1970s and what had become of those exotic new religions, the Moonies, the Krishnas, etc. He thought of one of the most controversial aspects of the whole fiasco: the "deprogrammers." These were self-educated "specialists" who had lost someone to this or that cult and were out to settle the score. While their own loved ones might be out of reach, they hoped to derive some kind of vicarious satisfaction by abducting other cult kids, isolating them, strapping them to a chair, and haranguing them till they agreed to drop their faith in Reverend Moon and return to the Presbyterians.

A guy named Ted Patrick had pioneered the trade and racked up a reputation that eventually landed him in jail for kidnapping. But others had followed in his footsteps, armed with "conservatorships" granted by the courts. The cult hysteria had long since given way to the "Satanic Panic" of the 1990s, and there weren't any deprogrammers active anymore. But, Jake was thinking, maybe that was a vacuum to be filled...

Jake had often heard anguished parents in the atheist meetings lamenting that their teen-aged children had abandoned the atheist "faith" to join church youth groups or campus evangelical organizations. It just might be that these parents would appreciate some specialized help from someone who had been there and back. It would take some preparation, familiarizing himself with the legal dimensions of deprogramming, the logistics, and, of course, case histories.

One of the first things he learned was that deprogramming had fallen on hard times partly because the turnover rate in the cults was amazingly high: over *ninety* percent of recruits dropped out in a year or so! So why not just wait it out? But Jake realized this had to be due to the extreme nature of these sects and the commitment they required. Conventional churches, even fundamentalist ones, were much less demanding. Atheist parents weren't afraid of their sons and daughters being starved and sleep-deprived, forced to sell flowers on the street. They regarded religious belief *itself* as a serious abuse from which their loved ones needed to be rescued. And Jake was, er, just the guy to do it!

He decided to ease his way into it. At first he just had the worried atheist parents invite him over to dinner with their newly

Christian son or daughter present. He'd pleasantly turn the conversation to his own experience, his conversion, then his deconversion and the reasons for it. If all went well, and the young believer seemed open to pursuing it further, there would be further evenings. This approach produced some results, but soon he had to decide what to do if the target put up a roadblock and wanted to hear no more. At first he marked these down as failures. But too many of these inclined him to think the old deprogrammers were right: it was time to get tough. Fewer parents would be willing to do this, but once Jake could point to a good record of success with these methods, he was sure there would be less resistance. And that's what happened.

Atheist parents tried to "protect" their children from religious teaching, since kids should be left to "decide for themselves." They didn't seem to realize that, in doing this, they were really catechizing them in atheism. And ask the Catholics; catechism usually amounts to vaccination; they'd get sick of it and rebel. No wonder so many atheist kids jumped ship. Well, that was more work for Jake. It wasn't long before he was able to quit his "secular" job and live off what he made from deprogramming.

Many of his charges didn't take a whole lot of convincing. Many converts missed the sexual freedom they had sacrificed to become straight-laced Christians. But then there were those like Charles Menninger, stubbornly committed to his faith and ready to defend it. With Charles, Jake saw, he'd have to get tough. He hated to do it, was almost embarrassed at the stunt he had to pull in order to lure his prey into confinement.

Right now Charles was strapped to a dining room chair, laughing at him, at the whole absurd situation.

"You know, Mr. Stubbins, this chair's not much of an argument! If you could make a decent case against Christ, you wouldn't have to resort to stuff like *this*! If not for the secular-progressive bias of the courts, you'd never be able to get away with this legally!"

"Maybe not, Charles, maybe not. Do you know what a 'tarrying bench' is, Charles? In the days of the old revivals, if somebody was praying to receive the Holy Ghost but nothing was happening, the guy would kneel at the tarrying bench, and several of the brethren would lay hands on him and pray real loud till there was a breakthrough. Well, that's what *this* is."

The young man was very like Jake in so many ways, it scared him. Charles was impressively well-read. He would soon graduate college and had been accepted to seminary. He had a winning personality and a sharp intellect. Jake hated to see him wasting it. And he was certainly Jake's greatest challenge to date. There had been several evenings of vigorous discussion at the dinner table, which Charles appeared to relish almost like a sport. But finally they found themselves going round in circles. It was a matter of pride now, and Jake refused to give up. Maybe it was because Charles was so much like him. It felt like he was once again going through the struggle of doubt and belief, and he didn't want to lose the fight against his old self, Jake the believer, who was now sitting in front of him.

"All right, Mr. Stubbins, hit me with your best shot!"

"Okay, I'd like to revisit the resurrection narratives. You've insisted that there are no plausible explanations for the empty tomb and the resurrection appearances that don't involve the supernatural, right?"

"Exactly. It's silly to think Mary Magdalene and the others would have visited the wrong tomb; only a couple of days earlier they watched where Joseph of Arimathea had stashed Jesus' body. They *knew* where he was buried."

"But you admit Joseph had put the body in his tomb only temporarily, planning to give it permanent burial somewhere else after the Sabbath. Suppose he got there before the women. Suppose he took Jesus' body away before the women got there? John's gospel actually says that's what Mary thought!"

"I guess that's possible. But wouldn't Joseph have set them straight once he heard rumors about a resurrection?"

"Sounds like *you* know what happened better than the gospel writers, Charles! You're writing your own gospel, aren't you?" Jake snickered. But Charles was undaunted.

"Next I suppose you'll be throwing the old 'Swoon Theory' at me, right? Jesus just passed out on the cross and woke up in the

51

tomb. So he didn't rise because he hadn't actually *died*, right? Good luck with *that* one, pal! He'd still be a sagging sad sack. They'd never believe he had conquered death!"

Jake was ready.

"That's no real problem, though, is it? Josephus the historian tells of a friend of his who was taken down alive from the cross. And hadn't Jesus' followers already seen him in pretty bad shape? Would that really have dampened their enthusiasm, seeing him alive after being crucified?" Jake was really getting warmed up now.

"And have you ever noticed that several of the Easter appearances are described as being the *first* one? How many 'first' ones could there have been? And how do you deal with the fact that some of the stories say the disciples didn't even *recognize* Jesus? Later they just decided it *must* have been Jesus. C'mon, that'd never hold up in court and you know it!"

These were oddities that had never occurred to Jake in his believing days. They jumped out at him only once he had taken off the blinders of faith. He had saved them till now. And it looked like he might be making a dent. Charles was, for the moment, out of snappy comebacks.

"Here's something that finally occurred to me, Charles. Why do we even bother trying to dissect these stories under the microscope? Because that's all they are: *stories*, right? I mean, why should we take it for granted that *some* elements in the Easter story are solid history, like Joseph of Arimathea, Mary Magdalene, the tomb being empty—and then argue on that basis that the *last* part of the story, the resurrection, must be a fact, too? You see what I mean? Why should we think *any* of it happened in the *first* place? Isn't it like saying Moby Dick must really exist because we know Captain Ahab was hunting him?"

Jake felt sorry for Charles. He could tell something was happening. A tear escaped the corner of the young man's eye. Jake resisted the temptation to gloat over an apparent victory. He knew what the poor guy must be going through.

"Ah, let me get you something to drink. Want a, uh, cup to pee in?"

Something was happening all right, but a lot more than he thought. A peculiar light began emanating from the nodding Charles. The man's head did not appear to rise to look at him, but suddenly the face, now glowing, was nonetheless staring Jake in the eye. It was quite strange, as if a translucent image of Charles had been superimposed over the slumping form of the actual man. The arms of this new Charles were not bound to the chair. The image was smiling broadly. Jake squeezed his eyes shut, pinched his nose bridge, and opened his eyes, hoping not to see what he knew he would see. It was still there. Jake tried to simulate some bravado.

"Jake Stubbins, I am Charles Menninger's guardian angel. I have followed your discussions with interest. It distresses me that his faith seems to be teetering on the brink, thanks to you. I am heartily sorry we lost you, and I am not willing to let this one be lost, too."

"Uh, so... what now?"

"Let us wrestle, Jake Stubbins, as one of my kind wrestled with another Jacob long ago. Verbally, of course. Shall we take up where you and Charles Menninger left off?"

Jake thought fast. He didn't know what to make of this ghostly Charles-substitute, but he figured he might as well default to habit and keep disputing.

"Why not? Let's shift gears. Let's look at it philosophically. Remember, I used to be where Charles is now, wanting to believe but unable to do it with a clean conscience. I came to see a glaring problem, well, a problem I'd always seen. But I got tired of sweeping it under the rug. Namely, how can the world be so full of suffering and evil if it's run by a good God?"

"Free will, Jake, free will. You must know that."

"Ha! I know that's supposed to get God off the hook, but it doesn't. Christians shift ground at this point. On the one hand, God is in loving control of everything. Not a single bird drops from its branch without God's say-so. But on the other, God is standing on the sidelines, watching as everything goes out of control. Which is it? You're switching back and forth between predestination and deism! Is God in active control or isn't he? We comfort ourselves with the belief that nothing happens without God's will—until something *really* awful happens, and we don't want to blame God, so it must be *our* fault! Look, *you* must know what goes on behind the scenes; where do you draw the line?"

No answer.

"I guess it's a secret, huh? The bottom line goes like this, *Clarence*: if God can stop evil but he doesn't, he's not good. And don't bother saying it would not be 'good' for *us* to allow evil, but that 'good' doesn't necessarily mean the same for God as it does for measly mortals. That's just equivocation. Say what you mean! God is beyond good and evil. Why don't you just *say* so? But if God *can't* stop evil, though he *wishes* he could, then he ain't much of a God, is he?"

Still nothing. But the self-styled angel wasn't smiling as brightly anymore.

"But it gets worse! Ever wondered what *makes* something 'good'? Socrates already asked that question over three hundred years before Jesus, and Jesus never gave him an answer. Let's see if *you* can. Is an act 'good' just because God *says* it is? That's 'divine voluntarism.' It means *nothing* is good, *or* bad, in and of itself. But if it is in*herently* good, and God simply *recognizes* it as such, then 'good' is independent of God and actually su*perior* to him! Like old Zeus!"

Super-Charles did have somewhat to say here.

"No, what you're missing, poor fellow, is that God simply *is* good. His nature is what 'good' *is*. Surely you see that, Jake?"

"No. No, I don't. Here's what's wrong with it. What you're saying, it's just a tautology: God is God. Yeah, big deal. We knew that. You want to say something about God that we wouldn't know just from the definition of God. God is this or that, some new information we wouldn't already know just from his being 'God.' And then we're back to characterizing God by something distinct from him, namely the moral law. God may be moral, but he's not *morality*. But if he *is*, then we're back to divine voluntarism."

No smile at all now.

"Here's another one. Christians always say God is in loving control of the world, even if it doesn't always look like that. You just have to *trust* him. You don't see the whole picture as God does. Well *you* do, don't you? Tell me what I'm missing! The real problem

54

is whether the claim that God is in loving control has *any meaning at all*. Like, what, if it were to happen, would be enough to debunk the claim? What would have to happen before Christians would say, 'Okay, I guess I was wrong! There *is* no loving Providence!'? If the answer is, '*Nothing* would debunk the claim,' well then, I have to conclude you're not making any claim at all! It looks the same whether God is in charge or not! You only know what a statement means once you can contrast it with what it *isn't* saying! Talk all you want: it's just speaking in tongues!"

The image was flickering. Beneath it, or behind it, Charles was still unconscious.

"You're his guardian angel? Well, you're not doing a great job guarding his faith! Mine sure didn't!"

A crazy thought occurred to Jake. He pointed to the seated figure and shouted, "Spirit of ignorance! In the holy name of Reason, I cast you out! Trouble this man no longer! Let him henceforth think for himself!"

Somewhere above or below him, Jake could not quite tell which, some turbulence echoed. Thunder? The earth's crust cracking? The golden light surrounding Charles's sleeping form went out, replaced a moment later by a new radiance, pinkish orange in color. It swirled around the man, whose head now arose, awake, his eyes springing open, filled with this infernal effulgence. He spoke thus:

"*There is a greater than God! There is freedom! There is liberty and there is light! I go now, Jake Stubbins, to seek the company of the Light-bringer!*" With that, he was gone, a very faint hint of sulfur lingering a moment in the air.

Charles Menninger was dizzily shaking his head as Jake loosened his bonds and helped him to his feet.

"You okay, Charles?"

The other man nodded.

"I guess we're done here," Jake said, dabbing sweat from his brow.

Charles looked him in the eye, then winked. "No, I think we're just getting started, partner!"

THE CALIPHATE OF CTHULHU

i. THE MADNESS FROM THE MANUSCRIPT

Sometimes I think the most tragic thing in the world is the unwillingness of people to correlate evident facts for fear of facing the alarming reality that would then emerge. They prefer to flee to the imagined safety of obliviousness and the false comfort of chronic denial. Even when that awful reality catches up with them, they will wish away what must seem inescapably obvious. The ability to combine fantasizing and rationalizing seems to have no limits—except death. And that is the point at which we have all arrived. Though we refused to see it coming, we will have no choice but to see it, and ourselves, going. It seems unlikely that any human being, at least in their present form, will lay eyes on what I am here writing. But I will write it for my own satisfaction, as my last testament.

For years I made my living as a scholar of Middle Eastern religions, which is perhaps less exotic than it sounds, since the major objects of research were the familiar faiths of Judaism, Christianity, and Islam. All three of them have an esoteric as well as the more familiar exoteric, or public, side. Of these, Islam has turned out to have a rather more esoteric aspect than anyone realized until very recently. I realized it earlier than anyone else.

I was certainly not the first to take a new look at Islamic origins. That research had been proceeding apace for a couple of generations. John Wansbrough made a good case for his theory that the so-called "history" of Islam, as well as its supposedly "original" doctrines, were fabricated, not even in Arabia, where Islam is said to have begun, but in Syria, and that the whole business of the Prophet Muhammad, his revelation, even the text of the Koran, was the accumulated product of a new sect triangulating itself between Christian and Jewish faiths, trying to come up with something new and distinctive. Günter Lüling had shown, through intricate textual analysis, with the aid of newly discovered Koranic papyri earlier than any previously known, that as much as one third of the sacred text had been rewritten from Arabic Christian hymnody. Patricia Crone and Michael Cook examined early Jewish and Christian accounts of Muslims (originally called "Hagarenes") suggesting that Muhammad was a kind of John the Baptist figure heralding Umar (familiar to "history" as one of the early caliphs who ruled the Islamic empire after the Prophet's death) as a messiah. Christoph Luxemberg drew attention to certain early inscriptional evidence suggesting that "Muhammad" (meaning "the Illustrious") was a title used for Jesus Christ by Arab Christians and was only later imagined to be the name of a new Arab prophet.

It has been difficult for this new thinking to gain any purchase in the wider world. There is always a predictable intransigence among veteran scholars, a reluctance to take seriously any revolutionary paradigm, acceptance of which would overthrow all their assumptions as well as reams of their work based on them. Indeed, most of the Western "experts" on Islam had traditionally accepted the contrived version of Islamic and Koranic origins promoted as pious propaganda by Muslim savants. In retrospect it seems hard to believe men of such stature would have been content to imbibe uncritically the catechism of the official guardians of an institution. It now seems like Galileo taking astronomy lessons from the Pope.

Nonetheless, the scholarly works setting forth some of these theories did manage to achieve publication, some by pretty obscure presses. Even then, they were like trees falling in a forest with no hearers present. Some were never reprinted because of threats against their authors by "offended" Muslims. Lüling, for instance, was told to stay out of Syria for the sake of his personal safety, and this was long before the apocalyptic war raged upon his own citizens by the bloody-handed Bashir Assad.

Surely the most shocking discovery of all was that of Alton Lindars, who had stumbled across another cache of primitive Koran pages featuring altogether different punctuation, that is vowel points added to the original consonantal text. He found the utterly unexpected: repointed in this manner, the Koranic texts leaped into new focus, revealed to be none other than the long-lost, half-mythical *Al-Azif*, better known to certain eccentrics in Europe and America, and largely through various hoaxes purporting to supply the text, as the *Necronomicon*. Professor Lindars had disappeared, and I had been allowed to examine his papers which contained the tale of his delving. And what a tale it was! Even with the events that have now overtaken the world, their true nature unsuspected at that time, some twenty years ago, I can scarcely credit much of what my colleague related. But the manuscripts were included in his papers, never having been photographed or sent to a museum. And these spoke for themselves. And quite eloquently.

I did not know what to do with the astonishing knowledge that I alone, at least among Westerners, now possessed. Apparently, Professor Lindars didn't either. But I knew that in any case I had more work to do. The discovery obviously necessitated yet another reconfiguring of Islamic origins. I reread the research I mentioned above, gleaned from it the bits of data that contradicted the orthodox story of the beginnings of the Muslim faith, and sought to formulate a new *gestalt* for them in light of the bombshell that the Koran must now be understood as a disguised version of the *Al-Azif*.

Of course, the primary challenge was that of chronology: Abdul Alhazred, a Yemeni from the city of Sanaa, was said to have composed the *Necronomicon* in the years or perhaps decades before his death in 738 C.E. Traditionally, the Koran was compiled after the passing of Muhammad in 632 C.E., collecting his various revelations. There was a century's gap. But here is where the previous researches of Cook and Crone, Wansbrough and the others opened up intriguing possibilities. "Muhammad" was no solid historical quantity. Far from the "new Moses" portrayed by Islamic hagiography, "he" might not have actually been more than a title. And then one must ask: *whose* title? Yes, it had been applied to the Christian savior, but even his title, "the Christ," had been applied to others before and after him. I was beginning to think that "the Illustrious One" referred to Alhazred, who was called by outsiders the "Mad Arab." I thought of a Koranic verse that was not changed in meaning with the new pointation: "No, your compatriot is not mad, nor is this the utterance of an accursed devil." But maybe it *was*.

And the time difference was really not insuperable either. Most of the newer theories suggested in various ways that the standard Muhammad tale was both fictitious and anachronistic anyway. Archaeology had shown that Muhammad's native city of Mecca, supposedly a vibrant commercial center of pilgrimage and guardian of the shrines of the Arabic pantheon, had been but a minor oasis in the seventh century. This fact alone debunked the orthodox account as ill-fitting in both space and time. And if, as had seemed clear from the work of Lüling, Crone and Cook, and the rest, the whole saga of the Prophet charged by the angel Gabriel to reveal a new Arabic revelation, was a complete fabrication, one might well ask what had been in so desperate need of masking? Perhaps the true origin of Islam as the cult of the Old Ones. The cult of Cthulhu, ever since it had come to light through a set of coincidences in 1926, had been regarded as a secret cult. And that it was, but it was a secret hidden in plain sight. And today it boasts more than a billion members.

The initial, largely accidental discovery of the Cthulhu cult was marked by what the tabloid press called a repeat of King Tut's curse, for all those men whose disparate testimonies to the vile rites of the cult had come to suspicious and tragic ends. But that need not be attributed to conspiracy-theory paranoia. Some religions will both dissemble to protect their faith from outside scrutiny and seek bloody vengeance on any who reveal them. Just think of the numerous *fatwas* pronounced again novelists, musicians, and even editorial cartoonists for their slights, real or imagined, against Holy Islam. And this is, I suggest, no mere analogy.

ii. THE CRAWLING CHAOS

I said it was, in retrospect, remarkable that Western scholars of Islam obediently imbibed the "official" story of the beginnings of Islam conveniently supplied them by the guardians of the Islamic institution. Most are still quite happy with the party line, despite the work of the critical revisionists I have mentioned and who have influenced me. But the old pattern has reproduced itself in yet another form. Academics, marching lock-step with the doctrines of Political Correctness, propagate in their classrooms the inaccurate notion that Muslims belong to a "religion of peace" and that the Koran teaches tolerance, that Muslims had always been the best friends of Jews until the Western powers colonized and exploited the remains of the Ottoman Empire after the First World War. Perhaps this rehearsal of a false history was a witting strategy: to teach the history that *should* have been rather than history as it actually occurred. The goal would be to shape the present by fabricating a past to which the present might conform. And, notoriously, to suggest otherwise would bring down upon one's head the wrath of one's Politically Correct colleagues, whose devotion to Islamic public relations begins to look like the Stockholm Syndrome.

And it goes farther than that, much farther. Militant Muslims, as is no secret, learned to take advantage of Western societies who crumbled beneath the burden of guilt laid upon them by Third-World demagogues like Franz Fanon, adopting the self-image of chastened former oppressors, ashamed of their patriotism and the achievements of Euro-American civilization. They accepted what their critics taught them about themselves and became frightened mice, intimidated by any allegation of prejudice, oppression, even "insensitivity." And all this in the teeth of ever-increasing terrorist violence. Cowed and cowardly American, Canadian, and British "leaders" tried their absurd best to deny that mass murders by suicide bombers, airplane hijackings, church burnings and human trafficking of non-Muslims were terrorism at all, maintaining instead that they were merely run-of-the-mill "crimes" on the same level with larceny or, at worst, violence done by disgruntled employees. There were even anti-blasphemy laws enacted, so that anyone overheard so much as criticizing "the religion of peace" could be arrested. Other religions? Mock them at your pleasure, by all means.

In the time of the twentieth-century Cold War, one used to hear the term "Finlandization." It referred to appeasement of, and accommodation to, the Soviet Union, especially by adjacent

Finland. The Finns knew they were helpless against the vast might of the Soviet Empire, and, though not quite a puppet state like the miserable Warsaw Pacts countries, "allies" of the U.S.S.R., the Finns knew what was good for them and did nothing to affront their iron-fisted neighbor. "When Russia gets a cold, Finland sneezes." And now the whole of the West is "Finlandized" in mute subservience to Islamo-fascism. One could almost forgive the cowardice if it were simply a matter of self-preservation against an overwhelming military threat ("Better red than dead"). But it is not. Instead, it is more contemptible still, being the product of a paralysis of nerve. The Western societies and their governments no longer feel they have any right to act, to stand up for themselves, as if fearing that any act, any protest, against the scolding, whining barbarians of the Muslim states would make them liable to cat-calls of racism and "Islamophobia."

These are things I could never admit to myself, much less speak aloud. Social and academic speech codes, both implicit and explicit, made it impossible to voice such opinions. To do so would meet the same reception as if one were to say, "What's so bad about lynchings, or rape?"

Though the leaders of the Islamo-fascist Jihad made absolutely no secret of their design to infiltrate the liberal democracies of the West by means of immigration, refusal to assimilate, and demanding the establishment of medieval Sharia law, complete with stonings, amputations, child marriages and all, we felt (or were made to feel) like Ku Klux Klan bigots if we balked. No one had learned the old lesson that there is a very definite limit to tolerance, namely, that one cannot affirm *intolerance* as another legitimate option, for it is a cancer cell that will sooner or later devour the body.

This is the only way to explain how the supposedly freedom-loving West turned against the only democracy in Southwest Asia, Israel, turning a blind eye to the ceaseless atrocities visited upon her by her murderous neighbors. When Iran made no bones about her intention to eradicate Israel, our leaders cared only to appease these planners of the Second Shoah. Ritually repeating the old assurances that America would defend Israel, we did nothing when Iran, aided by her partner Russia, rained nuclear annihilation upon our "friends" the Jews. The official American response was to regret that peace talks had never succeeded. In other words, it was the Jews' own fault for not saving Iran the trouble and allowing the Palestinian terrorists to exterminate them, as they had admitted was their intent for decades.

Western civilization had become decadent and effeminate, cowardly and delusional. It is the way of history that, when a great power so declines, it offers itself as prey to more vital, if barbaric, "civilizations." And so it has happened. This much I knew. But the discovery of the true nature of Islam as the humanity-hating cult of Cthulhu and Yog-Sothoth has supplied the answer to the long-standing enigma: how came Islam to be a nihilistic death cult? The answer: it only came out of the closet.

It was hard, however, to imagine that most Muslims in the modern day understood the true identity of Islam as Yog-Sothothery, of Muhammad as the Mad Arab. I had to believe that the vast majority knew nothing of this, as reflected in their seeming indifference to the ascendancy of Islamic extremism. True, few of them said much by way of protest, but one could hope that was due to their fear of deadly reprisals. Ironically, these were the Muslims who had more or less successfully assimilated to Western societies. They had learned both our modern ways and our kowtowing cowardice.

I was convinced that the truth about the religion was reserved for a small coterie of initiates. I remembered the complaints of Sunni Muslims of a few centuries ago to the effect that the Ismail'i branch of Shi'ism was ultimately nihilistic because, with ever higher degrees of initiation, the faithful learned that every traditional Islamic doctrine and pious practice represented only a symbolic veil of the highest truth: a quasi-Buddhistic Void. Now I had reason to believe that even *that* characterization was only another concealment: the object of final enlightenment was rather the Crawling Chaos called Nyarlathotep and Azathoth in the re-pointed Arabic text.

iii. BENEATH THE BURKHA

All of this, the new discovery, the new knowledge, though quite alarming, was still, in one sense, unreal to me. It had the feel of a "reality" existing on paper, like the many historical reconstructions with which scholars busy themselves. What I had pieced together did seem cogent, but in the sense that an academic paper or seminar presentation does. It was hard to feel it was part of the real world, the world in which Islamic extremism held increasing sway—even though what I had surmised made such good sense of those phenomena. One can scarcely ever corroborate a hypothesis about ancient history: the evidence is lost or fragmentary. So it remains a kind of educated guessing game. But if the plague of fanatical terror and international subversion were really the product of the disguised Cthulhu cult, there ought to be some way, at least in principle, to turn up some evidence, if only I could figure out some way to do it. That would bring the matter down to earth. And then maybe (who knows?) something might be done about it. I set about considering my options.

It wasn't long before something occurred to me. But before I could follow up on it, something else presented itself. It was a news item concerning a shooting incident in a mosque in Minneapolis where, improbably, given the weather, there was a large Somali community. These incidents are nowadays so tragically common that one hardly notices the reports anymore. But this one struck me as odd in that the killer was himself a Muslim and even a recent member of the congregation he targeted. True, religion might have had nothing to do with it, as when a church member starts shooting up his house of worship out of general frustration with his life's circumstances. But I had a feeling it was worth checking out.

I was scheduled to give a paper at the upcoming convention of the American Academy of Religion in an adjacent state, so I resolved to rent a car and drive over to the mental hospital where the shooter was still under observation. I would present my credentials to the authorities and offer my services. I felt sure they would welcome any assistance an expert in Islam might supply. I decided to call ahead and make arrangements before I got there. It saved me some time, since he had just been transferred to a larger facility with a bigger staff. And they did indeed welcome my visit.

The paper I gave was, as far as I was concerned, pretty much a charade in light of what I had recently come to believe. It was some tame thing on the identity of the mysterious "Sabeans" counted among the "People of the Book" in the Koran. The other papers in the section were similarly inconsequential. Of course I had some real news, had I dared to share it, but that was out of the question. I skipped a committee meeting and left the conference hotel as soon as I could escape. From one loony bin to another, I suppose.

I had no difficulty finding the facility. Signs made it impossible to miss. The parking attendant motioned me into the physicians' lot. He must have been given my information in advance and known to watch for me. I was quickly cleared at the front desk and had to wait only a few minutes for an orderly, who conducted me to the shooter's room. On the way he told me the man's name, withheld in the news report. He was a close relative of an important Somali government official, and it was understandably a sensitive matter.

Entering the room, the first thing I noticed was the padded restraints on young Mr. Rahmani's wrists. The second was the man's characteristic Somali good looks: the mahogany coloring, the high cheek bones and forehead, the chiseled features. He appeared calm enough and raised his clear eyes to meet mine. I introduced myself and sat down beside his bed.

"Are you another psychiatrist?"

"No, I am a different kind of doctor, a teacher and researcher. I specialize in the religions of the Middle East, including Islam. If it's all right with you, I would like to talk with you about the incident in the mosque. You seem like a rational person. I would like to understand what might have motivated you. It could be important in your case. I gather you lost your faith in Islam. You must have felt betrayed by those who taught it to you. Did you feel you had to get back at them?"

He turned away from me and looked ahead, silently considering his answer. I did not get the feeling he was reluctant to talk.

"Dr. McNair, I am going to tell you a story, not a long one, but one you will not believe. I have told the doctors my story, and I believe it would have been enough to get me confined here even if I had not done... what I did."

"Try me. I promise to take you seriously."

"Very well. Here goes. I had come late to the mosque for Friday prayers. We know not to disturb the service once it is underway, so I decided not to enter through the usual door. I didn't know much of the layout of the building, because I had only ever come right in and gone right out. So I went down an alleyway looking for a side door. I found one and tried the knob, not knowing where it might lead. It was a stupid thing to do. I'm sure you know how strictly Muslims separate men from women, lest the lust of the men be kindled. This, they say, is why our women go veiled. They are covered head to foot in the garment called the hijab or the burkha. You have seen them many times, I'm sure."

I nodded. While regretting that Muslim women had to encumber themselves in this manner, I had long thought Westerners misunderstood the reason for the enveloping garb. It was not due to a chauvinist belief that women were temptresses, but rather that men could not be trusted not to become enflamed with lust at the sight of them. Mr. Rahmani continued, seemingly encouraged by my lack of a patronizing tone.

"As soon as I crossed the threshold the screams began. I had trespassed into a women's dressing room of some kind. Their bodies and faces were on full display. I was not ready for the sight, which I had no business seeing."

I tried hard to suppress a smile. The story was not without a comical aspect, though I knew no Muslim, male or female, would see any humor in it.

"But how did this shake your faith? Were the imams too strict in their discipline? Did they excommunicate you?"

"No, at least not yet, though I do expect to feel their wrath. What I beheld was not anything that could cause a man to lust after the lovely form of the female."

He fell silent here, considering whether to go on. I reassured him he could speak freely with nothing to fear from me.

"The form of them was not that of a human being, Doctor.

They had been covered in black fabric to conceal their shapelessness, their... tentacles, their many eyes... Oh, it was terrible. It *is* terrible."

"I begin to see the reason for your targeting the women when you returned to the mosque. At least that's what they've said you did."

"Yes, and what I was trying to do was reveal to the world what I had seen. I knew I would never get away with it, and I didn't try. I just hoped the news would cover the story. And they did. But not a word of what the females proved to be. You know the media. It would be condemned as Islamophobia, even *this*! *Especially* this.

"Admit it, sir, you think me hopelessly insane. I half think so myself."

"Mr. Rahmani, I honestly don't know what to think. I can't assume you were hallucinating, though you may have been. I don't think the psychiatrists or the courts are going to take this seriously, but I do. And I'll do whatever I can."

A few days later I received a call from the hospital informing me that Mr. Rahmani was dead. He had been given a fatal dose of the wrong drug by an orderly no one could now find. I was sad for him, scared for me.

iv. THE STONE FROM HEAVEN

I was pretty confident that there was or soon would be a *fatwa* leveled against me by whomever had ordered the death of Rahmani. Given the situation, and what I now knew, that was obvious. I determined to make whatever time I had left to me count for something. I would try my best to do what young Rahmani tried to do: give the world a clue about the true danger ready to devour them.

Why not beard the lion in its lair? Even if it killed me. It would anyway, one way or another. I booked a flight to Saudi Arabia. I would visit Mecca, the holiest city of Islam, where unbelievers dare not tread. Non-Muslims are forbidden under pain of death to infiltrate the Hajj, the pilgrimage required of all able-bodied Muslims at least once in their lives. Few unbelievers had ever risked it. Naturally, not many would even be interested. A few who tried it did not get away with it. But the renowned nineteenth-century explorer Richard Burton (do I need to tell you it wasn't the actor?) disguised himself in Arab robes, dyed his skin, and grew a beard. He was of course quite fluent in Arabic and knew conventional Islam inside and out—better than most Muslims. He got into the city, performed the traditional rites, and joined the pious tourists in entering the Kaaba. This is the Holy of Holies, a gigantic pavilion draped by great black, gold-trimmed curtains, containing a huge and ancient meteorite. Islamic legend had it that this "Black Stone" was the very site where in biblical days the Patriarch Abraham had come to sacrifice his son, though Muslims believed it was Ishmael, the ancestor of the Arab nation, not Isaac, who at the last moment was reprieved from his father's obsidian blade. Burton saw all this, participating no doubt with real reverence and no cynicism. But he waited till he was safely back on his native soil before publicizing his feat. Needless to say, he was never welcome to set foot in the sands of Arabia again.

I am certainly no bold adventurer, but I felt pretty sure I could duplicate Burton's ruse. Given the advanced state of Western knowledge of Islam, I knew much more of the rituals and protocols than he had known. Naturally, I had long since gained great fluency in the Arabic tongue. And the disguise was easy to arrange, especially since all pilgrims to Mecca wear identical, simple white sheets to symbolize the spiritual equality of all Muslims. For the duration of the Hajj, there were no rich, no poor, no masters, no slaves. The sight of this is what revolutionized Malcolm X's understanding of Islam, leading him to break with the racist sectarianism of the Honorable Elijah Muhammad's Nation of Islam, popularly dubbed "the Black Muslims."

There is no need to tarry on the details of my flight, except to note that I was surprised to get there without incident. I admit I was suspiciously glancing about me in the airport and on board. The farther I got, the more nearly relaxed I grew, deciding that an assassin could have picked me off at any of several opportunities. If I had managed to come this far safely, perhaps I would not be hindered.

Once in Mecca, I joined the crowds in fulfilling the duties of a pilgrim, including casting a pebble into the sacred well of Zemzem to pelt the devils believed to dwell at the bottom. We venerated the tombs of various saints and sheiks, calling upon them to intercede for us on the Day of Judgment, disregarding the clear teaching of the Koran that every man must bear his own burden of guilt without intercession from the righteous. It was all quite touching. I could scarcely imagine that these dear souls had any faintest idea of the secret origin and character of their religion. But I was equally persuaded that an increasing number did, as scholars estimated that fully ten to fifteen percent of Muslims worldwide adhered to the bloodthirsty ideals of the Jihad, and dreamed of a universal caliphate. And I knew too well where all that came from.

It was with considerable relief, as well as a genuine thrill, that I, amid a great company of praying and chanting Muslims, finally slipped between the tall sable curtains and beheld the Black Stone. Fortunately, pilgrims are allowed to circle the object slowly and closely, so I had a fine opportunity to study it by ample torch light. I was taken aback to see that the stone cube was covered with pictorial bas reliefs as well as inscribed captions in no language I had ever seen. And the carvings! It was the last thing I could have expected in light of the strict Islamic prohibition of images of living things, as in Judaism, whence the idea was borrowed. For here were represented all manner of marine creatures, all attendant upon what looked like a colossal octopus on one side, a toad creature with bat's ears on the next, something like a crustacean on the third, and a shapeless mass surrounded by stars on the fourth.

As it was our turn to make room for others, I exited, amazed at what I had seen. And then a strange, vague sense of recognition gelled, and I recognized the thing. It had to be the fabled Abhoth Block, at which the Mad Arab had hinted wildly, a meteorite indeed, but one brought to earth by nameless creatures from the stars in the dawn age of the world. His infamous couplet, "In aeons past, some black fate brought it here / and left it for all men to fear," was equivocal in meaning no longer.

v. STARRY WISDOM

The next day I happily departed Mecca with much to think about. As I drove back to my hotel next to the airport, I weighed my next steps. I now felt absolutely certain the connections I had made were valid. But I was equally certain that there was no chance of getting anyone, whether in academia or in the government, to believe me. They would probably make sure I took Rahmani's bed in the psychiatric hospital. And in the end, what real difference would the truth make even if I managed to convince the authorities? Whether one referred to the Lord of Jihad as Allah or as Cthulhu, the insane hatred and the thirst for world domination posed the same danger, and the spineless governments of the West would expire like a sick man on his deathbed in either case.

There was one more surprise awaiting me when I opened the door and entered my hotel room. A man sat in the corner shadows waiting for me. At once, with anticlimactic resignation, I knew the assassins of the cult had caught up with me.

"Greetings, Professor."

The voice and the accent were American. The seated figure motioned me to the chair across from him, and I sat. I still could not see his features.

"Is this the end?"

"Do you mean the end for you, or the End in a collective sense? Very shortly now the world will witness a mutual discharge of nuclear weapons between this country and its Shi'ite rival, Iran. I believe that shortly afterward, Pakistan will press the Jihad upon heathen India. Then the faithful in Central Asia will sweep over their former overlords, Russia and China. Our America can be depended upon to hide its timid head in the radioactive sand. Did you ever see the film *On the Beach*? It was prophetic, believe me. But from the glowing debris a glorious new world will arise. You may take part in it if you wish."

My head was spinning. I began to feel nausea. My blood pounded in my ears.

"Dr. McNair, I wanted, as a colleague, to congratulate you on forging a path to this destination. You have ferreted out the truth of the matter. Soon you will know much more, perhaps more than you ever wanted to know. You will learn the secret of the Lost Tomb of Nephren-Ka, of the Host of Ekron, of the Pyramid of Koth-Serapis, and of how the pyramids were really built. You will learn of primordial Stygia and Acheron, and of the Lords of the Fire Mist. These are things not taught by that Western science of which we were both so proud."

I felt sure I knew this man. Not personally, but I must have heard him speak on more than one occasion.

"Let me turn on the light. I believe I will know you by sight."

"Very well. You may."

I was right: this was Professor Alton Lindars. He was the one whose papers had been given me. He it was who had recognized in the alternate pointation of the Koran the underlying text of the *Al Azif*—and then disappeared. I had been present for some of his earlier lectures at the American Society for Oriental Research. He now looked older, as expected, but also subtly altered in a queer way hard to describe. And I could swear I saw his beard *moving* slightly.

"Dr. McNair, do you recall what St. Paul said? 'Now we know in part and we prophesy in part. But when the perfect comes, the imperfect will pass away. Now we see in a glass darkly, but then face to face.' You and I have pieced together fragments and hints like the researchers who reassembled tiny fragments of the Dead Sea Scrolls. None of that is of any consequence anymore. Very soon now we will be seeing face to face. *Iä! Shub-Niggurath! Azathoth-ho-Akbar!*"

I had no alternative. If the world I knew was to pass away, it only made sense to take refuge in another. It would certainly be a very different world, one whose values would be alien, even repugnant to me. But what choice did I have? If there is a God even remotely like the one I grew up believing in, may he forgive me. I have, in the last days remaining, while waiting out the birth pangs of a new age, recorded my experiences along this road to the Apocalypse. Who knows if anyone will ever read it? You can answer more truly than I. Come, Lord Cthulhu!

❖

THE CASTLE OF THE HERETICS

i POUNDING THUNDER

The steed fairly stampeded over and between the vineyard-clad hills of southern France. No alteration of terrain, no obstacle, broke the pace of the horse, driven on by its rider, an impressively tall and broad man hunched forward, blue eyes fixed on the path ahead of him. The mounted man, named Cormac Fitzgeoffrey, was not abusing his faithful steed. Neither did he apply whip or spur; he had trained the horse to this mad pace. Cormac was a living engine of endurance, a born warrior who was accustomed to riding for days without sleep, not even while he paused to permit his steed to rest, preferring to brood in his black Gaelic fashion. In his early fifties, one might have estimated him as fully two decades younger. No gray faded his straw-brown mop of hair. Scars lined his face, but no lines of age. Close to seven feet in height, his limbs were massively muscled, the product not of calisthenics but of constant weapons training and physical combat.

Cormac Fitzgeoffrey, as a youth, had thrown in with the troops of the Third Crusade, caring little for the stated cause but eager to join in a grand conflict in exotic climes. No Christian, Cormac bore no grudge against the Moslems, but simply felt the challenge a hunter feels at the prospect of tracking some unfamiliar game. He had been eager to match his longsword against the crescent scimitars of Saladin and his hordes. The Crusade managed to drive the Moslems out of a few coastal cities like Acre and Jaffa but failed to achieve its primary objective, freeing Holy Jerusalem from the shadow of Mohammedanism. But it was all the same to Cormac. He had joined himself to a party of the Templar Knights, warrior monks stationed in the region to protect Christian pilgrims who felt

71

compelled to visit the ancient city like hapless moths drawn to the flame. There was fighting on the narrow, winding streets, finally breaching the Dome of the Rock, the structure erected on the site of the ruined Jewish Temple.

Though the Temple of Herod the Great had been razed a millennium earlier by the Romans and their local allies the Idumeans, rumor spoke of a subterranean warren of tunnels and chambers containing the treasures of the half-mythical King Solomon, he who had bound the very devils to his service gathering the vast stone blocks to build the Temple. The rumors had proven true, and the Templars had spirited away what they could carry from the torch-glinting heap of riches. A couple of the blood-drenched monks carried between them a golden chest surmounted by winged harpies. Cormac had assumed he should receive a share of the spoils when the party should win their way back to camp, but his eye at once fell upon a sword of strange workmanship, its blade engraven with sigils or runes in some language unknown to him. This he had seized for himself on the spot, deciding to be content with it as his portion of the booty. That was well, since the Templars, he soon discovered, considered the plunder sacrosanct relics past all monetary value, henceforth under the protection of the Templar order. But he kept the sword for himself. He was carrying it now.

The afternoon was waning. The reddening skies flickered with tongues of brighter orange as Cormac neared the site of the siege, the fortress of Monsegur, where the last of the notorious Cathar heretics were holed up, desperately battling toward a foredoomed end. Their foemen, the troops of the seneschal of Carcosa and the Archbishop of Narbonne, were Catholic Christians, no pious zealots of faith like the Templars, but a mixed multitude of mercenaries and laymen who'd been promised relief from Purgatory if they would undertake the holy butchery they were now engaged in. Cormac reined in his mount, then surveyed the situation. He was still outside the camp of the besiegers. He was not afraid of anyone seeing him. He intended to approach the largest tent he could see and offer his services as a mercenary. But first he turned the horse and made his way to the nearest village where he found a stable and paid a good sum to house the horse till his business was finished. He retraced his path to the camp on foot. He would have no use for the animal till it was done. Nor could he leave him among the horses of the besiegers. When finished with his work, it would not be wise for him to return to the Catholic camp. His intended exit from the fray lay along a different course.

Cormac passed the outer ring of the encampment, almost a transitory village in its own right with its collection of weaponers, blacksmiths, harlots, and mess kitchens. Despite their relentless activity, all the merchants and artisans could not resist sparing him a wondering glance, as Cormac towered over even the tallest of the French mercenaries and papal troops alike. No one sought to bar his way, however, feeling no threat from a man offering no aggressive gesture. All assumed he was what he pretended to be: a wandering adventurer looking to sell his sword arm. None had reason to suspect his real intention, or his mission. No Galahad, he had nonetheless come in search of the Holy Grail.

Once the greedy Philip IV had undertaken his persecution of the Templars, cloaking his lust for their massive wealth beneath fabricated charges of apostasy and heresy, many of the Templar Knights had sought refuge among the villages of the Gnostic Cathar sect, little suspecting they were jumping out of the frying pan into the fire. Of all this Cormac Fitzgeoffrey knew nothing until a messenger caught up with him in Northern France, bearing news from one of the Gael's old battle companions, Reynard, one of the Templars who had fought alongside him as they breached the hidden treasury of King Solomon. King Philip had successfully confiscated nearly all of the holdings of the Templars, who had become the greatest bankers of Europe, frequently lending huge sums to various kings and princes who habitually spent far in excess of their own resources. Reynard was one of the refugees among the Cathars, and with him he managed to bring the greatest of all the hidden relics, the chalice of Jesus Christ from the Last Supper.

Some legends told that Jesus' uncle, Joseph of Arimathea, had carried the Grail to Brittany and thence to Glastonbury, but in fact it was another of Jesus' sympathizers, Nicodemus, who had hidden it in the vault under the Herodian Temple, where the Templars had discovered it a millennium later. Reynard thought it his duty to keep the holy chalice out of the profane hands of the avaricious king. He had appropriated it and handed it over to the Cathari whom he considered more fitting inheritors of the precious object.

But of course this meant that the Grail, too, had passed from the frying pan into the flames. Reynard's message made it clear: the end was not far off. He knew the defenders of Monsegur were doomed. But he was determined that the Grail should not end up in the hands of their Catholic persecutors. There was a way one man might spirit it away, but he could not be that man, for his escape would amount to deserting the Cathari who had given him shelter. Reynard should tell him more when and if Cormac arrived.

Upon receipt of this puzzling message, Cormac had risen without hesitation, taking from the purse at his broad, nail-studded belt some coins, and told the messenger to take his room at the inn and rest up there for as long as the coins held out. Withal he was on his way.

ii. OVER THE RAMPARTS

Cormac spotted one of the huge dinosaur-like ballistas and approached the man in charge of it, a tall fellow who suddenly seemed to shrink when measured against the giant Gael. Cormac tapped him on the shoulder, whereupon the man turned and flinched at the sight of him. But the newcomer did not challenge him, only asking him a question. "Surely a mighty siege engine! I see you use it to hurl flaming missiles into the enemy's fortress. And to good effect! The tall flames attest that."

"Aye, I do right well. I have a good eye for it, or so they tell me."

"Friend, I wonder if you might be willing to help me. I need a ride—up there!"

"You mean," he looked suspiciously at Cormac, at the catapult, and back at Cormac, "you? In that?"

The giant chuckled, something rarely seen of him.

"Yes, my man. As soon as it cools down a bit from its last passenger!"

The man shrugged, then fetched a pair of buckets, splashing

their contents into the concavity to speed its cooling. Before long, Cormac judged it cool enough and crawled into the hollow ball, clutching his sword hilt before him. The arm of the great machine drew back and hurled its burden into the smoky sky.

Cormac had undertaken many adventures in his time, but none of them had afforded the opportunity of *flight*. It was exhilarating but short-lived. He experienced a brief panic as he feared the momentum of the launch might propel him past the Cathar citadel into the rocky slopes beyond. But his faith in the man operating the machine was justified. As Cormac found himself passing over the gaping heads of the Cathar defenders, he shot out his arms and legs, spread-eagled, in order to break his speed. He dropped to the ground in a crouch, sword in hand, ready to take on attackers though hoping he would not have to. Nor did he, for at once he heard the familiar voice of Reynard: "No, no, my brothers! He is a *friend*. He is come to *help* us!"

Cormac embraced his old comrade, who was clad in his threadbare, blood-spattered Templar tunic. Holes and rips in the white fabric had nearly obliterated the crimson cross on the breast, but Cormac recognized it from the old days. Initially nonplussed, the Cathars quickly turned back to their stations along the crenelated ramparts. One or two flaming arrows homed in on Cormac, by sheer luck, but their target easily batted them aside with the flat of his blade. He followed as Reynard motioned him down a set of steps to the interior of the fortress.

Soon the two men sat on either side of a massive fieldstone fireplace. The flickering firelight imparted a sinister cast to Reynard's weary features as he settled in his chair. Cormac stared expectantly at his old friend, while Reynard seemed to have difficulty gathering his thoughts. Finally he spoke, his tone apologetic.

"Thank you, friend Cormac, for coming to share in our hour of need."

Cormac, not impatient but eager, came to the point.

"What is the plan? You hand over the Grail and I take it... where?"

"I shall lead you to a secret door opening onto the foot of the mountain, whence you shall carry it to safety. Where exactly, I leave to your discretion. We are in the last refuge of the Cathari known to me, or I should guide you to another. As for the chalice itself, I... uh... I fear it is not in my possession!"

"*What?*" Cormac sprang to his booted feet. "Then my coming here was for *nothing?!*"

Reynard stroked his reddish goatee with one nervous hand, his eyes averted.

"Nay, nay, Cormac! The Grail is here, but I do not have it. It is... complicated. It will doubtless sound like folly to you. Only to the Cathari does it make sense. I am not one of their order, but perhaps I can explain it. Their beliefs are, shall we say, unusual. They see the world as a vast war between two rival forces, the powers of Light and the powers of Darkness. These they consider equally matched, hence the eternal stalemate. All good things in this world mark a victory of the Light. All plagues, earthquakes, famines, and crimes are reckoned as assaults of the Dark forces. They believe Christ came into the world to reveal all this, and to summon the righteous to marshal their numbers to aid him in the battle for the cosmos."

Sitting again, his brows knit and his eyes projecting a cold stare, Cormac replied, drily, "And how, pray tell, are they to do *that?*"

"Well, naturally, they teach that all good deeds are blows struck on behalf of the Light, and that the common believers should try their best to avoid sinning. But that is not sufficient. Few even of them know that the key to the hidden cosmic war is to *enact it in ritual form*. To this end, the Perfects, as they are called, divide their number into two dueling hosts, one representing the Light, the other the Darkness. They, ah, actually arm themselves and, er, fight one another in a designated set of chambers in this castle. If you listen closely you may hear the faint clashing of their weapons."

Cormac's bafflement was matched only by his embarrassment for his old friend, for this was the most outrageous notion ever to strike his ears.

"And what a grim spectacle *this* must be! Are not these men aging ascetics? Can they even hold their weapons steady? With what do the fools fight? Broom sticks?" He doubled over with belly-deep laughter. Reynard looked as if he had expected it, nor did the absurdity of the whole business escape him. Patiently, he waited for the Gael's barking hilarity to subside, then spoke.

"I fear there is a good bit more to it than that, old friend, and the rest is in no wise amusing. You see, their child-like pretense is designed to invoke real Powers from either side, devils and angels. For these are no mere wives' tales to frighten children as men like us have long believed. As the play-battle waxes and wanes, so does the violence between the warring spirits unseen above them. And to reach the Grail, Cormac, you must intervene in this battle. I believe you can break the stalemate that has so far resulted from the evenly matched warfare of pious weaklings."

Cormac found this newly and definitely intriguing. No humor in this voice this time.

"And exactly who would I be fighting? Surely not your spindle-shanked monks?"

This time it was Reynard's turn to laugh, though not so heartily, as the burden of dread and imminent massacre weighed heavily upon him.

"Nay, Cormac. I would not unleash a lion among rabbits. I believe your presence, and not least that blade of yours, will cause the demons to take solid form on this material plane."

"My sword? Why should that make such a difference?"

"I know where you obtained it. I saw you take it those years ago from the Temple treasure trove. You bear the potent Sword of Solomon, Master of Demons, Vanquisher of Asmodeus! It is no mere length of steel plated with gold. In all your conflicts you have never beheld its true power, for up till now, you have faced only mortal foes."

Cormac drew the sword from its sheath and looked at the inset sigils, no longer so familiar given the new light Reynard's words had shed upon them. His eyes narrowed, and his lips smiled. He was eager to be about his task.

iii. THE GOLDEN SWORD

After further instructions and directions, Reynard bade his friend farewell and returned to the fray atop the fortress, leaving Cormac to his own devices against the shadowy forces he must momentarily face. Undaunted, he paced down the torch-lit corridor that led to the war games, still skeptical. How could Reynard be so sure the Cathars were right about their role as proxies for unseen creatures? He said he was no Cathar initiate, but he certainly sounded like one. Nonetheless, it was best to be vigilant in case there should be any truth to it.

Cormac paused and peeked around a corner. The room was a long, bare hall. The walls were draped with very old tapestries. Whatever they had once depicted was indistinguishable now. No rugs softened the flagstone floor. A snicker almost escaped the Gael at the sight of the inept and clownish holy men behaving like children at play. One monk aimed a blow as best he could, swinging his wooden sword wide of his mark and stumbling with his momentum. Blows that did manage to connect were but glancing taps, but even these were sufficient to stagger the scarecrows who received them.

But an oddity up near the ceiling stifled Cormac's chuckle and galvanized his thews. He squinted to gain a clearer sight of what seemed a slow-moving mist or shadow drifting purposefully like a great vulture, though no actual shape could be discerned. Then another, and another, half-appeared.

Consternation gave way to real alarm when Cormac saw, or thought he saw, one of the things seize one of the monks, who dropped his wooden sword and seemed to be getting pulled up into an invisible trap door. But there was no door up there. There was, however, surely something here that should not be. And as he made ready to step into the chamber, in which both factions of the monks now stood motionless, staring at the ceiling, the Gael noticed the strange designs on his sword blade had begun to glow with a strange radiance. As if this were a signal, Cormac strode into the room.

He was amazed to see an altar set up at the far end of the room upon which rested what had to be the Holy Grail! Nothing about the chalice betrayed its historic significance. It looked to be made from some hybrid of silver and gold but bore no particular adornment or engraving. Apparently unprotected, it stood out in the open for anyone to see—and seize! Cormac barreled on through the stunned monks who scattered before him. But when he drew near the altar, he was stunned to collide with an unseen barrier. Shaking his aching head, he looked again at the cup, now thinking it had been secured behind some very hard and thick glass. If so, he would find some way to pound his way through it. He could hear murmuring and chuckling among the monks at the opposite end of the chamber but gave his attention to what was before him, which appeared to be nothing at all, nothing separating him from the object of his quest. No matter his angle of view, Cormac could see no light reflection, no glint, no empty likeness of himself such as a glass should offer. He felt no angry frustration, just confusion, as nothing made sense. He was a pragmatic man of action, and mysteries were not to his liking. What was keeping him from the relic? And why had Reynard not informed him about it?

Unless he *had*...

Cormac stood and looked at the sword in his hand. Perhaps Reynard's words had not been pious drivel. On a hunch (or was it an inspiration?) the Gael extended the sword and lightly touched the invisible barrier. Or rather, he did *not* touch it since it was now gone. The Sword of Solomon, if that was truly what it was, seemed to have been a key in a lock.

He started to reach for the chalice but thought it best to give a look behind him first. Good thing, too. Because he no longer saw the fidgeting old scarecrows in their threadbare habits. They had been replaced by, or even turned into, an advancing gang of horned and well-muscled battlers. For a split second Cormac thought they wore Viking helms until they came a step closer and he could see the horns came directly out of their skulls. And as for that, some had but swaths of fraying skin stretched over their skulls. Some possessed two eyes, or sockets, some with three. By Judas, some had the heads and hooves of beasts! And he would later recall the resemblance of one or two of the intact human faces to old foes he had slain in battle or brawl. So the pretend combat of the monkish

79

host was in truth more than it seemed. Supernatural forces were in play!

There must have been at least twenty of these devils, all armed either with weapons or scythe-like talons. Rarely had he faced such odds alone, but never had he shirked a battle, no matter how strong or numerous the foe. Cormac planted his feet apart for greater stability. A feral grin turned into a predatory growl as he instinctively welcomed the fray. They might in truth be demons from hell, but he was Cormac Fitzgeoffrey, reputed by most to be a demon in his own right. He did not know what might happen when his blade made contact with such alien flesh, but that did not daunt him.

Cormac raised his sword aloft in a gesture of defiance. The result surprised him, for his attackers instantly came to a screeching halt! One guttural, strangely echoing voice exclaimed, "*Behold! The Son of David!*" It made a bizarre spectacle, a horde of demons falling to their calloused knees like pious Christians at prayer. Was it some sort of trick? But none made a move. Nonplussed, Cormac was visibly confused, though none of those kneeling noticed, their hideous heads bowed low.

At once it struck him, and he lowered the golden sword and gazed at it. The sigils, which Cormac now began to realize must be inscriptions in the Hebrew tongue, were glowing again. Reynard had called the blade Solomon's, and called Solomon the Master of Demons. That power must have come from his enchanted weapon, or passed into it from the hand of him who had it forged.

"You must obey me, yes?"

A submissive muttering was sufficient answer.

"Then hear my command, devils of hell! I think you will not find it onerous. You shall depart and fall upon the besieging host below! Why do you wait? Be about it!"

All at once, the formidable fiends were just old men again, fainting on the stone-flagged floor. Cormac did not doubt that the spirits that had inhabited their physical forms had rushed to join the battle against the Catholic troops below. With a hearty laugh, he turned back toward the table on which the Grail rested, only to receive another shock. Another group of figures stood in his way.

This time, they must have been angels. And they did not look to be intimidated by the sword he held. They were one and all tall, strapping men, accoutered in the manner, Cormac judged, of ancient Greeks or Romans. They lacked the fabled wings of their species, but Cormac had no doubt as to their identity.

"The Grail is mine, as is this sword of holy power. Stand aside, friends."

The foremost spoke: "Nay, O man of sanguine hands. The cup of our Lord Jesus is not for such as you. You have already sinned grievously by loosing the hounds of hell on the men below. We go to engage them, but first you must repent your plan to lay unhallowed hands of the Holiest of Holies. I shall remain here to see that you obey."

"*Obey*, is it? Cormac Fitzgeoffrey 'obeys' neither man nor god, nor whatever *you* may be."

The rest of the heavenly host vanished, headed for the melee below. But their captain remained, facing Cormac and drawing his own sword.

"You dare much, man of sin. Such hubris as yours invites humbling." Withal, he rushed his mortal opponent.

"Ha! You are as sanctimonious as the perverts in their fancy dresses who make their faithful cower! So sure of your own righteousness!" The Gael raised his sword to parry the thrust of the angel. The divine warrior was no mean swordsman, having, they say, contested against dragons in the heavens. But that was not like close combat. This was.

The tip of Solomon's sword raked the other's brow, and some sort of golden ichor spilled into the angel's eyes. Cormac laughed, gloating, while his foeman staggered backward in astonishment. He wiped his eyes clear, regathered his composure, and returned to the fight. This time it was Cormac's blood that sprayed from a gash. But he was well used to such and scarcely paused in his attack. The sheer momentum of his assault was an effective weapon. This being's Master might be all-powerful, but the servant was not. He seemed as cowed by a human whirlwind like Cormac as the latter's mortal opponents had always been.

Cormac thought he noticed the angel glance skyward, as if

considering whether to petition his Lord for aid. Was it dangerous pride that made him reject the notion and redouble his attack? But Cormac now knew he had the advantage. Easily blocking the increasingly desperate thrusts, at length Cormac aimed not at his foe but at the latter's weapon, a sword that radiated a brilliance greater than his own. But it was waning even as its wielder's strength did. The Sword of Solomon proved more than its match, shattering it into dulling shards.

Disarmed, the angel slouched upon the steps leading to the Grail dais, his vitality draining away with the gushing streams of shining ichor. As Cormac stood over him, a strange notion entered his mind.

He leaped up to the platform and seized the Grail. Dropping back to the floor below, he jammed the cup against one of the angel's flowing wounds. As the creature expired, Cormac raised the chalice to his lips and quaffed the unearthly fluid.

The angel faded, then vanished, but Cormac did not notice, for his head was spinning as fantastic visions flooded his mind. At once he saw the ancient war in heaven. He saw cities and citadels fashioned from single, gigantic gems. He beheld a king on a throne at whose commands great brutes bore massive blocks and boulders on their backs through the air from distant quarries to the crest of Mount Zion. He saw thirteen men reclining around a low table, one speaking in doleful tones, twelve uncomprehending or asleep. In their midst, the very Grail. He saw a terrible Face, whether of God or of Satan he did not know.

Lucky for Cormac, no one attacked him while in this visionary state. Small defense he could have offered. He nearly passed out. Shaking his head to be free of the heavenly visions as if they were delirium tremens, the Gael looked about, saw that he still clutched the holy cup. He had what he wanted and knew it was time to abandon the place, and good luck to the Cathars.

iv TABLE FELLOWSHIP

Reynard had given his old friend Cormac directions to a secret fissure at the mountain's base. He was the only one who knew about it. Not even the Cathar brethren knew of it. Earlier dwellers in the ancient fortress must have known and used it. Reynard himself might have escaped that way but did not want to desert those who had given him refuge. Besides, the crack would have been useless as an escape route for a group of any size, as, once their movement were noticed, the Catholic forces could easily pick off the refugees one by one as they emerged. But the siege was still going on, and it was easy for Cormac to make his exit and to circle around past the besiegers' camp. He jogged to the village where his steed was lodged, found him and stroked his muzzle. The beast seemed glad to rejoin his friend and comrade. Soon they were on their way, to where the Gael knew not.

The next night, Cormac relaxed in a roadside tavern with a simple supper. He drank the local wine from the Grail. It looked like an undistinguished goblet, and Cormac felt it natural to use it as one. Brawls were breaking out around him, but he paid them no mind, merely amused that none of the drunken rowdies picked on him. No one even passed near him for fear of riling the man-mountain by some chance gesture.

Until someone close behind him spoke his name.

"Friend Cormac, I think you've had about enough for tonight. Your cup—hand it over, please?"

Had he not recognized the voice, Cormac would have wheeled about, offering a fist or a sword thrust in reply. Instead: "Join me, my friend."

It was Reynard. Somehow he had escaped the massacre of hundreds of Cathars that extinguished the sect.

"I never thought to see you again, sword-brother! I am glad I was wrong. And here is your Grail. You're the rightful owner. I'm no more than a courier. Where will you take it?"

Accepting the relic, Reynard smiled. "I shall take it home, where it belongs." Withal he vanished before Cormac's eyes. And now Cormac understood: Reynard had not survived the siege after all.

"Barkeep! I am in need of another goblet!"

❖

THE FEAR OF THE LORD

i THE SECRET IN SANDSTONE

I deem it the most pathetic thing in the world when we cannot correlate what our minds tell us must be true with what we would prefer to believe.

Readers are not unlikely to know me as a skeptical (and often political) essayist and literary critic. Most of my books and essay collections deal with great literature and political matters, though a couple have cast down the gauntlet to challenge religion. I held a child's belief in God, heaven, and the Church until university years, whereupon wider reading disabused me of my fairy tales and illusions. Having experienced this enlightenment, a simple matter, or so I judged, I was impatient with other students, equally sharp, who nonetheless held onto their puerile religious convictions. The more they learned, it seemed the more desperate and (I suspected) disingenuous they became in order to retain their faith, or the desperate pretense of holding it. Their arguments (for we used often to debate the matter) were so contrived that I suspected they were trying to suppress their own doubts and to convince themselves by rationalizing. Eventually I wearied of such sport, and after graduate studies, I set out on the literary career of which I have spoken. It was only a few years ago that I entered the ring again. The upsurge of religious obscurantism, as well as the flood of violence committed in God's name, moved me to begin writing on religion and its bluffing. This seemed to me in fact a moral obligation, for I felt someone had to point out that a philosophy of life based unstably upon an initial piece of self-deceit must sooner or later manifest the unscrupulousness at the heart of its zealotry. I did not believe that the Christian religion possessed the credentials its defenders affirmed it had: eyewitness testimony in the gospels, pagan attestation of a historical Jesus, and so forth, these supposed data

84

being matters of hot dispute even among Christians themselves. My principle objections were more in the philosophical and ethical vein. The gross arbitrariness of the doctrine of the atoning death of Christ, for instance: how could anyone possibly think it just for an innocent man to take on himself the punishment due a race of wicked offenders? Again, what sense can it make to claim that the world with all its horrors is supervised by a watchful, loving, omnipotent deity? One can defend such a deity only by redefining all these attributes away to nothing, and then what claim is being made? Not to forget the hell of eternal torment. What could account for a prescient deity creating a human race, most of whom he knew would be headed for everlasting torment? But I suppose the Christian tenet most repugnant to me was the outrage of demanding the sacrifice of individual moral autonomy – how degrading of human dignity! If this religion (or pretty much any other) is true, then the world is a tyranny, or worse, a mad house.

Religious believers of the more intellectual type, reminiscent of my debate partners in college, began to reply to my critiques in print and finally to challenge me to platform debates, some of them on public television. I actually debated a few opponents more than once, like a traveling road show, which held no surprises for us on stage but which tickled the curiosity of our large audiences. It was through this futile but enjoyable debating that I made a new friend, one Germaine Caulkins, a deservedly famous geneticist who had been instrumental in unlocking the code of DNA. He was, as it happened, a doctrinaire fundamentalist. One could not but suspect that his biblicist followers took vicarious pride in his scientific attainments, in that he seemed living proof that one need not sacrifice the intellect to serve Christ. But then he never really ventured to bring his scientific expertise to bear in debate, for how could he? He did not even claim that scientific research had led him to faith. In fact, he had been convinced by certain historical arguments for the resurrection of Jesus Christ which I thought held no water. He was, in my judgment, a Christian in spite of his great mind, not because of it.

But he was a jolly and great-hearted man, and I could not help but like him. It did not even offend me when he promised he would

85

pray for me. I knew he meant well, and I recalled a quip from Bob Harrington, the comedic "Chaplain of Bourbon Street," who used to cover the debate circuit some decades ago, facing off against atheist matriarch Madeline Murray O'Hare. Once, he said, a pious old lady who thought him too frivolous told him scoldingly that she would be praying for him, to which he replied, "That's fine, ma'am! I probably need the prayer and you probably need the practice!" My friend Germaine retuned a good laugh when I tried the comeback on him. A good fellow. Obviously, we had tacitly agreed to disagree. But this did not stop him from occasionally making tactful observations and reading suggestions that he hoped might lead me to embrace faith.

Accordingly, one day he enthusiastically handed me a journal article claiming that a collector in Jerusalem had purchased from a dealer of antiquities a remarkable ancient ossuary. An ossuary was a bone box. Jews in the early centuries of the Common Era often waited for the bones of their entombed dead to slough off their flesh, and then would gather the bones into a stone container about the size and dimensions of a shoebox. This one, the collector claimed, though now empty of all but dry dust, had once housed the sacred bones of James the Just, the brother of Jesus Christ. Actually what the chiseled inscription said was "James the son of Joseph, brother of Jesus" (the Hebrew equivalent, of course). The scholar argued, on the basis of ancient population estimates and the known occurrence of common names in ancient Judea, that a man whose name was James (Jacob) being both the son of a man named Joseph and the brother of another named Jesus virtually had to be the one famous from the Bible. Naturally, as the article admitted, there were scholarly dissenters, but the reasoning seemed pretty sound. At least to Germaine. I was suspicious.

Why was this not merely intriguing but rather important? If the ossuary had been identified correctly it meant that the long-standing debate over whether Jesus of Nazareth had been a real historical figure or only a mythic hero like Osiris and Hercules was put to rest. The most radical of skeptics would thus have been soundly refuted. As for myself, I did not have a dog in this particular race. It did not much matter to me, as an unbeliever, whether there had really been a Jesus or not. Some wise sayings had been attributed to him, nor would I deny that. But the notion of his possibly having been the Son of God was a non-starter if one believed, as I did, that there is no God to begin with. But Germaine seemed to regard the discovery as a blow struck for his side and fairly gloated over it, as did many scholars of religion, who were, alas, soon to be eating their words, just like those who scant years before had been fooled by the hoax of the so-called Hitler Diaries.

Serious objections to the James identification soon emerged. For one thing, it seemed that "brother of Jesus" had been scrawled by a different hand than that which had carved "son of Joseph." This meant there was no particular reason to believe the former was part of the original inscription at all. For another, the patina, the film of ancient dust and oil covering the sandstone box, stopped at the edge of the incised letters. Obviously, this meant the letters had one and all been carved into an old box in recent days. And then the Israeli Antiquities Authority, in a scene right out of *The Untouchables*, raided the home of the collector who claimed to have purchased the ossuary from a dealer. It turned out he had a miniature factory in the back room where he turned out fake relics to sell to scholarly suckers. This is why a supposed archaeological find doesn't mean much (or shouldn't) if the owner cannot tell you who found it and where and how it came to its owner. I need not tell you how deflated Germaine was. Nor did I rub it in. After all, the disqualification of this bit of "evidence" proved or disproved nothing. Even if it had been genuinely ancient, I thought, it was equivocal at best.

But not long afterward, a truly amazing, really uncanny, development occurred. This time I did not need Germaine to inform me of it. An archaeologist was exploring a site in Egypt which he believed to be the site described by Philo Judaeus where a monastic community of Jewish ascetics called the Therapeutae had dwelt. He hoped to find concrete evidence that might further illuminate the ancient sect. It had been the object, I now read, of much speculation. Some scholars, such as Christian Lindtner, saw in the name a version of that of South Asian Buddhism, the Theravada, or "Way of the Elders." That implied that Jewish monasticism was actually founded by Buddhist missionaries whom King Asoka had dispatched to Syria and Egypt in the third century BCE. Other scholars believed the Therapeutae to be an Egyptian branch of the Essene sect who inhabited the Jordan valley, among whom most numbered the community of the famous Dead Sea Scrolls. (Of course.these theories, though seldom combined, were by no means incompatible). The fourth-century church historian Eusebius had taken the Therapeutae (long extinct by his time) to be a band of primitive Christians and even suggested Philo had visited Saint Peter in Rome.

The explorer, one must say, hit the jackpot. I forget the rest of his tale, but he did find what he was looking for. While no tantalizing manuscripts came to light, some iconography did suggest Buddhist themes. But the real stunner was, yes, another ossuary ostensibly containing the bones of James the Just! If this one were genuine, or even if it proved to be an ancient fake rather than a modern one, the implications were major, at least if one were interested in these questions. And, given what my debating opponents might seek to make of this find, I had to follow the coverage as best I could. At one stroke, all the hitherto-competing theories were vindicated and merged: The Therapeutae must indeed have been Theravadins, as well as Essenes, with whom James had sometimes been associated. And if James had been one of these Buddhist-Essene-Therapeuts, could Jesus Christ have been far behind?

As the weeks went by, Carbon 14 dating, paleography, and tests of the telltale patina all checked out. And a closer examination of the inscription revealed a clear reference to "Jesus, King Messiah." There was no doubt this was the final resting place of James, son of Mary and Joseph, brother of Jesus, who had therefore really existed as more than a myth. My friend Germaine was, on one level, quite thrilled, as if a treasured possession, once lost, had been restored to him (and on this I congratulated him). The connection with Buddhism, however, was not much to his liking, offending his orthodox beliefs about Christian origins and his dismissal of all non-Christian faiths as simply false. I had to smile, hoping the unexpected revelation might push him toward a more tolerant stance. Little did I then suspect in what direction the discovery might begin to push me, however incrementally.

ii. *THE TALE OF INSPECTOR LEGRANDE*

A few months later, I chanced to catch a program on what once deserved the name "The History Channel" but which had, like its kindred networks, "Arts & Entertainment" and "Bravo," abandoned its original mission and sunk to the level of cheap sensationalism. I was about to click the button on the remote control, as I often had recently, to escape ludicrous spectacles such as the quack exorcist Bob Larson telling tall tales of the demons he personally had cast out, and which rock-and-roll songs each devil had penned. But this evening, the interviewee was a sober-seeming police detective from New Orleans, famous for his crackdown on organized crime in the Big Easy some years before Hurricane Katrina. I was surprised to see him subjecting himself to participation in such a sideshow, but soon I realized that no more respectable venue would have risked hosting him.

The inspector was recounting a raid on some out-of-the-way crack houses in the bayou country. He and his men were taken by surprise, to put it mildly, when they came upon, deep in the swamp, the low-lifes they had sought, and they were engaging in what looked to be a religious ritual. Religious devotion to anything but drugs was not exactly what one expected from denizens like these. So the police hunkered down in the reeds, which provided more than ample covering, while they watched the event unfold.

LeGrande, of Haitian ancestry himself, recognized some elements of the ritual from Voodoo and Obeah ceremonies witnessed as a boy. But whereas Voodoo was a syncretic mix of African traditional religion and Catholic slave religion, what he was now observing was decidedly more sinister. He thought he heard chanting invocations of Satan, Mastema, Semjaza, all names for the Christian devil. But these were by no means the harmless poseurs familiar from American pop Satanism, the make-believe cults of LaVey and his merry pranksters.

When LeGrande saw a sudden eruption of blood amidst the general chaos of leaping and diving naked bodies, he decided he must act. It might be an animal sacrifice, but it might be the blood of a human captive. He could not see which from his present vantage point. He had risen halfway from his crouch when what he beheld froze him where he was.

Above the howling pack of degenerates there towered a form of fiery, golden radiance. It had angelic eagle wings and the head of a goat. It was both beautiful and horrible. And it could not be some special effects projection. Not here. Not in these circumstances. Not with these idiots.

But now they had been seen! Though most of the cultists were focused on the rising apparition, some few men must have been posted as watchers. At the sight of LeGrande and his men, they shouted to one another and opened fire with the weapons they already had poised. This broke the spell; the image vanished with a blazing flash which set several of the thickly crowding trees afire. Given the swampy conditions, the fire did not burn out of control and even died down quickly, but it had achieved two results. The ensuing melee provided sufficient confusion for the revelers to escape, no doubt along secret paths known only to them. And the blackened branches and scorched trunks proved it was no hallucination that the inspector and most of his men agreed they had seen.

LeGrande, a man of stolid character, did his duty and reported precisely what he had seen. Not surprisingly, his superiors rejected his report and fired him, along with a couple of his men who dared to come forth and corroborate his wild story.

Apparently, LeGrande had supplied enough entertainment for the jaded audience, and the host summarily dismissed him with an insincere "thanks for being with us." But I for one had to hear more. At once I got up and retrieved my calendar book to see when I might be able to book a flight to Louisiana. For I felt I had to talk to this man. Maybe he was a fanatic or a lunatic, but he certainly hadn't seemed like one. And he had made a far more convincing case for the reality of the supernatural than Germaine Caulkins or his fellow apologists ever had. I was curiously disturbed by what this humble and sober-seeming man had said. I still cannot say why I did not simply dismiss it as if it were one more UFO abduction story from a gap-toothed hillbilly. I suppose my intellectual conscience was reminding me that that would have been unfair of me, that I would have been excluding evidence for that which I disliked to believe. At any rate, the bee was in my bonnet now, and there was but one way to get it out. I had to track down Inspector LeGrande.

The next day I contacted the show's producer through the History Channel website, phoning once I had the number. They usually shielded their guests from contact with pesky viewers, but I managed to convince them to put me in touch with LeGrande, or at least to supply contact information. You see, they recognized my name and my voice from my own several media appearances. I make a point not to exploit my notoriety, since I hate when others do it, but sometimes it comes in handy.

By sunset of the following day I had reached LeGrande and persuaded him to see me. He had plenty of time, given his forced early retirement. I felt I had to see the man in person to properly assess his own belief in his story and the likelihood that he had not unwittingly embellished it, as often happens when someone witnesses an odd event.

Three days later, the inspector, as polite a fellow as ever I had met, picked me up from the airport and drove us in his aging Buick to one of his favorite restaurants. It was nothing fancy, but they didn't mind you lingering for a long conversation.

As I sat across from him and absently munched whatever it was I had ordered, I was struck not only with the man's acuity but with his look of profound weariness and resignation. He did not so much mourn the loss of his job and his chosen work as he seemed utterly at a loss to assimilate his recent experience. I now had no doubt that he was not magnifying his story. If anything, the opposite was true; he several times hedged, suggesting that perhaps this or that detail was not quite as it seemed. But I could see he simply could not bring himself to dismiss his encounter as an illusion. If he wasn't going to lie to anyone else about it, he sure was not about to start lying to himself.

In fact, there had been *more* to the incident than he had dared to disclose, even on TV. He had feared incarceration as a lunatic. What he had not divulged, as he now told me, was that the looming, luminous figure of Baphomet grabbed up several both of the rioting cultists and of his own men, whereupon they blazed like flares in his scaly hands, and then he popped them into his open maw like blackened marshmallows. This fact helped explain his abrupt dismissal from the Police Department, since he could not account for the disappearance of these officers in any believable way.

As I sat there and listened to Inspector LeGrande, I found myself feeling that his crazy story was yet somehow plausible, given the evidence he had provided (the burning and charring in the swamp, which I verified for myself the next afternoon) and the testimony of his surviving men which had cost them so much. But I also felt a foreboding sense that, should I dare entertain the possible truth of his story, I should be embarking on a road I did not want to go down, to a destination I very much feared.

I thanked the inspector and commiserated with him on his treatment, and the next evening I returned home, all the while feeling I had been cut loose from any familiar moorings.

The next week I decided to meet with Germaine. I needed to know what he would make of the story. I knew pretty well without asking what my secular colleagues would say. At least Germaine had a wider frame of reference. I called him up and arranged to meet him for dinner the next evening.

"Well, Chris," he said, "I guess you can see the implications here. If there is a devil, and I get the impression you're open to that possibility, then there must be a God, too. Right?" The thought had crossed my mind, but I was not about to give up without a fight.

"Actually, I don't think *you* get the implications, my friend. If there is an archfiend who can counter God's moves, thwart his will, successfully defy him, what kind of God are we talking about? I mean, I guess I could almost see Spinoza's God, or Tillich's, more of an impersonal essence or something. But if there is a goat-hoofed devil – and he's God's opposite number, well, wouldn't even you agree that's raw mythology?"

He was quick with a reply. "I confess I never paid much attention to the Satan business. I figure man's own evil is enough to explain most of what happens in the world. But there *is* the Bible. And there's what LeGrande says he saw! Maybe things are a bit more like we learned them in childhood. Maybe we have made it too abstract. I don't know. But one thing does occur to me. If you try very hard, you could probably come up with some rationalization of this thing, but I'm willing to bet it would be like your friend Hume said: you shouldn't believe any report of a miracle until any rival explanation would itself be more far-fetched than the miracle itself!"

I had already decided I was not going to try to get out of a tight spot by using the kind of tortured reasoning fundamentalists use when they're trying to avoid admitting a biblical contradiction. I was getting a headache.

iii. THE WITNESS FROM THE SEA

I must admit I tried to put the whole crazy business out of my mind for the next weeks, but it was not to last. I was up late working on a column about the latest Mideast war when the phone rang. On the other end was a fellow skeptic who insisted I go to the television and turn on the Catholic channel. I knew which one he meant; sometimes, trying to escape Pat Robertson's squinting smiles I would hasten up a few clicks and find myself flinching at Mother Angelica, the head honcho of the network. She always looked like the witch from "Hansel and Gretel," if you ask me. But here was the channel, and some gray-robed monk was blathering on about the mercies of the Mother of God, the Blessed Mother of our Savior. "So what?" I thought. But I decided I'd best listen to a little of it, if only to understand the jokes my friend would be making about it next time I saw him.

Suddenly I could see what my pal had thought so funny, at least outrageous. The monk wasn't talking about the same old apparitions of the Blessed Virgin at Fatima and La Salette, but of something from a decade ago that had come to light only recently. A Norwegian sea captain had been about to go down with his ship in a terrible typhoon that had blown up out of nowhere. And *he'd* had a vision, too. Like LeGrande's, it had been a whopper! This time, a nimbus of light had formed (the story went) above the ship, cutting through the gray shroud of the driving rain. It formed an oval, and within it there appeared a three-dimensional image of the Virgin Mary. She said, in a ringing voice loud enough to be heard above the storm, "Peace be still!" And the wind and rain stopped almost immediately, like bad editing in a movie.

I figured it was a lot of pious nonsense. Who knew *what* had happened, if anything at all? But then two "details" made my ears perk up. *One*: all the sailors, like most Scandinavians, were Protestants, not likely to have visions, or even tell tales, of the Virgin Mary. *Two*: the captain, a man named Josefson, did not at the time understand what the voice had uttered, though he said he remembered exactly what it sounded like. When he got back to Oslo, he went to inquire of a linguist at the university, who told him the meaning of the words he had heard—*in Aramaic*.

You know what they say, "In for a penny, in for a pound." I started making travel plans again. On line I was able to dig up a couple of old and skimpy reports, one in a pretty derisive tone, about Captain Josefson's Mariological adventure. I already knew he had been located in Oslo, and these internet clips gave me a couple of new clues. I figured I'd probably be able to nail down a definite address once I got there, perhaps from the local police.

On the long flight over, I knew I wouldn't be able to sleep, so I brought a couple of books Germaine had loaned me, *Mere Christianity* by the venerable C.S. Lewis and *The Everlasting Man* by G.K. Chesterton. I had always inclined toward regarding Lewis as too clever for his own good and Chesterton as a pompous windbag with nothing cogent to say. But in light of recent experiences, I thought it might be worth reading them through again, with new eyes. But I found only my usual objections to faith coming to mind again and again, almost on every page. How could a fair-minded God condemn you to hell for flunking a theology exam? Not having the "right" beliefs? And how can poor mortals ever decide which of the competing sects *has* the right beliefs? How can reasoning adults be told just to put their own judgment on the shelf and believe what an old book says simply because the old book says it? I kept shaking my head and finally closed the books. Sleep came after all.

In Oslo, I went through customs and checked into my hotel. I didn't bother with the police after all, but visited the American embassy, and they were able to give me what I needed after two or three calls. Nice people. So I hailed a cab and handed the driver the paper slip with Josefson's address hastily penciled on it. It didn't take long till he deposited me on the curb in front of a tidy old cottage that bore the name *Josefson* on its freestanding mailbox. Up the slate walk I went, then knocked.

After a few moments the door opened a crack, and an eye scrutinized me from behind a thick lens. I thought it was a woman's eye. "Mrs. Josefson?" I pulled from my pocket one of those cell phones with the translation program. I thought I might as well try this first and go off to find a translator if I had to. I gave her my name and asked briefly if I might talk to her husband. I could understand enough of what she said in answer to know I had come much too late. Her husband, the captain, had died of a stroke some years earlier. Luckily she knew a bit of English, enough to tell me the bad news. I managed to convey that I was very interested in his vision of Mary. She motioned me to wait a moment, then returned with a videocassette. I gathered it was a recording of her late husband telling his story for the umpteenth time; he must have decided to tell it on tape and be done with it, just hand it to future inquirers. I imagined there had been a lot of them. But why a videocassette rather than just an audiocassette? I thanked her and left her, I hope, in peace. Back in my hotel room I ordered up a VCR and put the cassette in its mouth.

I expected to see an old man sitting in his easy chair rattling off a tall tale, and I thought it would probably be all in Norwegian. Surely I would have to get someone to make me a transcript in English. But no. Definitely not.

My scalp tingled. My arms went numb. I felt light-headed. One of Josefson's crewmen had brought along a video camera for any one of a number of possible reasons. He had caught the apparition on tape! Given the conditions, the camera work was pretty choppy, as you'd expect, but remember, the violence of the storm had abated suddenly, and the man was able to hold the camera pretty steady for long enough to catch the image of the giant woman up in the sky.

I suppose it was possible for the tape to have been an elaborate hoax, like that alien autopsy thing. But I cannot easily picture these old, poor, salt-of-the-earth peasants having the skill or taking the trouble. Again, that seemed about as unlikely as the truth of what I had seen on the tape. And I saw it several times. I still have it.

All during the trip home, the flight attendants kept asking me if I was sick. Not exactly sick, no, but I spent the whole flight in a state of near-shock. I felt utterly at sea, as if my sanity were slipping away.

Of course, once I got home I showed the tape to various experts, who all assumed it was, if not a hoax, a cinematic fiction, but none of them could find any trace of artifice. Whoever had shot it, all averred, was an unknown master whose skills none of these professionals could match. That's all I needed to hear.

By the way, there was an e-mail waiting for me on my computer, from the New Orleans police. Inspector LeGrande had been burned to death in his apartment, though nothing around the body was so much as singed. You know, like those cases they chalk up to spontaneous human combustion. Come to think of it, I believe I first heard about that on the History Channel, too.

iv. ANGEL STREET

I didn't sleep for a few days, and then I slept for a few days. My head was spinning. My world was tottering. Maybe I should have phoned Germaine, but I didn't. I guess I was afraid he might gloat, but of course he wouldn't. I guess I was too proud to admit I might have been wrong about everything all this time. I still can't stand the idea. But I don't think it's pride. I've always been willing to change my mind if somebody could prove me wrong. I've actually done it a couple of times, though never on anything this big.

I decided I needed a rest, so I took off for the mountains, after canceling a couple of major speaking engagements. I tried to put everything out of mind. Drinking helped, but not for very long. I located a Bible and glanced through the gospels, then the epistle to the Romans. None of it seemed very plausible to me, either the stories or the reasoning. I guess it might have been possible to admit the reality of the supernatural without having to swallow *all* this stuff, but then I thought of how the James ossuary, the visitation of Satan, the apparition of Mary – all of it was very specifically Christian, even Catholic. But how could it be true? And, even worse, what if it was? What would my life mean? What kind of a universe would I be stuck in? But the vise was about to get squeezed tighter.

I was hiking through the hills one evening, again trying to get my mind back in its usual groove, trying to plan out a new essay, maybe a new book, one on politics maybe. Nothing was coming, and night was rapidly falling. I stopped and built a campfire. I opened a can of beans. I dropped it, whole, into the fire as my fingers went nerveless.

Above me there appeared in a shower of light the form of a winged man. Yes, I might as well say it: an angel. He looked straight at me, and he said in tones that chimed like a bell, "Chris, you have been greatly blessed. It is time for you to stop running, to give your heart to our Father and his Son. Will you do it?" And he held out his hand to me.

Where another might rejoice at such a token of divine favor, I cannot rise from the slough of despond. Despite the light that nearly blinded me, I am mired in a darkness of soul, for I now know I do have a soul. I can no longer deny that Germaine and his friends are horribly correct. Only they are fools not to see the leaden weight of the thing. There is a capricious Jehovah who crushes the innocent to save the guilty, and who nonetheless shovels his children into hell like coal into a furnace. There is a Trinity which we cannot understand but must try our best to believe in on pain of damnation. We must bow and scrape and kowtow to a tyrant who demands unceasing flattery and blind obedience. We are to bend and twist our better judgment to believe that which we know to be stupid. We live in a cosmic insane asylum with the patients in charge. Under the burden of this knowledge I must try to live out my days.

And after that, will I be condemned for not doing what I cannot do: accepting a faith which every moral instinct bids me disdain? I cannot lose my soul in a bid to save it.

I shall know soon enough. I have just been diagnosed with inoperable cancer.

THE GREY RITE OF AZATHOTH

I write in great haste. I must needs set down my recent experience while I am able, for I do already feel the memory fading and failing, as a dream flees with the dawn, as I was told. While no man is entitled to expunge from his memory any knowledge, even if it be possible, I confess I shall not mourn the flight of that recollection which I am presently to lose. And yet the knowledge may someday prove of value, even of great necessity, for the good of mankind. I shall not consult this account again, but shall lock it away for any who come after, whoever they may be, as Providence shall decree.

My name, John Checkley, will likely be familiar to you. Upon my arrival in the Colony of Rhode Island and Providence Plantations, subsequent to certain much-noised difficulties in the Massachusetts Bay Colony, I waxed curious concerning a notorious resident whose acquaintance I could not make in my new congregation of King's Church, as he frequented the Congregational Church instead. The man's name was Joseph Curwen. By all accounts, Mr. Curwen, a prosperous but secretive merchant prince, was the possessor of a keen intellect and of numerous esoteric scholarly interests. I ventured to call upon him and was welcomed quite cordially, contrary to all I had been told of his supposed reclusivity. I was relieved to find him wholly congenial as a host and convivial as a companion. I soon learned how much we had in common, as we had each traveled extensively through the capitols of Europe, sampling liberally the rich opportunities there afforded to the seeker after knowledge of the unseen realms. I, of course, sought an education in the field of theology, of which I made ample use in my later controversies with the Calvinists of Puritan Massachusetts. Curwen's quest inclined him to more arcane pursuits of a medieval character. I should not hesitate to brand the speculations implicit in his cryptical hints as heresy, but I have long championed sectarian tolerance, and if Joseph Curwen could be persecuted for unorthodox beliefs, so could the Quakers and the Baptists, a thing I decried in print. I now know, to my chagrin, that even enlightened tolerance must draw boundaries.

Joseph Curwen's manner of conversation produced in me strangely mixed sensations of expectancy and of apprehension. There was no guessing what he might say next. One was eager and yet frightened to receive the next revelations, mercifully cloaked in ambiguity as they might be. But things were about to become altogether too perspicuous.

"Dr. Checkley, I am of course familiar with your theological polemics and with the courage which moves you to advance them against those less amicable than yourself. I should like both to reward and to test that courage. Indeed, I have reserved to you a great privilege accorded to no divine in the history of Christendom."

I confess that the grandiose character of this utterance at once took me aback. In truth, Curwen's words were so extreme as to compel their hearer to question their speaker's sanity. And he had not even got to the hinted disclosure. I replied, "Mr. Curwen, whatever you intend, I am sure there are many who are more deserving than I. I would only puff myself up with vain pride should I accept the favor with which you tempt me."

"So you compare yourself to our Saviour and me to his diabolical tempter."

He had taken me by surprise, and I knew myself for a woodland creature caught in a trap. There was naught for it but to laugh and to let my host proceed.

"I dare say, Mr. Checkley, that, as a clergyman in the Church of England, you are a believer in the resurrection of Jesus Christ; am I correct in that opinion?"

"Of course you are, sir. And what of it?"

"Then I fear a grave duty has fallen to me. I must inform you of the error of your sincere belief."

As Curwen himself had already mentioned, I was no stranger to polemic and debate on religious subjects. I had met more than one

Deist in public debate as well as in pamphlet wars. Their futile arguments, aimed at refuting the resurrection of our Lord, did not shake my faith in the least degree. I did not fear aught that Curwen, now seemingly revealed as an infidel, might propose. I braced myself to engage in the tiresome rhetorical motions entailed in these exchanges. But I quickly found that such was not after all what my host had in mind. He continued.

"Do you think me a religious skeptic? A denier of all things supernatural desirous of winning you to my opinions? Let me assure you: that is antipodal to the truth. In truth, I aim to confirm your faith, that and more! For in truth Jesus the son of Joseph did not return from his death sixteen centuries agone. But rise he will. Today. And it shall be done by your own word."

I glanced over in the direction of the door by which I had entered. My one thought was now to take my leave with as little offense and mutual embarrassment as possible. It had become inescapably clear that Joseph Curwen was beside himself. What he might be planning next I could not guess, but I did not fear violence. Nothing in his manner, his words, or his movements suggested such. But I had no desire to be the audience of a sad spectacle of pathetic madness such as now seemed likely to commence.

Wordlessly beckoning me with a wave of the hand, Curwen strode into an adjacent room. It would now be a simple matter for me to head for the opposite door. Yet to do so would be unconscionably rude, as foolish as this may seem. Besides, my curiosity had gotten the better of me. I could not resist the lure of whatever charade he might have in mind. So, yes, I rose and followed him. The trail led through several small rooms and down a twisting flight of crudely hewn steps. My apprehension was growing as I realized that, the deeper we descended, the more difficult it would be to escape should there prove to be aught from which to escape. Perhaps we all have a dangerous dose of Faust inside us; I only hoped, in vain, as it would prove, that Joseph Curwen did not possess rather too much of it.

At length we arrived at what looked like a workroom, a makeshift laboratory of some sort. The nitrous walls were lined with rough shelves laden with ancient-looking jars and flasks. There were two or three tall posts upholding beams designed to brace the stone walls, somewhat reminiscent of the walls of a coal mine, and these featured a series of pegs and hooks from which depended various kettles, tools, and pitchers. Most of the jars bore labels emblazoned with numbers, Hebrew characters, or zodiacal symbols. All were crowned with metal stoppers. Curwen reached for one of these and emptied out its contents upon the stained and splintered table surface. The stuff was a very fine dust, none of it clumping together but instead resembling fine sand. Curwen commenced to explain.

"As is commonly rumoured, I have engaged and in fact still engage in a clandestine traffic in, shall we say, archaeological specimens... for my private collection, as you might say. I have learned that one stands to learn far more of the vanished past if one bypasses the stone monuments, which conceal as much as they reveal, and instead seek the wisdom of the ancients from the ancients themselves."

"You mean," I countered, "from their writings. Have you then made important manuscript discoveries?" He must have suspected, as I suppose I did, that I was offering him a sane and reasonable alternative, hoping to fend off some terrible truth he seemed on the point of revealing.

He paused and smiled in a way I cannot say I liked. "In truth, Dr. Checkley, I have. You might find several of them to be of deep interest. But that is not what I mean. I mean the ancients themselves. It is quite possible, you know. Does not scripture say that the Witch of En-Dor invoked the shade of the prophet Samuel to converse with King Saul?"

"Indeed it does, Mr. Curwen, but that episode is hardly meant as an example for us to follow! It is properly called Necromancy, and people have been put to death on account of it, as I am sure you know from your experiences in Salem."

"Of course I do, my friend. But you yourself abandoned the Puritan kingdom because of its rulers' intolerance of heterodoxy. Are you still so fair-minded?" He had me.

"I hope that I am. Proceed, then. What have you in store for me?"

"As I say, the rarest of treats! What God the Father would not or could not do, you shall do, here and now. Another voice from of old set me upon the trail of perhaps the greatest discovery of its kind: the very remains, such as they are, of the Nazarene Jesus. They are my newest acquisition, and I mean to give you the honor of initiating... the process. It is surprisingly simple. Now if you would just read the words written on this slip."

"Curwen, 'thy great learning hath driven thee mad.'"

"Ah, that is what I like so much about you, sir! Ever a jest at the ready! But I am quite serious. Let me prove it to you. Read on."

What harm could it do? When nothing transpired, I should at least gain some particular notion of the manner of my host's dementia. Presumably he should fancy to behold some spectre of his own fevered imagination. Then I must play along as best I could, humouring the madman as convincingly as I might till I could manage a diplomatic departure. So I took the paper from his hand and scanned the strange syllables. I will not boast if I remind the reader of my competence in the biblical languages as well as a passable knowledge of several modern European tongues. But I had never beheld the like of these. They did not appear to be phonetic interpretations of words in any familiar language, but were foreign altogether. Nevertheless, I began.

As soon as I had enunciated the first complete line, I found my concentration distracted by a sudden change in the room's temperature, which was now quite cold. I looked up at Curwen, who seemed in no whit surprised. He did betray a slight grin, nothing more. As I found my place and continued, he listened patiently, stopping me once or twice to correct my pronunciation. He said he might have recited the formula for me to imitate but that he wanted the results of the chant to be in answer to my intonation, not his.

Y'AI 'NG'NGAH,
YOG-SOTHOTH
H'EE-L'GEB
F'AI THRODOG
UAAAH

I got through it, finally, with passable accuracy. Or so I must have, for there were indeed results. As Curwen clapped his hands with childlike glee, a fumarole of mephitic smoke began to spread and swirl in the room between us, as the spilled powder sublimated directly into the air. Within the slow cyclone a definite outline began to distinguish itself. The unwholesome odor subsided in direct proportion to the increasing solidification of the human form before me. Naturally the whole business was most impressive, but I was not carried away by superstitious credulity. Instead my amazement consisted in admiration for the fantastic ingenuity of Curwen's showmanship. The ancients were quite familiar with all the tricks still performed by charlatans and entertainers of our own day, and I imagined that Curwen was demonstrating some striking spectacle salvaged from one of the ancient documents he had acquired. On this I hastened to congratulate him, but he was having none of it. He began to exclaim, I thought a trifle sarcastically, "He is risen! He is risen indeed!"

A scrawny figure of a man stood shivering before us. He was about five feet tall and without a stitch of clothing. His drawn face bore bloodstains, while his beard and hair were matted and shaggy. His extremities showed raw wounds. He stood unevenly, one leg being plainly shorter than the other, though not by much. I thought of the Russian Orthodox cross, with its slanted bottom rung, denoting their tradition, apocryphal I should judge, that the Saviour was a cripple. And at once I recognized that I was taking seriously Curwen's blasphemous claim to be retrieving our Lord Jesus Christ from the mists of the past. Consciously, of course, I knew the whole thing for imposture, and I pitied this poor stooge of Curwen and the physical suffering he had plainly been put through in preparation for the present farce.

"Dr. Checkley, do you not know your Lord?"

"I have never seen a portrait of him not the product of an artist's fancy."

"I charge you, sir: do not squander this unparalleled opportunity! Have you no questions for the very Son of God? If so, you are a rare clergyman!"

I felt I was being made a fool of, but I thought to turn the tables. I did address the discomfited man, but I did so in the Aramaic tongue. I calculated that Curwen had expected me to forget myself and to speak my accustomed English, as if this "Jesus" should understand and reply in kind. Here is the translated sense of my question.

"What is your name, my poor friend? And how came you to suffer so?" I expected the man to stare blankly, uncertain how to proceed now that I had departed from the plan Curwen had designed.

But he answered me in the Aramaic. At first I thought he mispronounced the ancient words, but then I realized that my own pronunciation was derived from the speech of modern Syrians, and that this strange man must be speaking in the ancient accents. I was dumbfounded. Now everything looked completely different to me. The challenges to my thinking and to my composure were dramatic indeed. But this is what he said, again in translation.

"I am called Jehoshua, son of Joseph the Nazarene. I have suffered many things and climbed up the cross of Tiberius. The sun above me became black as sackcloth, and with it my eyes darkened, and I gave up my spirit. All this was mere moments ago. How came I to be here? In this cold place?"

Curwen had stepped away to retrieve a shapeless garment from a heap in the corner. He draped it about the chilled form. The man nodded in gratitude. For his part, Curwen motioned me onward, urging me to continue.

"Why, O Jehoshua, did men crucify you?"

"I wrought wonders once I bound the powers of Baal-Zebul, prince of demons. I bent them to do my will, and so I healed many sick and possessed. I was one of many, and my rivals gave false witness against me to the prefect of Rome."

The man shook his head with understandable confusion, as if to clear his mind. I hated to pester him further, but I must admit I was seriously intrigued. "But if you were the Son of God, why stoop to sorcery?"

His eyes had cleared and now fixed upon me firmly. "Amen, I say to you, my Father vouchsafed me the power wherewith I bound

Satan to despoil him of his goods."

"We have believed that you conquered death and rose from the grave, but it seems you did not, at least not until now."

His voice was acquiring a firmer tone. My own voice began to catch as I could no longer maintain a skeptical detachment. Good Lord, suppose Curwen had actually done as he claimed?

"My Father liveth, and all are alive to him."

"Bear with me, O Image of Jehoshua, and I will ask of you one question more. Did you come forth from the Godhead? Are you of a single nature with the heavenly Father? Mankind has shed blood over that question."

"You say that I am. Man, open your mind to understand the deep things of God, for he whom you call your God is a veritable Ocean of Light, and from him has wave after wave of angels gone forth to crash against the shore of crude matter. If you would seek my Father's kingdom, you must go up from earth and scale the Outer Spheres. The dark angels of Achamoth, who is also Azathoth, ever keep the gates. If you would surmount them, you must work the Grey Rite...'"

Just here Joseph Curwen interrupted our exchange, blasphemously silencing him who I was now on the verge of accepting as the very Word of God.

"Have I not given you a great gift, Dr. Checkley? Now you know what no Christian souls have known since the persecution of the ancient heretics! The churchmen of old were considerably less tolerant than you, kind sir. But you need not fear persecution for speaking the truth you now know, for you shall not know it for long. Are you feeling well, my friend?"

I took stock of my sensations and found that, in the excitement of the conversation just past, I had not noticed the entire ebbing of my physical strength. Indeed, I was virtually paralyzed! I tried to answer him but heard my own slurring speech. I realize now that Curwen must have poisoned me in some surreptitious manner, perhaps using some gas invisible to the eye. I was beginning to grow drowsy, and I understood that I should before long lose any memory of what had transpired here. The gift Curwen had given me he was not going to let me keep. I am very surprised to have retained even this much for this long. I know that I have lost some of the precious secrets vouchsafed me by the man Jehoshua, but I have managed to record what little has not yet flown.

One last thing I recall seeing and hearing in that subterranean den. Curwen took hold of the man and shook him violently. "Tell me the Grey Rite! For I would storm the heavens! I shall be as the Most High!"

This, too, was in passable Aramaic, as was the response. "I bestow my mysteries upon those who are worthy of my mysteries."

Whatever this Jehoshua might be that did not meet the eye of flesh, still, in the three dimensions that we occupy, he was a weak and wizened scarecrow; and it was with perfect ease that the doughtier Curwen seized and dragged him toward the wall, forcing him against the rough wood of the nearest bracing post. A blow to the poor man's forehead sent him into a semi-stupor. As the hammering began, the room commenced to spin around me. All I heard of whatever next transpired was one sentence apiece from each man.

"Prophesy! Who struck you!"

"Almighty, protect thy lamb!"

THE NATIVITY OF THE AVATAR

New manuscript discoveries, like that of the famous Dead Sea Scrolls, always cause a stir, at least briefly till the jaded public's attention flits away to some new momentary stimulus. Perhaps the last place one would expect to find a new cache of ancient documents would be the British Museum, where every scrap of antiquity has long been catalogued and filed away. But, as the reader may remember, a few years ago it was announced that a wealth of "new" documents had in fact been discovered, lying concealed on the very same sheets of papyrus which well-known texts were occupying. They were palimpsests, sheets already bearing writing but, given the scarcity of writing materials, erased to afford room for new texts. Various such documents had been discovered and deciphered before, but new infrared techniques now made it possible to recover the original layer of writing without removing the more recent ink. This scientific boon opened the vault, so to speak, of a whole unknown library of ancient works, and it has taken some years to decipher any significant portion of them. There were new copies of familiar Greek dramas, Platonic dialogues and other philosophical works, and what not. Many of these have been published in English translation, though only specialists are likely to have paid much attention.

My name is Alasdair McKenzie, Professor of Ecclesiastical History at Brichester University. I expressed my interest in the project early on and was happy to be assigned what appeared to be an apocryphal gospel of sorts. In particular, it may be classed among the Infancy or Nativity Gospels, whose better known members include the Infancy Gospels of James, Matthew, Thomas the Israelite, and the Arabic Infancy Gospel. Each of these has fascinating features well worth studying, especially the surprising Zoroastrian connections in the Arabic Infancy Gospel. But the new one, assigned to my care, was in some ways radically different. Having translated it to the best of my ability, I herewith offer it to readers, who may decide for themselves what to make of it. One note: it may seem out of place to employ the Sanskrit word "avatar" in the translation of a Hellenistic Greek document, but it represents *katabasis*, "descent," which is also the meaning of "avatar" (*avatara, anvantara*), denoting a god coming down to earth.

Finally, I have inserted chapter and verse numbers. Most readers will know the Bible was written without these divisions and that they were added many centuries later to facilitate reference. So why not here?

∗∗∗

1 [1] He who has ears, let him hear. He who has a mouth, let him bear witness to the truth of what we say. For this is the true account of the entry among men of the Avatar.

[2] In the last days of Herod the Blessed, three monks of Yian-Ho on the Plateau called Leng arrived in Jerusalem and gained audience with the king. [3] "O mighty Lord, we have learned from the midnight star that shines in the Cavern of the Elementals that the Avatar has been born in your kingdom, as a reward for your service to the cult of Set-Typhon.

[4] "The light of the Elder Pharos has shone upon us as we made our way over many miles and mountains. [5] We have come to worship him, to take him in hand and to prepare him for his mission. Where, with your permission, may we find him?"

[6] Withal did King Herod summon the brethren of the monastery of the Naassenes in the Judean desert. [7] These are they who maintain the secret worship of him who is called Father Yigael and Leviathan and Nehushtan, and whom Egypt knows as Set the Old Serpent. [8]And he put it to them, "Where may the new-born Avatar be found? I, too, would go and bow down before him."

[9] And the monks of Yig confessed that the One they sought should be found in the village of Beth-Lehem, chosen on account of its ancient shrine to the god Dusares. [10] For it was from there that Balaam had prophesied the Avatar should arise. Now this is he who in the latter days

should vindicate the Serpent and depose his ancient conqueror Jehovah. [11] Father Yigael had waited for many thousands of years, but soon he should regain his rightful mastery.

[12] And as he gave them provisions and horses and an escort of his troops, Herod told the brethren from Leng that he would offer all the infants of Beth-Lehem as a sacrifice to welcome the young Avatar into the world he should one day rule. [13] And Herod wept, knowing that he should never live to see the day of that final triumph.

[14] And as the company came near to Beth-Lehem, behold: the night was filled with the batlike forms of the gaunts of the night, and the number of them was so great that they blotted out the stars above. [15] And the gaunts chattered in no human tongue. But the men of Leng understood their meaning which, being interpreted, was, "Lo, the long night of Jehovah is ended, and the dawn of the Avatar is at hand! [16] And you, O men, see that you spread the tidings to all who cherish the secrets of the Olden Gods. But as for the rest, cast not your pearls before swine!"

[17] Thus they arrived at last where the child was. He lay in a manger between the dead bodies of his parents, for his birth was attended by many ill-omens, even the deaths of all the livestock in the place, [18] so that the owner of the stable and his servants had stoned the family. But the child they could not kill. [19] And now he lay wide-eyed, awaiting those who should take charge of him. [20] No childish cry did he make, but seemed to follow the movements of the men of Leng as a master observes his servants at work.

[21] As the company, carefully bearing the babe wrapped in swaddling, passed through the dark streets of Beth-Lehem, they were greeted by the sounds of violence and of the screaming of infants, [22] for Herod had sent his troops on the heels of the men of Leng and their guards. [23] The monks listened quietly, as if the screams contained some message that none but they could hear. [24] And thus was fulfilled the words of scripture, "Out of the mouths of babes and sucklings thou hast brought forth perfect praise."

2 [1] None hindered their journeying as they passed on into the land of Egypt after many days. Palm dates were their food, but also the lizards and scorpions of the desert. For these, too, may nourish the body when the soul is fitly prepared. [2] The men of Leng made their way at once to the great Sphinx, to the hidden adytum known but to the adepts, and it was to these that they entrusted the child.

[3] Within the deep chambers under the Sphinx and within the Pyramids did the child grow in stature and in learning. [4] For, though he

was in truth the fleshly embodiment of One whose ways are from of old, yet his fleshly mind must be brought to remembrance of those secrets he had known before.

⁵ There in the immemorial land of the asp and the viper, of the jackal and the crocodile, did the Avatar wipe away forgetfulness. ⁶ There did he learn again the arts he himself had created before the very foundation of the world. ⁷ The Pyramid adepts came to know him as Hermes Trismegistus, as their ancient forbears had. And they presumed to instruct him and to initiate him. ⁸ And this they did with fear and trembling lest they make some error that their disciple should recognize, and make them pay dreadfully.

⁹ Some days he would embark up the Nile, which he said was the extended form of Set-Typhon himself. ¹⁰ And he said that, just as the boat of Osiris would reach the end and sink down into Amente to resurface like an underground spring back at the point of departure, ¹¹ so had he gone down into the great Vault below, where the ghouls cavorted among the rock tombs of Neb. And these did teach him the mysteries of the worm.

¹² At length he was ready to return to the land of his birth. The men of Leng had grown old and died in the meantime, ¹³ but he did not depart Egypt alone, for it was said that great leopards followed him and licked his hands.

¹⁴ When he had reached the age of twelve, a second embassy from Yian-Ho journeyed to the land of Israel to observe and to guide him. ¹⁵ They asked no one the way this time, but proceeded unerringly to the temple in Jerusalem, where they found him in heated debate with the elders. ¹⁶ These explained to him how the temple had been founded on the great navel stone of the world, and that the world itself could not survive the destruction of the holy place, ¹⁷ since it was only the sacrifices offered there that dissuaded Jehovah from visiting the world in judgment.

¹⁸ But he said to them, "Do you see this temple made with hands? The day will come when I will destroy it and will establish another, in which you and your children shall be offered unto older gods. ¹⁹ The world you know will end when it returns to its rightful owners. In truth, you are like wicked tenants who took the vineyard for their own, saying, 'The master is long delayed; he will never return.'"

²⁰ The elders of the Jews were enraged at the saying, and they spoke no more with him. ²¹As he made to depart from the temple, the men of Leng came to meet him, explaining that it was time for him to come with them

back to the monastery, [22] where he should learn the secrets pertaining to his destiny. And he went with them obediently.

[23] They must needs cross the borders of Rome's empire and that of the neighboring Parthians, but none waylaid them. [24] Their provisions were renewed as needed as they were greeted by certain hermits and barbarian sorcerers who had been warned of their passing in dreams and premonitions. [25] The journey was long, and the company gained advantage in some places, losing it in others, as they followed ancient, hidden routes to the great plateau they sought.

[26] And he arrived at the monastery to the acclaim of all, seated upon a yak, as all the brethren spread their blood-red robes upon the rocky ground before him. [27] There the Avatar learned things which may not be uttered. [28] There they prepared him for the exercise of the office to which he was born, that of the High Lama of Leng, for the day he should be invested with the yellow robes and the silken mask. [29] But that day was not yet, for the one who then sat the throne would keep his post for a few more years before his successor should welcome the brethren to the sacred feast of his flesh.

3 [1] When he reached his thirtieth year he embarked upon the journey back to Israel, and this time he journeyed alone. [2] He suffered much along the way, but the time passed quickly as he meditated on all he had learned, upon that which he had been brought to recall, dispelling the stupor of the flesh.

[3] The Avatar commenced preaching in the meeting places of the Jews throughout Galilee, and each time he preached, he was cast out by the elders until word went around, and he was welcome nowhere. [4] For he brought a message strange and hateful to their ears. It was the tidings of a coming kingdom that would blot out all that came before it, even all that was. [5] "He that seeketh to save his life shall lose it, but he that loseth his life shall find it." And many other such things he told them.

[6] Once as he preached a man possessed of an unclean spirit cried out, saying, "What have you to do with us? We know who you are!"

[7] But he answered, "Blessed are you! Come, follow me!" [8] And the man passed through the crowd, who one and all shrank away from him, and he followed him.

[9] Another time he found a youth who foamed at the mouth and threw himself into the fire, and none could stop him. [10] The Avatar saith unto him, "Come, follow me!" And immediately he did so. [11] Again, he came to shore in the region called the Decapolis, as if he

had arranged to meet someone there. ¹²And there came out to greet him a man who went naked and lived among the tombs, gashing his own flesh and breaking every chain the people might put on him. ¹³ He was tormented by the earthbound souls of those buried in the cemetery, for, being in the Decapolis, it was unclean ground. ¹⁴Seeing him, he said to him, "Name yourself!" And the fellow cried out, "Legion, for myriads of us live in him!" ¹⁵ And he bowed before him, and asked that he might follow him. And the Avatar gave him leave to do so. ¹⁶ And they got into the boat and returned to Galilee. And many of the harlots and sinners followed him.

¹⁷ And the Romans sent spies to watch his movements, but he knew of it and cared nothing. ¹⁸ One day he sent one of his followers to the spies. "Be sure that you say to them, 'My Master says, "One day your proudest cities will fall to ruin and sink into the ground from which they were hewed. ¹⁹ In a single night they will fall, and all the tribes of the earth shall mourn when they behold their doom descending upon them. ²⁰ Sea bottoms shall be exposed to the gaze of men when the valleys are raised up and rough places are made a plain. And you will quail at what you see there.""" ²¹ And the Romans did not understand him, but they began to look for an opportunity to arrest him.

²² And it happened one day as they took their rest in the village of Chorazin, that he asked those who were with him, "Who do men say that I am?" ²³ And they answered, "Some say you are a false prophet. Others say Belial, and others the Antichrist." ²⁴ And he said, "But who do you say that I am?" And Legion said unto him, "You are Nyarlathotep, the Creeping Chaos."

THE RIGHTEOUS RISE

I have the privilege of membership as a Fellow of the Jesus Seminar, the most publicly notorious arm of the scholarly think-tank called The Westar Institute. Our research, shared in popular editions for over a decade with a hungry public, has brought us grateful praise from an audience of seekers dissatisfied with traditional church pabulum, and equal or greater indignation from the wider church public, including, one must admit, erstwhile colleagues who hastened to distance themselves from us once we began to expose for public scrutiny the long hushed-up conclusions of critical scholarship. Even within this scholarly fellowship, my own theories have tended to be so marginalized, influenced by the Dutch Radical School of the nineteenth century, that I have learned there is only so much I may share even with these beloved colleagues and fellow explorers into the shadowed past. This, probably destined to be nothing more than a superfluous note to myself, prefaces my translation of an astonishing document discovered a number of years ago by unknown persons, from whom it eventually passed into the hands of John M. Allegro, one of the first delvers into the Dead Sea Scrolls, and the only one not a devout Roman Catholic. Though my own academic career did not overlap with Dr. Allegro's, as a young man I came to admire his work, in some ways more radical than my own is now, and I was thrilled to shake his hand at a conference in Ann Arbor, Michigan, shortly before his death. His early books on the scrolls, some occasionally reprinted even now, are not controversial. His mature work was far more polarizing, even shocking: The Sacred Mushroom and the Cross, The Dead Sea Scrolls and the Christian Myth, etc. Having come into possession of the document that follows here, he had first thought to prepare a critical edition and make it known to the public, but failing health as well as discouragement over the universal repudiation of his work among the lock-step phalanx of conventional scholars led him to put aside these plans until it was too late. As practically the only admirer, I am sorry to say, of

Allegro's work, I easily persuaded his heirs to hand the project over to me. Once I saw what it was he had uncovered, I began to rethink my resolve. I now see that Allegro must have realized it would have been an utter waste of time to publish the manuscript, for the sheer impossibility that anyone would deem it more than a fiction and a hoax. Nor am I seeking publication now as I write. I suppose this brief preface is just to satisfy the curiosity of any of my own heirs who may in future days chance to pick up these sheets. Indeed, such a reader will most likely think the whole thing my own invention. Well, by the time you read this, I shall in any case be quite beyond caring.

These are the sworn last words of Joseph of Arimathea, member of the Sanhedrin of the Fifty, on whose account the Almighty Power does ever suspend righteous judgment from a sinful world. In the recounting I am about to write, I shall seek to leave out nothing of any weight from such recollections of my brethren as may be required unto the sense of the narrative. You will forgive an old man's inability to recover precise words, though many of them I could not forget if so I wished.

It was the day the death of Jesus the Nazorean was being accomplished, and I lay tossing on my cot. My wife and sons had hidden me in the inner court of the dwelling in case Pilate's men should seek me out during the tumult that shook the city, for not only mortal men but nature itself rocked and swayed with indignation. Yet of these things I lay oblivious as visions, fueled by the fever, rushed upon me like the nightmares of the wicked. Truly, it was not fever heat I felt but the very flames of Gehenna. I danced upon a merciless griddle, and my flesh seemed about to drop away from blackened bone, yet relief did not come to me. I felt as if I were one with that sow that Antiochus, may he be cursed, had caused to be sacrificed upon the altar of defilement. I shrieked, but there was no sound. It was all I could muster to remember my own name. But it was not my own name. In the grip of fantastic mania I believed myself to be Menandros the Essene. This was not a name unknown to me, but rather of a lamented friend, in his day a member of the Sanhedrin of the Fifty Righteous like myself. Here was a mystery: that one of the Righteous on whose account the world still stands~committed to the hell of fire! And yet I knew too well the reason for his, for my, presence there.

But suddenly, as my fever broke, and my forehead bathed itself in a crown of welcome sweat, the pangs of Tophet loosened themselves. And through the eyes of old Menandros I glimpsed, not the inside of my own house, but the dank and foul-smelling interior of a rock-cut tomb. The fit of the stone door was imperfect, and sunset rays gave some light to the scene within. My immobile form lay idle on a stone bench cut from the hill wall. My hands began to move first, and it was an easy matter to shrug away the rotting linen bands that had embraced me. I feared to extend arms and legs lest I look upon limbs ravaged by mold and maggot. But they were clear, bearing naught but the familiar wrinkles and spots I had grown accustomed to in life. A life to which I, or rather Menandros, had now returned. And then I awoke.

Beholding my fevered seizures on the cot, my family kept vigil around me for what remained of that dreadful day, now and again one of them creeping toward a window to receive a whisper of the latest tidings. So strange and distressing were these that I knew not what to credit. Had tale-bearers already been at work embellishing them? One said that mild quakings shook the earth, the which I, too, had felt, though at the time I did imagine these tremors to be part of my dreams. Pilate's men might still be observed roaming the narrow, cobbled streets, but they seemed now more intent on keeping general order than in rounding up those who had confessed faith in Jesus as King of the Jews. Of these I was commonly believed to be one, as so I was, save that I knew there was rather more to the Nazorean than most thought.

My fever returned about the third hour. I dreamed again, and once more I was not myself but took the name of another of my old fellows of the Fifty, another man whose loss I had mourned these last years, Abramelin of Socho. I felt no heat this time but instead a great parching of the throat, like a man wandering long in the wilderness. But wandering was denied me, for I was bound, my feet tied to some boulder or weight below me~in a depth of water stopping just above my wetted beard. The water around me was clear, clearer than the Lake of Genessaret, so that passing fishes were easily to be seen. Some paid me a moment's curious regard as they swam past my ungainly twistings and turnings, all in the effort to lower my chin and lap up some of the delicious water. But naught availed. Just above my head, like refreshing drops of rain, suspended by some magic, hung ripe and luscious fruits. I craned my neck till it pained me greatly, and still I found no means of satisfying thirst and hunger. And throughout all was the rueful memory that it might always have been so, and the leaden certainty that it should always be so, and the self-reproach for what I had done to put myself, or rather Abramelin, thinking with his thoughts, in such a place.

But at once there was a change, and I felt a welcome sense of free movement. I heard at some distance the common sound as of a clay pot shattering upon impact, as if thrown from a window, and then I felt no wetness and no binding of my limbs. Still I thirsted, but it was no more such agony. I sat up from the dusty ground, clearing away sharp shards of clay which pricked my back. And I saw through the gloom a line of irregular glazed jars, all about the same size, with names and holy symbols emblazoned thereon. They were ossuaries, containing the bones of the dead. I whispered thanks to the angels and got up, testing the strength of my spindly legs. The door was not hard to open, and I (which is to say, Abramelin) slipped into the night, heading instinctively for the Holy City as if in answer to some call.

My niece Tabitha caught me walking in my sleep and woke me from this dream. She was not much distressed, having learned over many years to expect the strange from her old uncle Joseph. The rest of my relations were just returning from outside, where the darkness had emboldened them to venture. And yet it was not night-time. From nowhere, it seemed, an eclipse had eaten the sun. Unwelcome in the season of Passover, when the full moon ought to be visible, the prodigy augured divine displeasure, but beyond this, whispered opinions divided: was the Most High showing his displeasure against the blasphemer Jesus or against those who had persecuted this prophet of God? That each man must decide for himself, or so Jesus would have said.

Helping me back to a bed whose clammy touch I would as well

escape, my sister and her daughter charged me to lie there and regain my strength. How could I, I tried to reason with them, when my friend must soon breathe his last atop the lonely gallows hill of Gol-Gotha, so named for the circle of standing stones amid which the latter-day Romans had taken to crucifying their Jewish subjects. Nonetheless, I drifted again into fitful sleep. As I did so, I thought I heard the fearful whispers of those about me that new and more terrifying reports had filtered in from passersby. For in the unnatural darkness that banished the day, the priests and Levites had in alarm sought the counsel of the Most High in the Temple Sanctuary, offering sacrifice and chanting psalms. And after they had so performed for an hour or so, as if in answer to their displays the great veil of purple, blue, and scarlet, whose topmost section was woven with gold in the form of laden grapevines, began to split open, without visible cause, from top to bottom, revealing the forbidden Inner Sanctum. Here none but the High Priest dares enter, and even then but once a year to offer the blood of atonement. The priests on duty, it was said, stopped in their tracks. They caught a glimpse of what lay within and fled in terror, precipitating a stampede of the gathered crowd, which not even the Temple police were able to stop.

More Roman troops were called forth from the adjacent Antonia Fortress to make sure the fleeing crowd did not ignite into riot. But they found themselves less than eager to intervene when reports began to reach them from still other panicked Jerusalemites that certain familiar faces of the sainted dead were being recognized here and there throughout the city. I knew as I heard these bedside mutterings that they must be the product of my fever-madness. And yet as I plunged deeper into sleep's enfolding layers, I felt that I understood even the strangest of what was happening on this fateful day.

Now I saw before me, sitting by her fire, the wizened, toothless face of a woman who was no relation of mine. No relation to Joseph, that is. But she was known to me at that moment, for she was the old mother of Nectebanus the sage, dead these last three years, and I was Nectebanus. Her distress showed widely across her face, and she asked me, asking Nectebanus, why the sun should be dark at such a time of day, and why her son should be alive again. I know not what he may have told her as I took my leave of their company at this juncture. But I was beginning to think I knew the answer to her questions.

***

Three *tau*-marks stood etched crudely against the sky, darker blurs against the gray void, drained of the sun at the very height of mid-day. Two silent forms gathered their strength to hold onto another useless hour of life. The man between them mumbled something, perhaps words of scripture to comfort himself on this, the crumbling ledge of eternity. The three of them were all but naked, mere strips half-protecting their forgotten modesty. Each alike was tied with abrasive rope to the crossbeam. What visibly distinguished the others from the man in the middle was the laurel wreath of nail-length thorns twisted gingerly into this peculiar shape and perched atop his pockmarked scalp. Mingled blood and sweat flowed down to irritate the wretch, so that he now and again shook his head feebly from side to side to shake off the stinging, salty fluid.

Watchful Roman eyes were fixed upon this man from below, where a centurion, despising his task, waited for these scarecrows to die. He had derived some small amusement a couple of hours before when the two men on the ends traded insults to one another, chiefly crude remarks about each other's genital endowments. Their bravado had ceased when the sunlight was eclipsed in some unnatural fashion. Now he listened carefully to the middle figure, who had begun to speak only once the light was gone. The Roman held his hastily lit lantern aloft and focused on the bruised lips of the torture victim, seeking to read the stammered Aramaic that fell from them now and then. He idly wondered if one so close to the lip of the next world might see something and try to forewarn the living. He could make out little. But he did notice, of a sudden, that with one of the man's periodic attempts to shake away the sweat in his eyes, his mock crown had almost been dislodged. For some reason the centurion felt this must not be allowed to happen, and he set down the lantern, tried to make sure of his mark, and hoisted his lance up to push the crown back into a more secure position with the sharp tip of the spear. What he could not see for the deep shadows was that his spearpoint had raked the forehead of the crucified man. Something else he could not see was a short line of what would have appeared to be healed scars, just at his hairline, forming the Hebrew word *emet*, "truth" or "faithfulness." Little did the Roman know his lancehead had nicked the flesh to the right of this scar, omitting the tiny rightmost letter. In an instant, the man slumped dead, no more fighting half-heartedly for breath. The centurion thought it odd and hoped Pilate would not think he had somehow killed the man before his sentence of suffering was complete. And then he noticed it was growing lighter.

***

Some measure of composure returned to my family once the light of the sun was restored about the ninth hour. The quaking of the earth had subsided as well, and word reached us that Jesus the Nazorean was dead, mercifully dead given the design of crucifixion to kill its victims from exposure over several days' time. Things seemed to be returning to normal~save for one lingering shadow of nightmare. Rumors persisted that many of the righteous of past days had been seen alive again in or nearby the places they had once dwelt, received alternatively with terror or delight, as at the return of one long prodigal. And every name was known to me. They were my brethren of the Sanhedrin of the Fifty Righteous on whose behalf the world continued, ever since the Holy One of Israel did swear unto our father Abraham that he should not destroy the Cities of the Plain if fifty righteous should be found within. The Angel of Death had thinned our ranks in recent years till I was the last left alive.

I rose from my sickbed, now in truth feeling much invigorated, perhaps from determination, and I brooked none of the attempts of my loved ones to hinder me. It was not the first such occasion. Now, as before, I wended my way as rapidly as my old limbs would take me through winding alleys in the oldest portion of the city, that in which the unclean ruins of the shrines of ancient Jebusite gods used to stand, and where rock-strewn passages yet opened upon nether secrets, provided one knew where to look for them. And I did. All the Fifty had known. And as I carefully sought each precarious step, I recalled the equally dangerous steps that had led to my previous course of action and its present aftermath.

***

Some three years before, when the Fifty Righteous were convened in prayer and advisement, I did mourn greatly, and another inquired of me, "O Joseph, praytell, wherefore is thy countenance fallen?" In truth I had grown thus sombre following the reporting of several of our number who, as was their wont, spent the year traveling to and fro through the earth. Our own lot was to act as salt savoring the world with a view toward making the same pleasing to God. If not, the world should still go on despite the magnitude of its sins, but our role would be little more than that of hostages, for whose sake, because of his ancient promise, the Almighty must needs spare mankind. And I for one was greatly crestfallen at the state of things, at the plague of evil and oppression that stretched like the empire of the Evil One across the boundaries of Rome, Parthia, Hind, Cathay, and whatever other lands might exist in God's wide knowledge.

I voiced among my brethren the hitherto unspoken fear that such a world might one day be found not to yield so scant a harvest as fifty righteous in a single generation. Our ranks were old and gray-bearded, with few on the horizon to replenish us. We must, I urged, undertake bold measures to purify the world in the sight of God, lest worse come to worst and all be lost. If God had ordained us as captains of a ship now tossing amid a great storm, surely our task was to find a means to see the ship safe into port, not to witness its final disappearance beneath the churning waves. All were weary, as I was, and though weariness often brings with it a paralyzing complacency, these were the Fifty Righteous, and they did not ignore my pleas. The question was what, precisely, we might do.

If my diagnosis was not controversial, the same cannot be said for my prescription. I had devoted much study to the scriptures until I concluded that much power might lie idle and dormant until some mighty man of valor should step forth to don the mantel of history, even as Saul, and Jephthah, and Gideon before us. They, too, lived in trying times, times when their people, though full of vigor, yet languished for the lack of any firebrand to ignite it. We the Fifty ought, I judged, to anoint such a champion, who might draw upon the forces with which God had endowed us, and to act mightily and heroically in ways closed to a group of aging and secret adepts. In recent years, many had instinctively looked to men of the stature of Athronges the Shepherd King and of John the Baptist to fill such a role, but these were struck down too easily by the mighty fist of Rome. Nay, the times required one with visible powers that should give a clear sign of the presence of God among men. And thus I proposed that we *create* us a champion such as we sought. There was a way, as all knew.

I had come to the meeting prepared, and now I brought forth the hoary scroll of *Yetsirah*, a collection of secrets surviving from before the flood, formulae bequeathed to the Nephilim by their fathers, the fallen Sons of Elyon. There were others like it housed in the repository where we met: the venerable *Book of Raziel* which Noah received from the archangel Raphael, containing cures for every illness; the terrifying *Stelae of Seth* of which none ever speaketh; the dreaded *Key of Shalmanu*, which Solomon stole away to summon the demons to build him a temple against the will of God. But I knew the *Sepher Yetsirah* held the secrets used by the Almighty Creator himself to make mankind, and which might with trepidation be employed likewise to repeat that endeavor.

And so I proposed to the assembly. Much debate followed. Several of the brethren begged time to familiarize themselves with the contents of the writing, which they had hitherto shunned, considering it blasphemy. It was a matter of months before we met again to reach a consensus, and yet more months before we had prepared the needful ingredients and arrangements, which I may not set down here. But at length, there beneath the streets of ancient Salem, even Jebusite Jerusalem, which once did echo the sandaled feet of Melchizedek, there lay before us the roughly molded clay *homunculus*, a puppetlike suggestion of the form of man. It reclined in a shallow tub of water enriched with divers substances. Chalk symbols ringed the basin, while corpse-fat candlesticks ringed these at a further distance. The head was propped so that the face from the cheekbones to the scalp-line was exposed. I had stooped down to engrave in the firm clay four letters, *e-m-e-t*, truth. This word of power should impart life and power to the Golem we had formed, and whom no man might stop save by effacing again the first of the letters, reducing the word to *met*, death. On this one we would set our hope. Into this one we had contrived to transfer our powers and vitalities, that he might succeed in saving a world which we had grown too old and tired to save.

I rose to my feet, and my friend Hibil-Ziwa handed me the text of *Yetsirah*, from which I read slowly. "And the mighty angels each did take of his own virtues and combined them into the form of a man which they had made from the clay of the bed of the River of Life. And they breathed life into what they had made, saying, 'He shall be called *Enosh*, for he is the first of men.' And a Voice did sound from the Four-Faced One seated on the sapphire throne, saying, 'Let all God's angels worship him!'" Whereupon I did make the final needful gesture, and all of us did kneel, our old bones creaking, to the rough chamber floor. And as we knelt, the figure within the circle did slowly rise, his eyes glowing with wisdom and power. And I feared much to speak now, but I must, saying, "You are like the man, though you are made by man, hence you shall be called *bar-enosh*, the Son of Man!" He turned to look at me with magnanimity.

***

Tripping only once or twice, distracted by memories, I succeeded in descending unto the adytum I sought, and once there, recollection melded seamlessly with reality, for here, as accustomed, were the restored circle of the Fifty Righteous, and I was unsure for the moment whether perhaps again I dreamed upon my sickbed. But no, the forms were real, their welcoming hands and words all too convincing. None knew precisely what had transpired in the world above, though many had some surmise to offer. We gathered in council as we had of old, the thoughtful gazes and wise words of Menandros, Hibil-Ziwa, Abramelin, Nectebanus, and all the rest a welcome delight in these most straitened of times.

I jested, apologizing for being the last of us left alive. But Eliadnor of Tyre corrected me, a gleam in his eye once he had brushed a clinging cobweb from it, "Nay, brother, you are no straying sheep, but you have returned to the flock."

"Rather, I should say that the rest of the flock has returned to me!" said I, still jovial. But this is not what my friend intended. Abramelin spoke next. "Perhaps, old friend, you knew not how very ill you were in these last days! How do you suppose you were able to visit with several of us in spirit and to witness the moment of our returning?"

Quoth Menandros the Essene, "Forsooth, you, too, became like us! You died, and your soul hastened to join us in the Pit of Tophet. But then *somewhat* intervened, restoring both you and us. Mayhap it was the clemency of the Lord, which causeth the prisoner to pine but which cometh at last." Here the man closed his eyes and lowered his head, meseems, in prayer. But I could no more hold my tongue.

"Nay, it was not as you suppose! But it was mine own will and working that regathered us here, though I am no less surprised than you at the result!" Here I explained to my brethren, all more astonished than hitherto, if that were possible, how we had come to this pass.

***

The appearance of the Son of Man amid the multitudes of Galilee and Peroea was marked with great acclaim. At once he was a sensation, healing both the bodies and the souls of those who sought his ministrations. And as he sought to rid the world of its affliction with evil, he scrupled not to beard the beast of sin in its lair.

And it happened one day that Jesus entered a village called

Magadan. And on the street he chanced to recognize some who were highly praised for their righteousness in the synagogues of Bethany, of Caphar-Nahum, of Nazareth, and of Chorazin. And he asked what business brought them here. Now the chief occupation of the men of Magadan was that of fishing, but none of these men had any employment in that trade. Now one man, dismayed to see Jesus, answered him some false excuse, and so did the next. And Jesus waited and saw where they went in. And he inquired of one of the men of Magadan, of what business might be transacted in that dwelling, and he was told, "Yonder is the house of Mary Magdalene, she who is known as the Great Harlot who hath grown wealthy on the trade of the nations, for all do come to see her ply her trade." Jesus gazed in the direction of her house, which was large and fronted with Greek pillars, and he said, "She seemeth to be the veriest embodiment of Lilith, who causeth God's servants to go astray." And withal, Jesus, too, went to her door and entered. And he began to overturn the tables of those who took payment and the couches of the harlots. Beaded curtains he seized and wielded as whiplashes to turn the flutegirls and the sinners out half-dressed into the streets, where they were much discomfited. At the ruckus, the Magdalene herself emerged from the inner chambers like Goliath alerted to the arrival of his mortal foe. "What have you to do with us, Jesus the Nazorean? I know who you are, O son of dust!" And Jesus replied, "And likewise do I know thee all too well, Magdalene, for that thou art not the harlot in the brothel, but rather even that very brothel in which seven wicked spirits cavort despite thee!" And he said some words invoking the Prophet Elijah, whereupon the Magdalene pitched over in convulsions as seven dybbuks fled from her supine form. And as they fled, one knocked over a pair of hanging lamps and set the place ablaze. As Jesus took Mary Magdalene to safety, now in her right mind and free of the band of devils, he uttered these words: "So shall the fire of untoward lust at length consume itself! He who has ears, let him hear!"

Not long afterward, these tidings reached my ears, and soon I heard also of the sad passing of my colleague Abramelin. I thought not to connect the two events at the time, but upon reflection, I was able to determine that the death followed hard upon the heels of the deliverance of the harlot, even in the selfsame hour, though many miles removed.

And Jesus came with his growing circle of disciples to the house of Simon in Caphar-Nahum, where Simon's daughter had long consumed the resources of the family with lingering illness, for she was sorely crippled since birth. And Simon had told him about her, hoping he might see fit to heal her. But as they entered the house, Simon's mother-in-law told him, "Trouble not the teacher the more, for the child is dead." And she wept much, but Simon only looked at Jesus. And Jesus said, "Where is the child?" And they showed him to the inner room, and he took with him Simon and Andrew and Jacob, and he bent over the girl's twisted form and said to her, "I tell you, daughter of Simon, get up!" And the girl arose and made to embrace her father. And all rejoiced, save Simon himself, so that Jesus asked him, "What troubleth thee, Simon?" And Simon replied, averting his gaze, "Forsooth, master, I hoped you might heal her of her affliction as well, yet she is no better, albeit she lives again." And Jesus said to him, "Do you think the Son of Man came to make men's lives easier? Nay, rather, harder, for only so may they learn endurance and compassion."

This I heard from Simon himself soon afterward, who had in the interval come to accept the wisdom of his lord. On the same occasion it was Simon who reported to me the death of Hezekiah ben-Imlah, another of the Fifty. He saw no connection.

One day Jesus entered a village of Judea, where a beggar approached him from a narrow alley, saying, "Jesus the Nazorean! Have mercy and heal me! Surely such is the will of God, is it not?" Jesus stopped in his way and looked at the man, answering him, "It may be. Let us see." And he touched the withered leg of the man, who said, "I injured it while I slept, I know not how." In a moment, his leg was sound like the other, and he went on his way rejoicing, leaping with the very leg that had hobbled him. Now Jesus lingered in that village, teaching. And it was not long before men told him of a rash of thefts and burglaries. And Jesus said, "Be vigilant, for if the master of the house had known in what hour the thief would come, he would not have suffered him to carry away his goods." And so Jesus himself kept watch that night and, sure enough, he caught a man looking though his things. No longer feigning sleep, he said to the robber, "What seek you? Have I not already given you such as I possess?" For in truth it was the lame man he had healed a few days earlier. And at once the man's leg withered up again. "If it is the will of God, it is better to beg from others than to steal from them."

I smiled when they repeated the episode to me, but at once my spirit was quenched by the news of another old friend's death, this time Hibil-Ziwa of the Rechabites. I began to fear.

When next I met with my brethren of the Fifty, there was great rejoicing at the seeming success of our endeavor, for they had all heard similar stories, and yet there were fewer gathered than in former days. And as the weeks and months went on, and the fame of Jesus the Nazorean grew, our numbers declined proportionately. If any besides me understood the linkage, they remained as silent as I did, reckoning that the price we were paying was a small one in view of the good we beheld accomplished on all sides. I gladly acquiesced in what seemed to be happening to us, since it was plain that the saving role of the Fifty had been transferred to more capable shoulders. The world might go on quite well without a crowd of old men huddling in secret. Our Golem would succeed, was succeeding where we had done nothing save to delay the inevitable slide into the Abyss. So Jesus increased from strength unto strength, while our number dwindled.

Oh, I knew well enough that when all of us whose powers energized him were exhausted and dead, Jesus' own powerful deeds must cease. All things must come to an end. Our wager was that, when that time came, Jesus should have effected so much good in the world as to have fended off the advances of darkness and of the Evil One. One is so often blinded by the glow of optimism, alas. Little did any of us foresee that, as Jesus weakened, leaving miracles behind and devoting more time to teaching his disciples, the crowds would begin to grow cooler to him, missing the bread and circuses he had first provided them, as they must have regarded them. At length, they should play into the hands of our enemies, Rome and the Powers behind their masks, and our defenses spent, the Darkness should rally for one last assault.

All this came home to me with resistless clarity once all the Fifty

127

but myself had passed away and, as I subsequently learned, entered the torment which our blasphemous usurpation of the divine prerogatives had earned us. Once the word arrived that Jesus had been arrested at the Olive Press of Gethsemane, I knew I must act quickly if there was to be any chance at all of undoing the damage my brethren and I had done. In the silence of the tomblike cavity beneath Old Jerusalem, I stood without witnesses and chanted softly from the *Sefer Yetsirah*, seeking to unleash and direct a bolt of the primeval life-force like unto that we had at the first released to make the Golem stand up. I hoped to revivify the Nazorean at the moment of his death, or as near to it as I might venture. I finished as much of the ritual as I could, without anyone to take the antiphonal part. My spirits still low, I crept back up the way I had come and retired to my cot, suddenly enervated. And so my fever dreams began.

As I now told my old friends and fellow-workers, my spell had gone astray. I had unleashed the Power of Creation, for which no doubt I should be doubly damned, but I had been a modicum too early, and the effect was unanticipated. Instead, it was the disintegrating forms of the buried Fifty which returned to life, creating havoc in the city as they ventured a hesitant return to their accustomed domiciles, then sought refuge in the last place it remained to them, even here. Our Jesus was dead, but we lived, for how long none might say. And no longer could we claim the distinction of the Sanhedrin of the Righteous, since we above all other men had transgressed the laws of God, relying upon our own rashness, mistaking it for wisdom. Surely our mere presence in the world could no longer serve to stave off its doom. If anything, we appeared to have hastened it.

But then, as the tattered form of Dositheus the Samaritan now observed, Jesus himself had done nothing but good. He could not have attracted to himself the damnation of a righteous God. And where I alone had failed, and died, might the restored college of Fifty succeed? Might we not again pool our life-forces, our knowledge of the arcane elements, to bring back the Nazorean from the dead? Miracles would likely remain beyond his grasp, but it was evident now that such had never been the strength of his ministry to the heart and the soul in any event. If we could but secure him a few added years in which to complete his teaching! Who knew? Perhaps he might succeed in building a new Sanhedrin of Fifty Righteous. And if he did not, if the world no longer possessed a guarantee of salvation despite its depravity, perhaps that was just as well. Perhaps the children of men would finally understand the gravity of their need. Perhaps the long stalemate of good versus evil, which the cumulative weight of the Fifty had only served to maintain in balance, would issue in a final struggle, for better or for worse. That might even prove to be the real will of God.

With no alternative available, the risen sages agreed to pursue my course, and we made as many of the ritual preparations as we could. The thing took some hours, but at length we were done. At once I left for Gol-Gotha, hoping that I might prevail upon the hegemon Pilate, a man not unknown to me from better times, to let me take charge of the corpse of Jesus, lest it be cast, as seemed likely, into a common lime pit. As I returned to the surface, I mused that I should never more see the Fifty, that already they must be collapsing again, this time in an unknown tomb that should hide their mysteriously missing corpses forever from the sight of men.

Despite the day's tumult, or rather perhaps because of it, the usual official barriers were easier to make one's way round, and finally I gained audience with Pilate. He was thoroughly exhausted with the strange business of the day. He had heard the superstitious rumors and sought to calm the fears of those who spread them, applying force as needed, and he was most heartily sick of it. With my request scarcely out of my mouth, he waved his permission and dismissed me with a paper hastily inscribed by one of his attendant scribes. I needed but give it to the centurion on duty, and he would assign a soldier to carry the body to my own nearby tomb.

Once the body of Jesus lay prone on the stone shelf of the tomb, I gave it a cursory examination, then noticed the torn flesh on the forehead. At first mistaking it for another wound of the thorny crown, I soon recognized the incidental effacement of the crucial letter, without which the mark of divine truth had changed to the mute seal of death. I was no surgeon, nor had I any tools to repair the wound, but I felt that the flesh of the Golem had begun to return, almost imperceptibly, to its original clay, something I had not anticipated. So it was a simple matter merely to smooth the flesh and reinscribe the torn letter. And at once the skin was warm again beneath my fingertips. His eyes opened. His mouth said one word. "Joseph." Then his glowing eyes blinked, and he spoke again. "I am he that liveth and was dead."

I put my finger against his lips and whispered, "No, master. Not now. I have but little time. You may not have much more. And we have much to accomplish. Let us go forth."

***

Where, you may wonder, did they go? Allegro said he had bought the manuscript from a trader (many of the Dead Sea Scrolls came into scholarly hands that way), not from an Arab smuggler, but from an antiquities dealer who swore the thing came from Nepal. Make of it what you will.

The Savage Sword of Jehu

i. Whispers from the Shadows

"But, Jehu my brother, how can you continue in the service of the witch-queen? How can a man sworn to Yahweh pledge allegiance to that priestess of Baal, and thus to Baal himself? I fear for your soul!"

With these tearful words, Tamar buried her face in the mighty chest of Jehu, weeping. Returning his sister's embrace, the guardsman Jehu rested his bearded cheek against her forehead and sought to reassure her.

"But I've told you before, I don't know how many times, of my plan. I have worked my way up through the ranks so that I may find myself close enough to Queen Jezebel to strike and to dispel the shadow she has caused to fall upon Israel. This is the land of Yahweh Sabaoth, and he will not share his worship with another! Do you not believe me?"

Suppressing her sobs for the moment, Tamar replied, "Of course I believe you, my brother! But great is the danger you face! King Ahab is a weak-willed child, putty in her hands. He has not lifted a finger to stop his foreign wife from spreading the cult of Baal where it does not belong. It falls to others to do it. And it will be done! The Prophet Elijah has pronounced her doom already! The wild dogs will lick up her foul blood from the gutters. It is the will of the Almighty! Do you think he requires your sword arm to strike for him? Let God act in his own time!"

"But that's just it, Tamar. The time has arrived! We faithful remnant of Yahweh dare wait no longer. For I have heard whispers in the palace that Jezebel is close to offering a final sacrifice, mustering the power needed to open the Gate to Baal and to bring him from his cursed domain into our world. And I for one doubt if

Yahweh will save us if we do not undertake to save ourselves! I tell you, do not worry, for it must be over soon, and the arm of Yahweh and the sword of Jehu shall prevail!"

Withal the towering figure kissed his sister's tear-damp cheek and stooped so as not to bump the doorway with his head. He squinted as he left the modest structure with its thatch roof and emerged into the blazing morning sunlight. He had walked his way, baked by the sun's oven, his entire life. His hide was deeply bronzed, his black mane lightened to brown. His brawn was barely bridled by his guard's harness. As he neared the palace, he hailed a couple of his comrades, coming off their shifts. Had you leaned very close, you might have heard something more serious than vacant pleasantries. Scant syllables, coded signals, portended great developments impending. Feigned smiles masked the subversive truth.

In the very shadow of the palace roof lurked a gaunt, wiry form, almost as tall as Jehu. The figure's sudden whisper startled the younger man, a hard thing to do. Jehu caught himself in a flinch, then recognized Jonadab, well-known leader of the ancient Rechabite Brotherhood. Rumor made the old man much more than a sage. Many feared the sorcerous powers they imagined he wielded. Jehu himself was not sure what abilities the old man might be concealing, but Jonadab was so imposing, even ominous, a figure that any wild speculation concerning him seemed plausible. He wore sackcloth gathered with a broad leather belt. He leaned on a gnarled, seemingly iron-hard staff, taller than his own spare frame. Its surface was inlaid with sigils which might have glowed softly when in shadow, though Jehu could not be sure.

"Is your heart right with my heart, as mine is right with yours?"

That is all the elder said. Jehu's only response was to clasp forearms with the other. Then he continued into the palace to assume his post. Standing to one side of the throne room door, he exchanged knowing nods with his counterpart on the other side.

ii. DEVIL'S DEVOTIONS

But the queen was not sitting on her golden throne. King Ahab slouched on his golden chair, the smaller of the two, and he appeared both bored and cowed. It had not taken long after his marriage with the Philistine princess Jezebel to learn, to his great chagrin, that he would henceforth be occupying the back seat. His hen-pecked plight did not earn him the contempt of his subjects, though. Instead, they seemed entirely sympathetic to him, seeing in Ahab a fellow victim of his demon bride. Few suspected it, but their characterization of Queen Jezebel was no mere metaphor. They could not know what the palace staff knew, that, on certain occasions when the counsel or the signature of the king was required, their monarch comported himself in unaccustomed style. Some thought, without daring to voice it, that Ahab's bearing, his expression, his tone of voice were all reminiscent more of the queen than the king. On such occasions the queen was nowhere to be seen, being "indisposed."

But today, though Ahab was not accompanied by Jezebel, he did not manifest her steely haughtiness. His queen was about her business elsewhere. Of this, the Yahweh priests feared and suspected terrible things, unprecedented abominations. In those days no one in Israel believed that their ancestral deity was the only deity. That day was yet a long way off. In the meantime, most believed that each country had the right to its own tutelary deity, even if only a totem. Their worship deserved respect from those whose countries served other gods. But Queen Jezebel had another philosophy. Great was her devotion to her native deity, Baal Melkart, and she was driven to spread his empire throughout her adopted land. And her efforts were meeting with surprising success. How had she managed it? It was simple, really: her Baal was a fertility god. The Israelite Yahweh was a storm god and a warrior. Queen Jezebel claimed that, the greater the kingdom's devotion to Baal, the greater the harvests, the larger the livestock herds. And the people had to agree she was right. It was not that they were repudiating old Yahweh; they just felt that God, like they themselves, could get used to a new arrangement, with two deities sharing the nation's adoration. But there were some, perhaps many, who remembered that Yahweh was a jealous god.

What form did Baal's worship take? It had its unique charms, for it was based on the magic of imitation. If a farmer desired to increase his chances of a good crop, he would visit one of the high places, the hilltop shrines, where he would patronize the attendant priestess, a sacred prostitute. As the farmer planted his seed in her receptive ground, Baal should inseminate his fields with his plentiful rains. Yahweh worship offered nothing like this! It was this seduction, this corruption, against which Elijah the Tishbite had railed. But there were deeper secrets, more shocking rites performed in the inner circles of Baalism. And that was the business that occupied the queen this day. Her husband knew nothing of it—and wanted to know even less.

Somewhere in a torch-lit cavern beneath the palace you would have witnessed strange sights. The rough hewn wall and smooth-worn cobbles underfoot showed very great age, perhaps from the days before the Great Flood. Even the queen did not know how her priests had discovered the place, but little did she care. The great depth, and the tons of rock separating the chamber from the surface, were all that mattered to her, for there was no danger of anyone hearing the screaming echoes of those being tortured and vivisected in Baal's name. These depredations were preparatory to the invocation of Baal planned for one midnight soon when his impatience would end and he would cross over to this world from some foreign dimension unimaginable to man. Pain caused the veil between the spheres to grow thinner and thinner.

Jezebel was busy fortifying her own powers because it took more than human energies to make the needful rites effective. Already her communion with the Other Side had endowed her with considerable potencies, but these she sought now to heighten to the ultimate degree. As much as her depraved priests relished their sadistic labors, few could resist a furtive glance toward the supine queen. For she lay gorgeously naked atop a pile of corpses, some human, others hard to identify. Her sweating body jolted forth and back as one after another hulking figure took his turn mounting her, then pistoning her frantically, finally leaping away to make

room for the next one. Closer attention than the priests dared give
the spectacle would have revealed that the queen's rough lovers were
not precisely *human*. Some had asymmetrical horns, some three
arms of different lengths, others covered with scales or dense fur, or
both.

At last, the exhausted, exhilarated despot found herself without
her welcomed rapists, who seemed to have vanished into thin air.
She sat up, wiping the blood from her eyes, nose, and ears. A pair of
her priestesses rushed to her side, each bearing towels and unguents
which they applied to her lacerated back. But in all this Jezebel felt
no pain, only power. Her eyes showed it; they glowed like coals
amid the shadows. The Baal priests, seeing this, formed a circle
about her and fell prostrate. As for their queen, now their high
priestess, she threw her head back and laughed.

iii. THE SUN OF RIGHTEOUSNESS

Miles outside the capital city of Samaria the faithful of Yahweh were
gathering on the plain. Though Jehu had summoned only the men
of fighting age, he was gratified to see that many had brought their
families, showing how deeply the heart of his people was grieved by
the growing corruption of the nation at the clawed hands of Queen
Jezebel. On Jonadab's advice Jehu had sent messengers even to
Judah to the south. Jezebel had as yet no real influence there, but it
required no oracle to see a short distance into the future. The curse
of depraved Baalism must surely spread there next. Jehu's
messengers had sought to convince the Judeans that the danger,
though still on the horizon, was real. But relations between the
once-united Hebrew kingdoms were always tenuous at best, and the
princes of Judah were ill-inclined to undertake what must become a
full-scale war. Nonetheless, a number of individual soldiers, zealots
for Yahweh, heeded Jehu's desperate call. Many had managed to
make their way to this gathering.

They knew not Jehu by sight but were enthusiastic in their
welcome as he climbed an outcrop of boulders to address them.
Jonadab joined him there; his strength obviously not diminished by

age, he easily made the ascent. Already something of a legend, he was at once recognized by the crowd, who quickly fell silent at his presence.

The Rechabite nodded but said nothing. Jehu, too, was silent as a third figure appeared. No one saw him making the climb, though surely he must have. At sight of this man the multitude gasped in awe. Who did not know the Prophet Elisha, son of Shaphat, by sight? He had once been the disciple of Elijah the Tishbite but now was reputed to have surpassed him in deeds of power. Though Elisha made himself available to the faithful, journeying from village to village, hovel to hovel, none could predict his movements, and for long periods no one saw him. His legend grew as his own disciples speculated as to his whereabouts, whether in this world or others. But here, today, he was.

The prophet of Yahweh, his bald pate reflecting the blinding sun, wordlessly took Jehu by his hilt-calloused hand and pointed downward, whereupon the young giant knelt unselfconsciously before him. Still saying nothing, Elisha drew from the folds of his enveloping robe a small vial of balsam oil. Unstoppering it, he proceeded to pour the contents on the bowed head of Jehu. The crowd gasped again, perceiving all too well the significance of the act. As Elisha stepped back, the other, wiping runnels of the oil from his eyes, stood erect. And Jehu lifted his face to the burning sun and flung his corded arms wide.

"By the one God of the Hebrews, I will drown the House of Ahab in a sea of blood and fire!"

iv. TEMPLE OF NIGHTMARE

The day arrived, and the conspirators were ready—as ready as they could be, though none really knew what to expect. There were guards posted around Baal's temple, several of them Jehu's men. Jehu was a captain of the royal guard, and he arrived early to inspect the troops, exchanging knowing glances with those he could trust. The temple was no great distance from the palace, and Jehu had various preparations to make for the great ceremony, necessitating several chariot trips back and forth between the two buildings, ferrying temple personnel and extra guards, transporting delicacies for the post-ceremonial banquet, and so forth. On the last such trip, he caught sight of Jonadab emerging again from the shadows. Looking around in all directions, he brought his team to a halt before the old man and extended a hand to help him into the chariot. Looking his patron in the eye, Jehu exclaimed, "Come and see my zeal for Yahweh!"

They arrived at the sprawling temple compound, now swarming with Baal's devotees as well as the merely curious and the many country folk hungry for any variation in routine. Jehu dropped the sage off as inconspicuously as he could. He handed the chariot off to the business-like attendants who detached the cab from the team and led the weary animals to the stable. Jehu, resplendent in polished finery, took his place at the head of the guard detail. After tedious long minutes, the more vexing because of mixed anticipation and foreboding, they received the signal and began their measured procession up to the dais, while the royal party emerged through the doors behind the elevated platform.

Jehu stood at attention at the side of Ahab the king. He very nearly did a double take at the close-up sight of the royal couple's costumes. He had seen the king and queen plenty of times in their service, but never had they decked themselves out in such a manner as this. Their matching robes were so thickly encrusted with emeralds and rubies that it was impossible to guess the color of the underlying fabric. Each wore headgear that hovered somewhere between a crown and a priestly miter. The sight was so distracting that Jehu scarcely noticed the uncharacteristic demeanor of both. Something was very much amiss. It only added to Jehu's foreboding.

Things only turned stranger when Ahab arose from his throne and strode with unaccustomed swagger to the front of the platform. After sonorously pronouncing a formal invocation to the god Baal, the king announced dramatically that in order to actually summon Baal into their midst, they must needs offer the highest sacrifice, no mere human, but the king himself! At this all present gaped as with a single mouth. Jehu was as astounded as anyone. He had not known what to expect, though he knew some dreadful thing must be afoot—and that it would be the turning point. He and his partisans would act, and may Yahweh give them success! Events were even now unfolding, nay, hastening to their climax!

Jezebel quaked with terror as her husband allowed himself to be trussed up by the priests and laid on the altar. In a moment, it occurred to Jehu that such binding must be superfluous if the victim went to his death voluntarily. Jehu began to unsheathe his sword as he beheld the bound king convulse and commence screaming. Things were clear now: poor Ahab had been displaced, taken over by his witch-queen who had abandoned his flabby form just in time to avoid the descending sacrificial blade. Ahab crumpled with a whimper, and the air inside the temple grew electric with new tension, the air filled with strangely-hued auroras through which everything appeared unstable and distorted. In the midst of the dizzying chaos, the dimensional gate began to open to Baal. Squinting at the eye-burning vista, Jehu thought he could make out a pulsating mass which somehow seemed to be sentient, though no recognizable features signaled the fact.

The priests commenced a peculiar limping dance, hopping from foot to foot while revolving at ever-increasing speed. In this way they sought to enter an ecstatic trance, insensible to pain. Accordingly, as Jehu watched with disgust, the dervishes produced wavy-bladed daggers and began gashing their bared limbs. The spraying rain of blood must have been intended as an offering to the awakening Baal. They chanted a mantra of "Come, Lord Baal! Come, O Baal!"

The light in the place was changing again, getting dimmer and partaking of some unnatural spectrum. Jehu found himself passing into a dreaming state without awareness of falling asleep. He came to himself with a start at a light tap on the shoulder. It was Jonadab wielding his inscribed staff. As Jehu shook off the haze, Jonadab waved the staff to indicate the whirling cultists. Jehu nodded and sprang from the dais to begin cutting a path through the mass of nonplussed dancers. As the bite of his blade awakened each one to his last moment of life, priest after priest dropped to the stone floor. As more and more succumbed, each fallen body made a splash in the deepening lake of priestly blood.

By this time most of the Baal priests had been awakened from their trance by the noise of the slaughter. Those farthest from the dais made for the doors, only to meet the thirsty swords of Jehu's men as the guards poured in from outside the temple. Those not in league with Jehu and Jonadab hesitated in confusion: what was going on? Why were their fellows attacking the priests? At first they supposed a party of assassins had slipped past them, attacking the priests trying to get to the royal couple, but, no, it was fellow guards who were striking them down. Should they come to the aid of the few remaining priests? They stood frozen until distracted by what was happening up on the dais.

Flashes, then blasts, of brilliant light erupted, unleashing waves of intense heat alternating with the terrible cold of interstellar space. It was difficult for the observer to tell what was transpiring. Jehu managed to make himself heard over the ruckus, calling the guards to rush the stage. Now all could see that their queen needed no protection but that, on the contrary, all the terrified congregation who remained needed protection from her! For the eerie swaths of alien light emanating from the opened portal began to take on physical solidity and to grab up struggling human figures, guards, priests, and worshippers alike, drawing them, screaming, into a cavern-like maw.

As his eyes grew adjusted to the bewildering fireworks, Jehu saw that not all the weird lights came from the dweller in the gulph. Many of the mystic bolts were generated like an exchange of spears or arrows between Jezebel, now revealed as a powerful magician, and none other than old Jonadab who plainly possessed powers beyond even those ascribed to him by popular rumor.

Jehu, sword in hand, leaped to the attack, hoping to add his all-too-mortal efforts to Jonadab's now-waning energies. Jezebel, Baal's whore, gave him an ominous glance which, lasting but an eye blink, effectively stopped Yahweh's champion in his tracks. Jehu had half-expected something of the sort, but he hoped he had lent Jonadab however narrow a window in which he might be able to regroup and summon any reserves he had remaining. Jonadab, too, gave his young protégé a quick look, his hint of a smile implying Jehu's gesture had done some good.

v. HELL'S CHAMPION

Such was his fleeting thought, cut off by the sudden, loathsome embrace of one of Baal's tentacles reaching through the portal! A shock of numbing cold passed through him, but it passed just as quickly, causing Jehu to breathe rapidly and heavily as he tried to comprehend the scope and nature of That which had seized him. He felt now a questing tendril of psychic menace, an imperious command to worship him. His head was spinning, but his mighty arm and instincts, his most trusty weapons, took over. The coiling appendage was perhaps double his own girth, necessarily no larger, so as to hold him like a single finger hooking a smaller object. Jehu's sword chopped hard, two, three, four times, finally severing the boneless arm.

As he dropped to the solid but rubbery ground of this awful space, Jehu was astonished to behold the cut-off limb quickly changing form. He felt his best choice would be to strike again while it was in flux but found himself paralyzed by curiosity. The thing bubbled and shifted its mass, finally settling into a roughly humanoid shape, like the demon lovers of Jezebel, had he known it. But this one was possessed of a rather different lust, the lust for battle and for murder. Jehu brought his own warrior fury to the match. He charged at his foe, very glad he had earlier received Jonadab's blessing (or magic spell?) on his blade. The demon appeared solid enough; a sword could connect with it, but it might be invulnerable to mortal armaments. Still, that no longer described the sword of Jehu.

Jehu opened, and hoped to close, with a powerful blow to the creature's skull, evenly between the two mismatched horns. As he had hoped, the head split like a coconut. But in a moment his grin of exultation yielded to slack-jawed shock as each half of the ruined head expanded into a whole new head, both with laughing mouths!

Time to switch tactics! The two-headed devil advanced upon Jehu as quickly as he could, yet hampered by an apparent lack of coordination due to the makeshift character of his body as well, perhaps, as the novelty of his newly individual consciousness. It was a simple matter to evade this foe despite his obvious might and fury. The Baal avatar would rush and stumble, punch and claw with poor aim.

It occurred to Jehu that the thing might in fact be confused by conflicting impulses from his two rival heads! The ancients located the faculty of thought in the heart, not the brain, but Jehu had never believed this. Were not the senses at home in the head? Then thought must dwell there as well. So Jehu decided to experiment. Again and again he chopped with his now-glowing sword, splitting each newly emerging head as soon as it emerged. Sure enough, before long the demon's scaly shoulders could scarcely accommodate the overburdening fruit of that infernal tree. Jehu's last blow was to the heart, assuming the thing had one. At any rate, the freakish thing fell to the ground. It began to lose coherency and quickly *soaked* into the barren ground.

The young warrior decided not to wait to see what else the anti-god might throw at him. He made for the open mouth of the gate of Baal and hurtled through it in a single leap. The supernatural battle still raged without, but Jehu was horrified to behold the sight of Jonadab suddenly turning away from his opponent and kneeling in prayer! What was he doing?

Could he be making his peace with his God, having surrendered all hope of defeating the witch-queen? That spelled doom for sure, as the ectoplasmic tentacles from across the void continued to sweep the interior of the sanctuary. With every life it devoured, the Baal-thing visibly grew more solid, more defined, more *real*. And more fatally dangerous. What hope was there if even the mighty Jonadab had failed? Jehu dreaded to imagine the devastation to be unleashed should the monstrous entity Baal pass completely over onto the earth plane, ravening unhindered. It must not happen! But where was Yahweh? Had he forsaken Israel? Worse yet, had his Lord's enemy Baal actually vanquished him? The very thought seemed blasphemous. But no more so than the things he had seen this day.

But perhaps the warrior's faith was not as strong as his great thews. For things changed in an instant. In answer to Jonadab's supplications, or so Jehu surmised, a flood of sane and natural light, albeit very brilliant, penetrated the temple through the entrance hallway. A lone figure walked calmly along the path thus illumined. It might have been any bald and bearded man, but Jehu knew it must be the Prophet Elisha. He turned his head to see Queen Jezebel standing still before Baal's altar, her arms no longer gesticulating but hanging at her sides. She, too, must have recognized the new arrival.

As holy Elisha, whom most deemed no mere prophet but something more than human, approached the dais, he raised his hands in the same moment Jezebel did. Both sets of hands began to smolder, then to ignite, then to blaze, with light. Jehu took advantage of the pause to hop off the platform again and to shepherd those left alive out of the building. They stood, stunned by what they had witnessed, passive like cattle awaiting the butcher, but they did not resist Jehu's firm hand as he led them to safety. He remained vigilant, not wanting to lose anyone else to the greedy grasp of Baal's incarnate fury, but the thing's flailing arms seemed to have stilled simultaneously with those of its priestess.

With Elisha taking up the fallen standard relinquished by the exhausted Jonadab, the contest was no longer evenly matched. Plainly, the prophet was drawing upon a far more powerful source of mystic energy than that employed by Jezebel. The two traded blows of divine force only the least traces of which were evident to human senses. But it did not last long. Jezebel collapsed like a limp rag. Elisha paced over to her inert form. Life remained in it, as spasmodic shivers attested. Behind her the portal to Baal's hellish realm was swiftly contracting. Before it could close entirely, the prophet made a gesture of beckoning, saying, "Let the word of Yahweh through Elijah be fulfilled!" His words crashed like lightning, nor did they go unanswered, for at once there sprang through the opening a pair of apparitions whose outlines were vague but whose motions recalled the gait of hyenas. They fell upon Jezebel as she sought to regain her feet. One tore at her throat, the other at her abdomen. Her corpse fell back onto the floor, but the fiends were not done. As they eagerly licked up her freely flowing blood, Jonadab whispered to the returned Jehu, "They are lean and athirst!"

"Save your strength, my lord Jonadab!" said Jehu as he held the old man's form in his own mighty arms. "Here, let me take you to safety, for this fane of the damned has but few minutes left!" Great cracks were loudly fissuring the temple's ceiling.

He looked around for Elisha, concerned for the prophet's safety, but there was no sign of him.

vi. KING AND MESSIAH

The sun was the benign eye of God looking down upon the coronation of Jehu, the champion of Yahweh. His sister Tamar, weeping with pride and gorgeously clad in one of the late and unlamented queen Jezebel's gowns, was at his side. They stood before the high altar of Yahweh's temple at Bethel, in the shadow of the great golden bull once erected by his predecessor Jeroboam to represent the invincible might of the God who liberated Israel from the house of Pharaoh's bondage. Many present, including the Princess Tamar, could not help thinking that perhaps their new king was a better symbol of the divine power.

But just now, that statuesque figure was kneeling before the sage Jonadab. The old man, who for the first time appeared to be weary and frail, defied the decorum of the occasion, refusing the elegant robes offered him in favor of his usual threadbare smock. But, really, this was by no means unexpected, however stark the contrast with the golden circlet-crown he now set upon Jehu's brow. He intoned the traditional formula: "May Yahweh's Spirit come upon you to establish your throne in righteousness like unto his own!"

King Jehu held the sceptre of Jeroboam in his left hand and, with his right, raised up his sword, recently scrubbed clean of blood, toward the heavens. "I will tell of the decree of Yahweh! He said to me, 'Thou art my Son; today have I begotten thee!'"

The gathered congregation broke into shouting and clapping. The acclaim died down as soon as the king resumed speaking, this time his own words, not those prescribed by ritual.

"You are my people, my flock. As your ruler, I shall tend to your welfare with a gentle crook to lift you up and with an iron rod when it becomes needful to enforce the Law of Moses and Joshua. You shall not serve me, but I shall serve you, as Yahweh has commanded. Know this: my love for you, the people of God, will be matched by my hate for his enemies. We have won a great victory over the abomination Baal. But that victory is not yet complete, not as long as there lurk in Israel more of the followers of the false god. They must be eradicated if the cult of Baal is to be eradicated. We have had a small taste of the reign of Baal and of his servants. That is enough for me. Will you join your king in this crusade?"

Again the roar of acclaim. King Jehu dismissed the rejoicing crowd, secure in the knowledge of the will of his God. Princess Tamar took herself back to her royal apartment, while her brother lingered in the holy shadows to meditate on his new responsibilities. Suddenly he found he was not after all alone. He saw no one but thought he heard the familiar voice of Jonadab—or was it Elisha? These were its words: "Beware, O King, lest you become that which you hate."

He turned about in an instant, hoping to catch sight of him who had spoken, but there was no one. Jehu shrugged and dismissed the matter. He had greater concerns to ponder.

t

THE SEVEN THUNDERS

Apollonius of Tyana had entered Ephesus to teach and to heal. It was true that most of those who flocked to him, for he was well known, were more desirous of being healed in body than uplifted in soul, but the sage knew this was the way of children, and he looked upon mankind as children. Fools perhaps, but with the foolishness of children, as well as some, it had to be allowed, with the stupidity of beasts. But then this was the reason for metempsychosis, so that souls might climb the ladder of perfection. Apollonius taught the precepts of the great Pythagoras, and indeed some deemed him the very reincarnation of that worthy, while others hailed him as the son of Proteus, as Pythagoras had been the son of Apollo.

A weary-looking woman came to him, dragging a pallet on which lay her son, who was paralyzed in both legs. Apollonius pointed to her and waited for her to speak. She did. "O master, I brought to you my poor son, who has never been able to walk. I love him and carry him, but I grow old and tired, and I fear I cannot carry him much longer. I beg you to heal him. Have mercy on us, son of Proteus." Withal, she lowered her eyes before him.

The sage closed his eyes for a moment, then replied, saying, "What if the cost for the cure you seek were for you to take his infirmity for your own? Would it be worth it to you?"

Without hesitation, she answered, "In truth, it would, O lord. I am ready!"

Apollonius said, "O mother, great is your devotion! You have already paid the price." He stooped by the side of the young man and whispered some words in his ear. The man shuddered as if with sudden cold. And at once he climbed easily to his feet. His mother wept for joy as the two walked away, this time with her leaning upon him as they went. The crowd gasped, then rejoiced with much shouting.

The wonder-worker went on from there, and his disciple Damis accompanied him. The two came upon a well where a man was beating his slave for some perceived disobedience. Damis flinched as if he had received the blows in his own flesh. Would his master intervene?

Apollonius knelt on the ground and gathered a pile of pebbles and withered leaves, holding them in a fold of his robes. Then he approached the two men, both of whom turned to face him.

"Sir, I would purchase this slave from you. Would this sum suffice?"

Looking at what the sage held out to him, the slave-owner's eyes widened, and he said, "Most certainly, my good man! Here, let me record the transaction, and you may keep the note as a bill of sale."

Damis looked on in bafflement as the man cradled the trash Apollonius had traded for the silent slave. As the man strode off with his newfound "wealth," Damis gazed at his master, his expression asking his question for him.

"This man has eyes but for gold. He can see nothing else. And so in this case, though when he reaches his home, things may look different to him. And if he is fortunate, he will come to realize that gold is of no more value than what I gave him. As for you, my friend," and here he turned to the waiting slave, "you may go your way, henceforth in servitude only to your own conscience."

A few days later, the philosopher and his disciple heard the sound of great mourning as they approached the gates of another city. One standing at the edge of the crowd told Apollonius what it was all about. It seemed a young woman of a noble house had died in the very hour she was to be wed. The groom headed the funeral procession and wept the loudest. Hearing this, the thaumaturge made his way through the multitude and motioned for the bearers to set down the bier on which the dead girl lay.

"I shall stay the tears you are shedding on her behalf."

Murmuring went through the crowd like ripples through a pond. Most thought Apollonius presumed to deliver a eulogy of comfort, but he placed his hand on her exposed throat, whereupon the maiden commenced to cough, spitting up an evil-looking bile.

She lived! Her mother rushed to embrace her. Her father appeared relieved but as if it were he who had escaped some misfortune.

Apollonius raised his voice to ring out above the acclaim of the multitude. "The maiden took poison rather than wed a man she did not love." At this her father and her would-be groom both grimaced. "She was to join the fortunes of two houses, but she could not abide the man her father chose. If she is forced to wed him now, she will only drink the potion again."

The girl got up, as a young man forced his way to the front and embraced the maid with joy. Evidently, it was he to whom her heart belonged.

Apollonius the sage did numerous such feats wherever he and Damis journeyed, but Damis urged him to conceal himself, for it was rumored that the Emperor Domitian was looking to slay him. But he continued undeterred. At Hierapolis, he was met by an embassy of men carrying torches and swords. They recognized him and beseeched him, "O son of the gods, our city is beset by violent men. They murder without reason or goal, like wild bears. Our streets run with blood."

He considered their words, then asked, "Are these men native to your city? And are they led by a single man?"

"They are men of the city, and known to us, but there is no mob. Each acts alone, and in turn. Another arises as soon as the last is slain!"

"Then it is a demon with whom you deal. He casts off one body for another, as a man changes his tunic. I see you are pursuing him now. Permit me to join you."

Apollonius, clad in simple robes, barefoot, wearing no helmet but a skull cap, seemed an odd volunteer for a vigilante force, but he would soon prove their greatest weapon. The group passed down street after street until they found their quarry at the end of a blind alley. He had none of the look of a cornered beast. Instead, he looked as if he were waiting for them. The torchbearers paused to see what Apollonius would do.

He stepped calmly toward the murderer, foolishly endangering himself, as it seemed to the witnesses.

"Come out of him, unclean spirit, I adjure you by the numbers

147

153 and 888, and enter none other in this city!"

At this command, the demoniac sank to his knees and began to writhe and to cry out. The words were punctuated by the sounds of crackling flames, though none were to be seen. The possessed man collapsed in a heap, and the echoing voice of the demon, now seeming to come from no single source, spoke: "Pious fool! I gladly depart, for I must prepare for the triumph to come! The coming of Leviathan who sleeps in his house at R'lyeh! Then it is *I* who shall be banishing *you*!" There was no more.

The sage graciously refused the reward offered him by the city and urged them to give the money instead to the widows of the many murdered by the demon and by those he had possessed, now dead. He did, however, accept the price of passage from the Asian mainland to his next destination, the Isle of Patmos.

On board ship, Damis waited till his mentor had finished his daily meditation, then asked, "Master, are you now heeding my urgings to hide yourself from the Emperor?"

"I am not, my friend, for he cannot harm me. But there is great danger ahead, and not just for us. We go now to inquire of an old friend of mine. It has been many years, and he may not recognize me. But I think he will not turn us away. In this form, I cannot see certain things that he can. I believe he can be of great assistance to us."

***

They had no trouble finding the aged seer. The island was home to two major concerns. One was a tin mine, the other a penal colony. The Roman overseers pressed the prisoners into service in the mine, at least the able-bodied ones. The man the visitors sought was under house arrest adjacent to the main prison. He had arrived on Patmos months before to preach his doctrine to the prisoners. The Romans would not tolerate this and imprisoned him. But he was so old and frail that they decided to treat him gently. Some said he had recruited a few secret believers among the guards, and they allowed their mentor special privileges, such as writing materials. They would bring him letters from the mainland congregations over which he presided, and pass his own epistles to the messengers who awaited them outside the prison.

The guard to whom Apollonius and Damis were directed turned out to be one of those friendly to the man they sought, and he led them to a small, spare cell. Its occupant had done his best to make it as pleasant as possible, but it left much to be desired. The furnishings consisted of little more than a straw pad, a crude chair, and a writing table apparently fashioned from a shipping crate. The old man slowly rose and gestured welcome. "Who are you, my friends?"

"Damis, this is the Elder John, or John the Revelator. He possesses great prophetic gifts."

"You are well met, friend Damis! And who may you be, sir?"

"I must confess to being Apollonius, from Tyana. Some consider me a sage. But it is your wisdom we seek." Withal, he bade John return to his chair, while he and Damis happily sat cross-legged on the floor. The Elder listened patiently and with rising interest as Apollonius recounted the recent episode of the demoniac and his ominous parting words.

"You are widely known for your second sight, O John. You can hear the trumpets of angels and the chitterings of devils. I am very much hoping that you may know more of these impending horrors and the rising of Leviathan. Can you enlighten us?"

The Elder sighed. "'I shall open my mouth to speak mysteries hidden from the foundation of the world.' The end is the return of the beginning, so I must go back to the beginning. For in the beginning was Leviathan, the father of the Elohim, which is to say, the gods. They trembled at his thrashings in the depths of Chaos and Old Night. They feared that he who had begotten them would turn and devour them. Then one of the Elohim, Yahve by name, stepped forth to issue a challenge to his elders: he would face the Dragon in pitched combat if they would vow to reward his victory with the divine throne. Being much afraid, they readily agreed.

"Yahve, who is also called Marduk and Indra, Aliyan Baal and Nodens, armed himself with many lightnings and went forth to harpoon the Dragon, he who is called Leviathan and Rahab, Tiamat and Vritra, Lotan and Cthulhu. Long did they struggle, until at last the warrior god imprisoned him in the Great Abyss, in his house at

149

R'lyeh. Kings and priests and sages have sought to blot out these things from the memory of men.

"But scripture speaks of 'those who are skilled to rouse up Leviathan.' Certain cults have long wished to destroy a world in which they have no share. They crave a freedom from all restraints. When their ancient god returns, they, too, will be destroyed, but, being fools, they do not know their foolishness."

Damis ventured to question the old saint, giving him a chance to catch his labored breath.

"Are these wicked men, then, leaguing themselves with the unclean spirits to bring about the awakening of this Leviathan?"

"And," added Apollonius, "who are these men?"

"Let the wise man reckon the number of the Beast, for it is the number of a man. His number is 666."

Apollonius was quick with an answer. "I have learned from Pythagoras the deeper meaning of numbers. This is the sum of the name 'Neron Caesar," is it not? But he is dead these forty years."

"That is not dead which can eternal lie. Many believe that Nero's foul spirit has retaken the throne of the Caesars under another name."

Damis gasped, "Domitian!"

The Elder nodded gravely. "I have heard that it was he who gave the order to confine me. And the angels tell me he is soon to unleash a great persecution against the saints. I have made an account of what I saw and heard and sent it to my seven congregations, directing each to make a copy to retain and to study during the terrible days to come."

The wrinkles lining Apollonius' brow deepened as he pondered. "Tell me two things, Elder John. Why would the Roman Caesar seek to destroy his own realm? It is his world. He cannot desire the ruin of his own kingdom. And how does he know the means to rouse up Leviathan?"

"Remember, O Apollonius, though he is called Domitian of the house of Flavius, the spirit that animates him is that of the Antichrist Nero. He was struck down by his own guards who cut his throat. His desire now is for vengeance against the empire of the Tiber.

"As to how he knows the secret of releasing the monster," and here a tear traced down his wrinkled cheek, "I fear I am to blame. May Christ forgive me on the day he comes in power to vanquish the Beast I have helped to unleash!"

Little surprised the sage of Tyana, but these words shocked him. "You? *How?*"

"I told you I wrote down what was revealed to me. There were many, many revelations that day. One of the most frightful was that of the Seven Thunders. I heard great thunderclaps, and in my spirit I discerned their meaning, and it was terrible indeed. Here was the secret of Leviathan and how to summon him. I hastened to write it down, as I had all the rest. But after I had sent my scroll to the seven congregations, my angelic guide rebuked me, saying, 'Seal up what the Seven Thunders said! They are the crafty interjections of Satan!' At once I sent word to the leaders of my congregations, ordering that they strike out the revelation of the Seven Thunders. I thought I had succeeded, but later I learned that one of them defied me, a man named Diotrephes. He recognized the great danger of the forbidden oracle. But, being a man who enjoys nothing more than pre-eminence, he saw here a rare opportunity."

Here the tired old man paused and covered his face in shame and pain.

"He promised his copy to the agents of the persecutor Domitian in return for protection and patronage. I am told Diotrephes remains in Pergamum, where Satan has his throne, but he will make for Rome as soon as his new master summons him there."

"Then," said Apollonius, turning to Damis, "we must find him before he gives the incantation to the Emperor."

"I will pray for you, my new friends. You may have success, for, as you know, Pergamum will be in easy reach once you return to the mainland. I would offer you such accommodations as I myself enjoy, but I fear that, if the wrong guard should discover you here, you might become my permanent companions!"

***

The voyage was short and the journey took but a few days once they begged a ride with a wine merchant who had room in his wagon. Apollonius thanked the driver, once he and Damis reached Pergamum, by laying hands upon his spine and relieving his chronic pain. They found an inn willing to let them bed down in the stable for as long as they needed shelter while they sought out the man Diotrephes. He was known as a tanner and a maker of sail-cloth, and they had no difficulty locating his place of business, only to find it closed. That boded ill. Apollonius assured Damis, however, that there was another avenue they might pursue. The two of them trod the dusty streets, examining the ground in front of every door.

It was a good two hours before they found what they were looking for, a figure made of two intersecting curved lines, coming to a point on one end, crossing at the opposite end and continuing to form only the beginning of a second oval. It suggested a fish.

"You recognize this, Damis, do you not?"

"Yes, master. It is the secret sign of our fraternity, whereby the brethren may know that a friend dwells here. But why do we seek another Pythagorean?"

"We do not, my friend. It happens that Christians have adopted the sign of the fish for similar reasons, desiring secrecy at a time when the clouds of persecution gather. It affords occasional confusion, as one of our brethren may find himself amid Christians, or a Christian among Pythagoreans, but neither has aught to fear from the other, as ought to be plain from our recent interview with the Elder John. I am hoping that a Christian of Pergamum, one of John's flock, may help us find this Diotrephes."

Damis nodded and said, "Allow me," giving the door a vigorous knock. When the door opened, a woman's face peeked out from behind it.

"Whom do you seek, sirs? I do not know you."

Apollonius answered, "I am sent by John of Patmos. My name is Apollonius."

She opened the door wider and allowed her face and form to be seen, a matronly woman with long silver hair piled atop her head and held in place by jeweled combs.

"I have heard of you: the wizard from Tyana."

With a chuckle, Apollonius replied, "I prefer the term

'philosopher,' but yes, I am he. I seek him who shepherded your congregation till recently, as I understand it."

Suspicion darkened her expression. "You are not in league with him, are you?"

"No, my sister. In truth, we aim to prevent him from doing great mischief."

She seemed relieved. "Now I know why Diotrephes forbade us to receive wandering strangers. Come in, good sirs."

They reclined at table, looking about them as their hostess retreated to the kitchen and directed her servants to prepare a meal and directed another to round up a few of her Christian brothers and sisters. Apollonius and Damis were happy to rest their travel-weary bones and to take some refreshment as they waited.

When an hour had passed, three more Christians, two young mothers, their babies in tow, and an elderly man, arrived. Others must have been busy as laborers, slaves, and shop keepers. Servants brought a modest spread of foods, mainly fruits, cheese, and bread, with one pitcher each of wine and of water. Apollonius and Damis, Pythagoreans, eschewed meat and wine and were delighted with the repast.

"It is a shame," the old man offered, "about Diotrephes. A proud man, and in the wrong way. You know what I mean."

Damis came to his aid, "Yes, the pride of arrogance, not the pride of dignity."

"That's it. He began with a servant's heart, but in time, as he was entrusted with ever greater responsibility, he lorded it over those who allowed him to. Come, let me show you the man's folly."

He rose and led the group to a closed room which housed the space in which the tiny congregation of Pergamum's believers met each Sunday at dawn. There was a kind of cupboard containing a few scrolls, each in its own pigeon hole. Wall murals depicted scenes from the scriptures, and in front, on a pillar beside a lectern, was an expensive-looking marble bust.

Apollonius, admiring the workmanship, inquired, "Does this represent one of the old patriarchs or one of your prophets? Um, Isaiah, perhaps?"

"No," the old man replied. "It depicts the vain Diotrephes

153

himself. He had it made and placed here." Everyone laughed.

Their hostess quipped, "It's a good likeness, for what it's worth. I think I may use it for a scarecrow." This prompted more laughter.

Apollonius came to the point. "And where is he now? I saw that his shop is closed. John the Revelator believes Diotrephes plans a trip to Rome." He thought it best to reveal as little as possible of what was at stake.

"Planning?" said their hostess, whose name, she finally told them, was Maximilla, "He has already departed."

Damis looked as if she had slapped him. "When did he go?"

One of the young women, Paulina, said, "No one has seen him for two days."

Apollonius, rising to his feet, said, "Thank you, my friends. You have been a great help. Our quarry has a head start on us, but we may yet overtake him, I think."

Kissing one another's cheeks, the party broke up and returned to their daily routines. When well out of sight of the house, the sage motioned Damis to follow him into an alley between two tenements.

"Diotrephes means to deliver the papyrus to Domitian in person, as we supposed. There is no time to waste."

"I understand, master. But how are we to overtake him at this point?"

"You will seek passage on a ship, as he did. As for me, I have other plans. And you cannot go with me now. Rest assured, I would take you with me if I could. We will find one another in Rome."

Damis' puzzlement turned into utter amazement when, away from all prying eyes, the son of Proteus vanished from his sight! Damis reminded himself that his mentor was not averse to employing stage tricks on occasion, so he hurried to the mouth of the alley and looked up and down the littered street but saw no one. In that moment he felt he had woefully underestimated Apollonius of Tyana, whose true nature he had now begun to suspect. With a strange hybrid of confusion and renewed purpose, Damis made for the inn, to see if the innkeeper might help him make the necessary connections for the voyage to Rome.

***

Apollonius appeared, though invisible to others, on the road leading into the city. He wanted to observe the people going into and out of the great city, blissfully unaware of the dreadful events about to befall them, that is, unless the wonder-worker could use his talents to prevent it. In his unseen form, really a kind of mesmeric aura that simply kept all near him from noticing him, he passed through the gates of Rome amid a group of chained slaves destined for gladiatorial training.

Most of those entering Rome were headed toward the great marketplace, but Apollonius continued in the company of a set of white-clad nobles on their way to the Senate. Before the great structure with its huge columns, like those which held up the heavens, stood a mob chanting, "Increase the dole!" These amplfied the volume and fervency of their shouting once they beheld the handful of senators approaching. But these paid their complaining public no mind as legionaries appeared from nowhere to safeguard their masters' passage into the gleaming halls of the legislature. Apollonius tarried here for a few moments, unobserved by the senators, their guards and pages. He watched the self-important mortals sitting on their marble benches and fine purple cushions and thought how like children playing games of pretend they looked. But he had business elsewhere.

There were inevitable limits to his abilities when in his present form. He could maintain his concealment, but it would be some time before he could repeat his teleportation feat. Thus he could not simply appear in the Emperor's presence, but such measures were not necessary. He circulated among the senators once the session broke up, listening to discover who might have business with Domitian. There must be a steady stream of them, seeking favors for themselves or their home villages. It did not take long to locate what he sought. A tall, gaunt man with iron gray hair and a confident stride left the building, accompanied by a soldier. Apollonius followed him as he walked.

They passed a number of fine statues of previous Caesars as well as of the heroes and deities of Rome's myths. There were Romulus and Remus, then another depicting Romulus in his exalted form as the god Quirinus. Next was Minerva, then Jupiter, Juno, Mercury, Hercules. Even the ancient Etruscan god Tinia found a place in the ranks of the petrified immortals.

At once, Apollonius halted and nearly collided with those around him who of course could not see him. He almost lost the concentration enabling him to evade their notice when he caught sight of him who had posed for a marble bust in far-away Pergamum: Diotrephes! How could the man have preceded him here? There could be but one answer: He, too, must have had some magical means at his disposal. It could only be that the papyrus of the Seven Thunders held revelations from its diabolical revealer beyond that which the Elder John had implied. Diotrephes must have studied the Satanic verses in some depth before arriving here. Had he already delivered it over to his patron Domitian?

Entering the palace, the senator, his bodyguard, and an unseen third man proceeded to the station where an officer of the Praetorian Guard screened visitors. The tall man was expected; his name, Publius Janus Garba was at the head of the list. The centurion assigned a guard to escort the senator into the presence of the divine Domitian. Had Apollonius not long ago eschewed the taking of life, this would have been a prime opportunity to rid the world of the wicked tyrant and the cataclysm he threatened to create. He was obliged to take a more indirect approach, and, for this, too, he faced a prime opportunity.

Domitian sat on his throne of judgment as they walked in. His countenance was stonily impassive, as if it were only a ceramic vessel for an alien consciousness that had been poured in. Swathed in late afternoon shadow, his staring eyes were nonetheless easily visible. At first his unseen observer thought a stray bar of setting sunlight lay across them. But on closer scrutiny, Apollonius saw that the Emperor's eyes emitted their own, rather baleful, illumination.

When the tyrant recognized his visitor he descended the steps from the dais and motioned Garba to join him on a luxurious couch. Domitian was very obviously disturbed, despite the neutrality of his expression. He glanced at his attendants who were just then lighting the bracketed torches around the audience chamber. When they were finished and left the room, Domitian again faced his confidant and resumed speaking his worries.

"I knew I should not have trusted the Christian apostate! My spies have learned that he plans to deceive me. He has decided to keep the true papyrus for himself and to give me a forgery that vitiates the crucial lines of the incantation! I confirmed this out of the mouth of the scribe whom the cursed Diotrephes paid to fabricate it. My torturers got to the truth quickly enough. They always do."

The senator considered what he had heard, then spoke. "My lord, I believe I understand your own intention, and you know that I am at one with you. As the high priest of the secret cult of Pluto, my goals are very much the same. I, too, wish to see the Titan Saturn, whatever we like to call him, rise from Galiyeh to sink the dry lands and raise up the sunken realms. If this man Diotrephes wishes to chant the invocation himself, how does that harm our plans? The same result will follow, will it not? Such is the expectation of my informants on the spirit plane."

"Let me tell you, my brother, what difference it will make! When Leviathan, or Saturn, what have you, arises in his ancient glory, the man who releases him from the Bottomless Pit will rule the world as his vicar on earth! That must be me! Of course, you will reign at my right hand. The Titan will rise in any case, that is true enough, but you and I must rise with him. So you see..."

The Emperor stopped mid-sentence and gaped at the sight of Apollonius the sage suddenly standing before him. Senator Garba leaped to his feet and tried to call for the guards, who stood on duty outside the audience hall. But the senator found he could not speak. That was Apollonius' doing.

"Gentlemen, give me a moment and hear me out. You have naught to fear from this old man. But I think you will want to hear what I have to say."

Domitian set aside the outrage that should have moved him to have this interloper seized and killed on the spot, along with the guards whose incredible laxity had permitted him to infiltrate. He reasoned that a man who could thus reveal himself was likely someone privy to secrets he needed.

157

"Say on, wizard. We will hear you."

"My lords, forgive me, but I fear you have fallen into the same error which has captured the upstart Diotrephes. Do not let yourselves take offense, but learn from your mistake. The Being whose advent you avidly await cares naught for any mere mortals except insofar as he may use them as pawns for his own ends, even you, the mighty of the earth. If Leviathan returns, there will be no one to rule, no one human at any rate. He will have no need of you or of any viceroy. Do you not see that? You are seeking but to hasten your own obliteration."

Both Romans sat in silence for a long time. Confusion and dismay marked their faces. It took no prophetic telepathy to see that the warning of Apollonius was nothing that had not occurred to them before, though neither had mentioned it to the other—or even allowed themselves to face the possibility. If justice is blind, it is no more blind than ambition.

Finally Domitian stood to his feet. His face, finally animated, registered an attitude of good-fellowship, which was almost certain to be a feigned pose. A man in his position never displayed his true feelings but wore whatever mask each situation seemed to require. He placed a powerful hand on Apollonius' shoulder and spoke to him, looking him in the eye.

"I believe you are the renowned Apollonius, the magician from Tyana. You are a man with great knowledge of secret matters. I will consider what you have said. Meanwhile, allow me to provide you with an apartment here in the palace."

By now the senator had regained his voice and gone to summon the guards. The Emperor pointed to two of the men, saying, "You, Septimus, and you, Gaius. Attend our distinguished guest. He will be with us for a few days." Apollonius understood the purpose of the guards assigned him was to keep an eye on him and to control his movements. Domitian said to him, "I will speak with you again when I have decided my next step." Then he turned to Garba, placed his arm about the senator's thin shoulders and walked away.

Some weeks passed as Apollonius, essentially under house arrest, redeemed the time with meditation to strengthen his abilities. He surmised that Domitian, paying no heed to his words of caution, was frantically searching for Diotrephes, hoping to seize the papyrus from him before he could use it himself. And why had he not? Perhaps the incantation was in some strange, glossolalic tongue difficult to pronounce correctly? If so, Apollonius could imagine Diotrephes' fear of experimenting with the formula.

***

And it was even so. Shortly after his arrival in Rome, the scheming Diotrephes had sought out the Sybil, whose famed oracular prowess seemed to offer his best hope for getting the conjuration right. But the would-be awakener of Leviathan came away from her grotto with only a cryptic prophecy:

> *Apollo's spirit speaketh now:*
> *To work the work he'll show thee how.*
> *Be sure thou speakest without fear,*
> *And if thou dost, the god shall hear.*

But Diotrephes reflected how this left him exactly where he was before! He supposed the Sybil meant to assure him that the exact pronunciation mattered less than the earnestness with which he uttered the spell. But how could he not be filled with apprehension that he was speaking with no grain of doubt? Ah, it was all quite maddening! Just like that baffling promise of Christos that one might gain any desired boon if he prayed without doubt! As if it were possible to banish all qualms. A cruel joke, and so was this.

Did he dare go through with his plan? It might be too great a risk, and, come to think of it, perhaps an unnecessary one. Had he not already gained formidable powers with the aid of the papyrus, even from the lesser mysteries it contained? Perhaps this world need not pass away to usher in a new one for him to rule. Perhaps this one would be satisfactory...

***

Apollonius had the honor of a private interview with the

Emperor, several such meetings in fact. Invariably Domitian's polite conversations eventuated in offers to pay the sage to teach him the art of going unseen, as well as other abilities he rightly suspected his guest possessed. But Apollonius was steadfast in his refusals. Today, however, the tyrant tried a different lure.

"I believe, sir, that you have an assistant called Damis. At least I hope I am not mistaken, for I have gone to some considerable trouble to locate him. He is at present being held by my guards, awaiting your decision, even as I do. You are in a position to do a good deed both for your disciple and for your emperor, who himself asks only to become your disciple. Teach me what I wish to know, O Apollonius, or I cannot be too optimistic about your apprentice's future. Septimus, you may bring him in now."

The Praetorian Guards appeared with a manacled Damis in tow. He had plainly been pummeled, though recently washed, his cuts and bruises treated. Apollonius was both delighted to see his young friend and dismayed at the treatment dealt him. Damis made to greet his master, but one of the guards dealt him a silencing blow.

Domitian began again. "Now we will see if..." But a commotion outside preempted his threat. "What is it? Guards! Give me a report!"

As the doors opened for some of the men to leave and investigate, the sounds became louder and more distinct. There were crashing noises as well as the roaring of a conflagration, and also much screaming as of a panicked crowd stampeding here and there. The guards pivoted and reentered the audience chamber, having been intercepted by other soldiers on their way in to tell their lord what transpired without.

"By Hecate, will no one tell me what is afoot?" Domitian slapped the face of a stammering guard.

The shaken man replied, voice uneven, "Your majesty, you will call me mad, but here it is! The very streets of Rome are erupting! Fire rages everywhere! But the worst is... the worst is..."

"Damn you! *Tell* me, or I will strike off your head this very minute!"

"My lord, the gods have returned!"

"I knew we had waited too long! The accursed Diotrephes has

completed the chant, and the terror has begun! If you fools had been able to find him, it would have been I who..."

Just then Publius Janus Garba rushed through the cordon of soldiers, breathlessly exclaiming, "No, Lord Domitian! It is not that! He means the gods of Rome! Their stone statues have stepped off their bases and are wreaking havoc with their marble thews! The soldiers are no match for them! Some sorcerer commands them!"

Domitian's gaze turned away, and he stared at nothing, the light dawning within.

"It is Diotrephes nonetheless! And it is good news for us, Garba! It means he has been unable to master the spell to rouse up Leviathan. Compared to that, what is going on in the streets is mere trickery. Our next move must be to wrest the papyrus from him."

"Yes, my lord, but something must be done to stop the present chaos! The people may rise up! Or," and here he looked worriedly at the soldiers with them in the room, "the Praetorian Guard!"

"Of course. Of course, senator, you are right. Other matters must wait. But what to do?"

Apollonius spoke up. "I believe I may be of some help, your highness. Let us go outside."

Domitian looked both puzzled and relieved. He gestured to the soldiers, who formed a protective ring around their Emperor, the senator, and the two philosophers. The party exited the great building and descended the marble steps to the street. About this time, an astonishing sight emerged from around the street corner. An insignificant-looking man, whose balding, chinless likeness Apollonius and Damis had seen before, drove a golden chariot drawn by mighty griffons. He, too, was flanked by fearsome defenders, only these were ten feet tall and bore the traditional images of the Olympian gods. Even the Emperor recoiled at the sight.

Apollonius stepped through the ring of Praetorian Guards as if he had parted a flimsy curtain. "Most impressive, Diotrephes, for a beginner! But haven't you frightened these poor Romans quite enough?" With a display of complex gestures, the sage caused the massive illusion, for that is what it was, to drain away. And then it could be seen that the shivering Diotrephes rode only in a miserable apple cart pulled by a pair of goats.

There had been no damage, no destruction, no fire. Only panic induced by mesmeric phantoms. Domitian looked amazed but was not paralyzed by astonishment as his soldiers were. His barked orders snapped them out of it: "Seize him! Search him!"

The guards secured the no longer impressive little man with ease, then stripped his clothing off him, as if he were a slave on the auction block. A few moments of turning pockets inside out and ripping seams disclosed what Domitian was looking for. In triumph, he held aloft a sealed scroll, small in size and easily concealed.

"I have it now! And with it a greater throne than Rome's!"

Apollonius dared interrupt the madman's exultation. "But, sire, you forget! Your monstrous master will by no means honor your service! He will cast you aside as a man dismisses a harlot when he is done with her!"

Domitian's eyes blazed with the light Apollonius had glimpsed when he first saw the man in his throne room weeks before.

"You do not fool me, you old charlatan! You never did! You wanted this power for yourself, but you shall not trick me! What Diotrephes could not or dared not do, I dare!"

Damis was alarmed, but Apollonius seemed to expect some outcome and patiently awaited it. The Emperor fingered the seven waxen seals and saw that one had already been broken, no doubt by Diotrephes, who must have feared opening the scroll any farther. Domitian fumbled with the second till it broke apart and crumbled.

He paused for a moment, waiting to see what might happen next.

What did happen was the rapid spraying out of a stream of black smoke which expanded till it formed the cloudy outline of a great black warhorse which reared menacingly over the Emperor. To his credit, Domitian did not cower.

"Is this another of your parlor tricks, charlatan?"

At once the figure of a featureless rider appeared astride the still-solidifying steed. Wordlessly, he unsheathed his blade and swept it back and forth through the air. Blue lightning flashed from it. At the sight of this, Domitian's bravado fled from him, and he made to run. But one of the levin-bolts caught him right between his shoulders, and he fell headlong.

His guards were afraid to approach him till the dark horseman dissipated into fading mist. Then one knelt beside the body, turned it over, and regarded the face.

"He *lives!* Great Caesar lives! Hail Caesar!"

Apollonius had stooped down, too, and retrieved the papyrus scroll from the ground. No one made a move to prevent him, not even Domitian, who was returning to full consciousness with surprising swiftness.

"You are... Apollonius of Tyana? I seem to recognize you, though I am sure we have never met."

Apollonius took his offered hand and helped him up. "Do not trouble yourself, my lord. You have not been... yourself for some time. Let us talk when you have recuperated."

***

Apollonius and Damis were soon on their way again, making for the harbor where a grateful Domitian had arranged for a comfortable voyage back to Asia and then passage overland to Pergamum, where they felt obliged to inform the Christians what had befallen their one-time leader, now assigned to stable duty in Caesar's palace. And to spread the news of the Emperor's pledge no more to persecute them or the followers of any religion.

Apollonius reached into the folds of his robes and drew forth the cursed and coveted scroll. "This shall no more trouble the world of men." He hurled it mightily into the salty air. In mid-arc, the rolled papyrus exploded into blinding flame, a miniature comet.

Damis could contain himself no longer. "Master, I have to know what happened to the Emperor! To all appearances, was he not struck dead? And yet he was taken up alive! And his madness had been driven from him! This was your doing, was it not?"

"Alas, I cannot take credit for the feat. It was the scroll itself that struck him down. At least poor Diotrephes, despite being such a fool, had the sense to study what little of the text he dared to read before attempting to draw upon its power, and you saw what he did with even its lesser mysteries. He must have feared he would not have been equal to the challenge of the greater arcana. But Domitian, or the entity we knew as Domitian, was by no means so cautious. Accustomed to commanding at a whim, he ventured to wield the scroll like a magic bludgeon, and it destroyed him."

Damis was not satisfied, however. "What do you mean, master? Destroyed? But he lives!"

"Domitian lives, but that which possessed him has been destroyed. Do you recall what the Revelator said concerning him? Domitian had been taken over by the vengeful ghost of the bloodthirsty Nero. The dark horseman has banished Nero's spirit to the Pit from whence it strayed. It was he who moved Domitian to his crimes and persecutions."

Quoth Damis: "We owe a great debt to the Christian seer John. With his help we have turned back the predicted Tribulation. And yet it was that reign of terror which was to usher in the return of their Christ! That will be a blow to him, surely?"

"We have not cheated him of the return of his lord, Damis. For, if you are willing to accept it, I am he."

THE SON OF JEHOVAH VERSUS THE CYCLOPS

"Master, why do we cross the Sea of Galilee, just to visit this desolate place?" Simon Peter spoke for all the disciples, breaking the silence that had prevailed hitherto. In a few moments, the capacious boat would be beaching at the water's edge.

Emboldened, Andrew could nonetheless not manage to keep a quaver out of his usually hearty voice, saying, "Yes, is this not the Decapolis of the Gentiles? What business can we have among the uncircumcised?"

Jesus turned from surveying the shore and answered his two chief lieutenants. "We are obliged to do the will of my Father while we may, for the night is coming, when no man can work." This quizzical answer that was no answer set the Twelve looking silently at one another (and hardly for the first time).

Once a few of the men pulled the craft up onto the beach far enough that the tides could not seize it and let it float away, Jesus called them to himself and motioned them to sit in a circle on the warm sand. Then he commenced to tell them more.

"Brothers, we have come to the ruins of Gergesa, long ago the dwelling of the mighty Girgashites."

Lebbaeus raised his hand, and Jesus paused. "Did not your namesake Joshua vanquish them in olden times? And before that, did not he and Caleb warn Father Moses of their great stature? Men knew them also as the Rephaim, or do I err?"

Jesus was visibly pleased at his disciple's knowledge of scripture. "Blessed are you, O Lebbaeus, for he who knows not scripture's commands cannot obey them, but woe to him who knows them and disobeys them." This left the disciple puzzled: he knew not whether his Master meant to commend him or to warn him. But, he reminded himself, it was the way of the Nazorean to leave one guessing, lest one grow complacent. But Jesus had returned to his topic.

"I have come to seek and to save what was lost. That is what brings us here, as you are about to see for yourselves." Withal, he turned away and indicated a tall form running towards them. The disciples one and all shielded their eyes, squinting in the sun to make out the onrushing figure. He was almost upon them and did not appear to be slowing down. The Twelve arose as one man, assuming a defensive stance. They would shield their Master from attack or else perish in the attempt!

The savage bellowing of the wild-eyed fellow was not the only thing that made him appear like a dangerous beast, for he was quite naked and tattooed in dried blood, whether his own or another's. Manacles with hanging fragments of iron chains enclosed his wrists. None of the disciples carried weapons, but loyal Simon grasped one of the oars and launched it at the howling maniac. The muscled mountain of a man collapsed like a fallen tree, his yelling now become screams of pain. Jesus fixed Simon with a look of disappointment and scorn as both knelt beside the man. Peter's crude javelin had gouged out one of the madman's eyes. Jesus tore a strip from his shawl and wiped away most of the blood, then took another to use as a bandage. By this time, the strange fellow had lapsed into unconsciousness.

Simon Peter, now well abashed, knew not what to expect from his Lord. To test the waters, he piped up and asked, "Rabbi, will you now restore his sight, his eye?"

The question only made Jesus more furious. "You think as men think! I tell you, your blindness is darker than his!" The whole band of disciples cringed, sensing that Jesus meant to include them all in this stinging rebuke. What might come next? Oh, why had they followed him across the lake?

"Do you not say, 'Let the pig return to the mud and the dog to his vomit?'"

Peter and the rest braced for whatever was next to befall them. But in another moment the ground on which they had stood no longer bore their tread but was instead draped in discarded clothing amid which a dozen grunting swine rooted and nuzzled.

"Truly, I have thrown my pearls to you long enough!"

Jesus left the pigs to their business and turned again to the brute beside him. By this time the man was awakening, setting aside not only his fading agony but also his former rage.

"Who are you, man? And how came you to this awful state?"

The man now possessed a surprising clarity. Propping himself upon one elbow, he wiped more blood away with his leathery forearm; then answered evenly but softly, "Once I was called Polyphemus, but now men whisper and call me 'Legion,' for I carry the souls of the Rephaim of this ancient place. I am their beast of burden and their slave. It is my task to keep them satiated with offerings of flesh and blood, that of the nearby villagers, especially of their children. I like not to do such deeds, but if I am slow to obey, they torment me with bouts of madness, of frenzy and the rending of my own poor flesh, as you see. Come, sir, and I shall show you."

Men say that once upon a time Jesus descended into Hell, but they have forgotten when and where. The truth of it is that, leaving his squealing pupils to forage, he followed the steps of his erstwhile enemy to an open tomb and entered in.

Dry and crumbling bones of the ancients festooned the shadowy recess. Vague impressions in the thick layer of dust indicated where the man Legion slept, and how little rest he got, flailing and convulsing in demoniacal nightmares. There were animal bones, too, some with rotting shreds of meat still clinging to them, the remains of his irregular repasts.

Yet all this formed but a kind of antechamber, and Legion beckoned him further, into a steeply declining shaft. It was no long journey to the bottom. Arriving there, Jesus could see that what appeared on the surface as an extensive, ruined cemetery was in truth the fragmentary outcroppings of a small city, buried here ages ago by an earthquake. The expanse was not completely shrouded in inky darkness because there remained great rifts and chasms through which daylight entered in random patterns.

The man who had the Legion spoke as if he were a tour guide addressing holy pilgrims. "This is the ghost of Gergesa, once a city of powerful warriors and petty kings, glorious till their arrogance and perversions forced the hand of Jehovah to grind them into the dirt. Now the whole place is little more, really, than a vast tomb. And I,

167

may God spare me, am its caretaker."

"What keeps you here, O Legion?"

"You know well enough, O Lord. The evil shades will not let me go. Once I dwelt as a young man in the village which now whispers my name in fear, the name they gave me. All their children are warned from the cradle not to venture near this woeful place, but I was so foolish as to see for myself what frightened them so. And see I did. Much as you and your men did, I encountered the ragged guardian of Gergesa. He was old and feeble, so the ghostly inhabitants replaced him with me."

"But what keeps *them* bound to this necropolis?"

"Their necromancy taught them many black truths, and they knew how to prolong their stay upon earth, albeit not in their proper flesh."

By this time, the pair of improbable companions had arrived at the half-wrecked fane of Molech, the devil-god once worshipped by the Rephaim. The place was, as expected, in a state of great disrepair; any efforts to restore the former glory of the blasphemous temple must be quite beyond the capability of the malnourished wretch who offered sacrifices when he could get them.

"But why linger? Surely it is a miserable existence, not to be desired!"

"That is so, but Hell is worse, and well they know that Hell must be their last destination. They are able to linger here so long as blood offerings are fed to them. And for that, I am needed... or one like me. O Jesus, I believe that God in his mercy has sent you here to take my place!"

Dim and seemingly distant voices, some moaning, some snickering and giggling, made themselves known. Their wretched servant was silent, torn between relief that his bondage soon would end and self-reproach that he had lured Jesus to his awful fate.

But Jesus, finding himself in the Valley of Death's Dark Shadow, was not afraid.

"Nay, my hour has not yet come. But it is high time you ancient sinners vacated this abode of foulness and the haunted victim you possess! Leave him!"

Now the echoing chorus of the damned returned: "Lord, do

not send us out of our accustomed land! Send us not into the Abyss!"

"Very well, devils. Outside you will find a small herd of unclean pigs. You may enter into them, and after that, I guarantee nothing!"

The dreary expanse was at once filled with the sounds of whipping winds, amid which eerie voices could be heard shrieking. But Jesus did not feel any wind.

Silence ensued, then broke again with the sobbing of the man now vacated by the Legion.

"Weep not, O Polyphemus! Come with me to the sunlit surface before this place is razed, no stone to stand upon another!" Jesus placed his arm around the scarred shoulders of the other, and they made the climb.

Once they emerged, blinking, the man besought Jesus that he might join the company of his disciples—if they still lived! For none were in evidence.

But Jesus shook his head. "No, my friend. I have other plans for you. You shall go forth among your Gentile compatriots, spreading the word of what the Lord God Jehovah has done for you. Your testimony will be the saving of many! You are Polyphemus, but henceforth you shall be known, in shorter form, as 'Paul.' Fare you well!"

Polyphemus, or Paul, at once went on his way rejoicing, no longer naked, but well-clothed.

For a short space Jesus waited alone by the boat. It was not long before twelve naked men emerged from the lake, coughing and confused but glad to be alive. Ashamed at their nakedness, each quickly picked out his cast-off garments As usual, Peter spoke for the rest.

"Master, I know not what befell us! I dreamed my brethren and I were a herd of swine, grazing hereabouts, until, of a sudden, we were consumed with madness and furious panic as some force overtook us like a cyclone, driving us helpless into the lake! And then we were once again men, as you see. Was it a vision from God?

"And has any man among you seen my clothes?"

***

I buffet my body, and lead it captive, lest, having preached to others, I should be myself rejected. (1 Corinthians 9:27)

I bear you witness that, if possible, you would have plucked out your eyes and given them to me. (Galatians 4:15)

Here indeed we groan, and long to put on our heavenly dwelling, so that by putting it on we may not be found naked. For while we are still in this tent, we sigh with anxiety; not that we would be unclothed, but that we would be further clothed, so that what is mortal may be swallowed up by life. (2 Corinthians 5:2-4)

THE SURAH OF THE MAKING OF MANKIND

O Alhazred! Hearken to the voice of thy Lord, him who hath assigned to all the worlds their binding laws and fixed the date of their demise. For I shall reveal unto thee a secret history which thou knowest not, even the tidings of mankind's creation.

In days so long ago that thou canst in no wise reckon them, the Elder Ones who settled your earth and raised their castles amid the frozen peaks did fashion all manner of servants for themselves, for the Elder Ones were wise and filled their days fashioning marvels of design, and they liked not to spend their strength on labors better suited for brutish strength. It is for this reason that they created the many-formed race of the shoggoths. Great weights did they bear; great toils did they accomplish.

But the shoggoths were as simple as the Elder Ones were wise, and it was not unknown for them, from time to time, to fail in a task. When such a lapse became known, the shoggoths' masters would bathe the transgressor in the rays of their devices, and the shoggoth would shrink down and lose all power to change form. No longer were such able to trade one shape for another. Their great strength did wane. Little could they accomplish henceforth. And yet they became clever in their infirmity. And ere long their masters found that these beings, which they called Man, were after all useful for certain tasks requiring dexterity and small size.

Fission was lost to them. They could not multiply after their own kind, but their creators were content to fill their ranks when needful by the same means as they had first made them.

In this manner did the history of thine own race begin. But as yet, mankind was little more than a stable of trained beasts. Things continued so until one day Something in the form of a man appeared in their midst in the temperate zone where several of the humans dwelt. All rose as one to confront the Stranger, the waking arousing the sleeping. Many a whisper and grunt made the rounds of the clearing until the murmuring yielded to the words of the newcomer.

"I am Nyarlathotep. You, too, shall have names henceforth. I have come that you may rise above your servile state. I shall teach you proper speech, and you shall speak to one another with your mouths as I now speak to your minds."

Here the tall, black figure produced a piece of fruit, swollen with juice or mayhap with corruption. "Eat the pulp; drink the nectar, and you shall know even as your foolish masters know. For I am wiser than any of them, and I have taken pity upon you."

And the small group of men did eat, crowding around their benefactor, eagerly grasping at the fruit. The one called Nyarlathotep, herald of unknown gods, brought forth, from no visible source, as much of the fruit as they desired. "It will be sweet to the taste, but sour in your bellies, for such is the way with knowledge."

All of them slumbered very deeply and woke together, they knew not how many days later. At once their eyes were opened, and they saw that they had become male and female, with organs like those of the beasts of the forests, who bred their own young. And with their new members came the lust to use them, and each turned to the other, aflame with unknown passion. And as they became a sweating, quivering mass of bodies, the tall black figure retreated into the shadows of the trees and ferns.

Now the Elder Ones saw that their human creatures had changed, and that it was not their own doing. They sent out a silent summons to work, but none answered. And so one of them betook itself to the dwelling place of men to know the truth of the matter. All the men and women slept in a rough circle around a fire as the towering Being loomed over them, silently observing. It stood upon a tripod of tentacles, its trunk like a great barrel. From this sprouted five fern-like wings, fanning gently. At its peak rested a starfish head with a single eye at its center. It made no sound but, like the black man, sent a lance of pain into the sleeping minds, causing their owners to start awake in a panic.

"Who has changed you? Have you eaten of the fruit of wisdom which only the Elder Ones may eat? You shall answer for your deeds, as shall the One who deceived you."

The men and women, however, did not cringe in fear, nor did they beg forgiveness, for the fruit had wrought other changes as well. And mankind at once took up sharp stones and broken branches, and they set upon the Elder One with bestial fury. With might greater than the men of thine own day possess, O Alhazred, they smote and slew the winged one.

Wearied and soaked with yellow-green slime, they stood and regarded the work of their bloody hands. And when they beheld his approach, they parted to make way for the black man who stood again among them. And he spoke to their minds once more.

"I am Nyarlathotep, messenger of the sleeping gods. I have freed you from the bondage of the Elder Ones, and henceforth you shall serve me, you and your children. I shall show you ever more ways to rejoice in killing, in riot, in blood, for this is the worship due to Those we serve. And in this way you shall strive to awaken Them from their slumbers. Together we shall clear the earth of the Elder Things and prepare it for its rightful masters. Come, I shall show you where you may find refuge from the star-heads' vengeance."

And this, O Alhazred, is the origin and the destiny of thy people. See that thou pursue it. Take care not to forget these revelations I have vouchsafed thee, and have faithful men write them down for the sons of men to read. For thy book shall be as the fruit of knowledge unto them. *Iä! Shub-Niggurath!*

THE PARCHMENT CHASE

"Murky." That was the word that came instantly to mind for Jim Hart when Professor Kingsport asked the students around the seminar table to free associate: "Don't be shy, gentlemen and ladies! We're going to do a bit of psychology. What pops into your head at the mention of 'Medieval Metaphysics'?" It was the first day of the course, and Jim didn't want to make a bad impression. But he realized that, whatever he blurted out, it would have to be less embarrassing than visibly hesitating when the prof asked for spontaneous reactions. So "murky" it was. Everyone laughed, including Professor Kingsport. This was to Jim's considerable relief.

"Actually," said the dry yet mellow voice of the septuagenarian scholar, "I was waiting for someone to say that! But murky isn't so bad. It shouldn't deter you or discourage you. Murky marks a challenge." (He almost pronounced the word "mucky.") "It invites you on a journey to a Dark Continent of philosophy that most are content to leave in mothballs. And thus they cheat themselves. It is true our Schoolmen of the Middle Ages, both Catholic and Muslim, dwelt on topics mostly alien to us, but that is all to the good. One of the chief goals of a philosophical education is to train the muscles of the mind, and the less familiar the subject matter, the more we have our work cut out for us. And before we are through, I dare say, you will find that some of these irrelevant old issues will take on a new life and reality, perhaps even urgency, for some of you. Welcome to the course!"

There were a few more remarks, mainly dealing with course mechanics: grades, assignments, exams, and so forth. Most of the grade would be based on each student's seminar presentation of his work, the more arcane, and the better explained, the better grade. Professor Kingsport passed out a list of suggested paper topics, but

174

he explained that, rather than choosing a topic now, when they would seem like gibberish, each student should make an appointment with the professor during the next week to consult about a choice. With that, Dr. Kingsport let his tiny flock, five advanced graduate students at the Miskatonic University School of Divinity, out early. They had been sitting at a long table a yard or two away from the professor's own desk in his oaken paneled office. Gathering his stuff, Jim left the room and walked over to the Student Commons with a friend, an earnest fellow named Frank Ford.

Jim and Frank took a look at the menu board in the Commons and decided to hit the streets instead, where in tacit agreement they made their way directly to a favorite haunt, the Arkham House of Pizza. Jim was gangly without being particularly tall. He sported irrepressibly frizzy hair the color of straw, that shade of dirty blonde that could be called a color by analogy if at all. He was a native New Englander, hailing from Rutledge, Vermont, while Frank, better dressed, bow-tied, black hair immaculately trimmed, was from Connecticut, which he thought was part of New England, but which Jim maintained was not. It properly belonged with New York and New Jersey, he said. And the fact that the House of Pizza chain did not extend into Connecticut only proved his point, or so he averred. But why argue when one's mouth might be put to better use, munching the distinctive toasty crust of New England Greek pizza?

As the two young men neared the finish line, neck and neck, with one slice left to each, and neither apparently destined to go to waste, Jim asked Frank, "Just what attracts you to this seminar? It's not your usual fare, is it?"

His friend replied with an instant readiness that signaled much previous thought on the matter, "I can't completely explain it. Partly, I guess I want to know what theologians and philosophers were saying in the Dark Ages. You don't hear much about that stuff in the standard Church History courses. You know—from the Book of Acts to the Protestant Reformation with nothing much in between. I'm curious about the bigger picture."

"That all? I mean, that's enough, but..."

"To come clean, I guess I expect it to be a safety zone, so weird that it won't directly challenge my faith. I'm getting enough of that in my Post-Modern Theology course and my Biblical Criticism course. Really, my head's spinning. So what about you?"

Jim could empathize with his friend. His faith had undergone a similar shake-up, and nothing was that easy for him to believe anymore. But by the same token, he felt he had snapped the chains of dogma and now found his education a voyage of discovery. He was curious about all sorts of ideas he never would have entertained only a semester ago.

"Just the name of the seminar, 'Medieval Metaphysics,' hooked me. I hope it's not all hype. I mean, I gather we'll be looking into some pretty esoteric stuff. I guess it's just a mind game, but I'm up for it! In fact, I'm going to pick the most far-out topic I can for my presentation." With this, Jim pulled out the list Professor Kingsport had distributed, already dog-eared and smudged with pizza sauce. "This one, I think. *Confessions of the Mad Monk Clithanus*. Can you beat that?"

"I'm not that venturesome. I'm trying to decide between Saint Bonaventure and Richard of St. Victor. I like that stuff about proving the Trinity from three-leafed clovers!" They both laughed at this, then began to consume the last pizza wedges. And a stray platelet of pepperoni Jim almost didn't notice. "Say, Jim, I heard this course was offered for many years but was discontinued. They only brought it back a year or two ago. It became controversial for some reason. Do you know anything about that?"

But it was news to Jim, who could not imagine what controversy might attach to a survey of dusty-dry philosophers from the Middle Ages. What was the big danger—falling asleep in class?

A couple of days later Jim met with Dr. Kingsport. He was hesitant mentioning his choice of a topic, fearing the old academic would think it too deep for him. But he was surprised; the professor approved, and then some. "My young friend, let me make a suggestion. Clithanus was not exactly a model of clarity or organization. You'd be well advised to focus on one particular section of the work. Have you looked through the text?"

"I've only scanned it so far, but most of it looks interesting. I'm open to recommendations, sir."

"I hoped you might be." Dr. Kingsport gave Jim a sidelong glance from beneath his bushy white brows as if to appraise him. "I'm thinking you'd be just the man to tackle the old eremite's 'Five Proofs of the Existence of the Devil.'"

Jim's bespectacled eyes widened. He had not even noticed that section. But it sounded fascinating! He readily agreed.

Exiting the professor's book-lined office, Jim headed for the University library, settled down in a vacant study carrel, then unzipped his book bag and pulled out the copy of the *Confessions*, which he had already checked out. Now for a closer look at those five proofs!

A quick survey of the italicized section headings supplied by the editor revealed the Proof from *Corruption*, the Proof from *Degradation*, the Proof from *Despair*, the Proof from *Lying Wonders*, and finally the Proof from *Manifestation*. A lot of room for head scratching there! Jim resolved to give a read to the first of the arguments, and then, he remembered, he had made a date for coffee with Liz Logan, another of the intimate cadre of students in the Medieval Metaphysics seminar.

> *The men of old taught that Jehovah created and sustained all things by his mighty word alone. Whence then corruption? It availeth not to plead that the Deity alone hath being in himself, and that accordingly, all created entities must needs fall into decay since otherwise they should not partake of the finitude intrinsic to created things. For if it be true that the mighty Lord upholdeth them directly from moment to moment, even as his Son saith, My Father worketh even now, then how can they lapse into weakness and fade into corruption? Hence there must be an antipodal Power which interposeth corruption like a poison spewed into a wound. And this Power all men know as the Devil.*

Jim thought, or hoped, he had picked up some of the thinking of the old heretic, but his head was beginning to spin with the unaccustomed doctrine, and so he slapped the volume shut and shoved it back into his book bag. That coffee was looking better and better, and come to think of it, so was Liz. He was off to see her, out the tall doors of the Library and across the quad, tickled by autumn breezes, pelted by leaves whose bright hues the early sunset hid.

There was Liz, talking with a small group of students, none of them familiar to Jim. But he introduced himself, shook hands all around. "Listen, Liz and I were just going to sit down over some coffee. Feel like joining us?" But all begged off. Seemed they should have buckled down to their books a couple of hours ago, and now were determined to make up for lost time. Most were Law School students, though what they were doing on this part of the Miskatonic campus, Jim did not know. Probably liked the food better. Anyway, he sat down with Liz after squirting the coffee into a Styrofoam cup and grabbing a pastry.

"Have you had your conference with Professor Kingsport yet, Liz? Got your topic?"

"Indeed I do," she said with an ocular twinkle. "And I think I may have you beat for weirdness! He suggested I take a crack at *Aradia*, the so-called 'Gospel of the Witches.' Surprisingly little critical work has ever been done on it. Even the name. Is 'Aradia' supposed to be Herodias, who had John the Baptist whacked?"

Jim chuckled. "I can see the professor is using the term 'metaphysics' in a pretty loose sense! I doubt there's much philosophy in a book like that, though I suppose you could always fake your way through the philosophical underpinnings. Like, does it show evidence of Manichaeanism?"

"Wait a second," Liz interrupted. "That's not bad! Let me make a note on that!" And she did, with no worries of anybody stealing the idea from her as she had pilfered it from Jim: nobody else could read her hand writing.

As she scrawled, Jim told her, "I've been talking to Will Bell. He's an old pal of mine, you know. He's thinking of giving Christian thinkers a break and dipping into Judaism. Kingsport approved his doing something on Merkabah mysticism."

"Which is...?"

"The *Merkabah* was the royal throne chariot of God. It was drawn through the heavens by twin storm clouds, personified as cherubim."

"Cherubs? You mean like Valentine's Day?" She snickered.

"No, more like winged bulls with human faces. That's how they described them next door in Babylon. The whole thing's pretty strange. Anyhow, these Jewish mystics would meditate on the beginning of the Book of Ezekiel, the story of the prophet having a vision of the throne chariot coming out of the sky, drawn by these cherubs. God was seated on the throne, with an emerald rainbow around his head."

"That begins to ring a bell. Doesn't it have something to do with flying saucers? I saw this thing on the History Channel..."

"You mean the Hysteria Channel."

A laugh. "I guess so. But it was pretty convincing. Some NASA engineer said the description of the thing fits the design of a workable flight vehicle."

"Maybe. If you've got enough imagination, I suppose. Anyway, these old sages used to meditate on that scene, and they hoped it would spark the same vision in their own minds. Then they could make a day trip to God's throne room in heaven. I wouldn't be surprised if Will's project is to try it himself!"

"Any, you know, *substances* involved?"

"Apparently not, but he says Kingsport did warn him, almost discouraged him at first."

"Why on earth? Does he need to be able to read the Bible chapter in the original Hebrew or something?"

"He probably could if he had to. I think he's gotten his biblical language requirement over with." Will was overweight, a bit rumpled, but his lower-class demeanor concealed a sharp mind.

"So what's the trouble?"

"I can't tell if the prof was serious or not, but it seems the rabbis would forbid anyone studying this stuff before they reached forty. It was too dangerous!"

"Dangerous how?" Liz said, and sat back to listen as she sipped the coffee, now cooled sufficiently.

"There's an old story called 'The Four Who Entered Paradise.' These four mystics agree to meet one day and to meditate as a group, I don't know why, on the throne chariot passage and see what would happen. It worked. They all tripped out, all right. But

179

when it was over, only Rabbi Johannan ben Zakki, this famous rabbi, came out of it safe and sound. I forget the names, but the other guys didn't fare so well. They couldn't rouse one of them at all. He had died during the vision. You can't see God and live, and all that. Another became a notorious heretic; he couldn't understand what he had seen and started ranting about two gods in heaven or something. The third went crazy. Whatever he had seen proved too much for the poor bastard. It's a cautionary tale, you see."

"Wow. I guess it didn't scare off Will, though, huh?"

"Not that I know of. I'm not sure when he's planning the launch. He may even have already done it, but I think he'd come running to tell me if anything, good or bad, had happened."

Jim was starting to fancy Liz. She had long, straight brown hair, cascading over her strong cheekbones, framing eyes full of thunderous intelligence. She always had much to say and yet seemed willing to let him talk all he wanted. There probably wouldn't be any future with her; who knew where your careers would take you after you got your degrees? But, hell, seize the day. They agreed to meet again soon.

It was a few weeks, half the semester later, when student presentations began. In the meantime the learned Professor Kingsport regaled his students with his famous lectures on some of the more standard-brand medieval thinkers. The seminarians listened respectfully, scribbling notes or else clacking as quietly as they could on their laptops. All but Tom Anderson, who was absent most sessions, a fact impossible to overlook with so few students around the table. One could easily tell Dr. Kingsport was displeased, irritated. How dare a mere student show disrespect this way? What better could they have to do? Jim and Liz heard rumors that Tom had departed from his former diligent habits and could be found playing, and losing, at poker much of the time, at least when he was sober enough to participate. The rumors were confirmed when Tom, his blond mop disheveled, showed up at their dorm rooms at odd hours stinking of booze and asking to borrow money.

How remarkable then when the day arrived for his scheduled presentation, and he was present. He displayed a day or two worth of stubble, and his eyes were a bit red, but his voice was steady, and he seemed ready to go. All listened, impressed, as their mutual glances showed, as Tom read his paper aloud. His subject had to do with Alcuin of York's interpretation of St. Augustine's *City of God* and whether he had wrongly interpreted it to further Charlemagne's imperialist aims. Most scholars thought he had, but here Tom was arguing, with surprising knowledge of the range of scholarly opinion, that Alcuin had been correct after all. The main thing his classmates were learning, however, was that one ought not underestimate Tom.

But this was shortly to prove a lesson they would have to forget. Tom finished to light hand-clapping, but the professor did not applaud. He did comment, though.

"Quite a fine paper, Mr. Anderson. I thought so *when I wrote it*, and I think so now."

Stunned silence descended, all eyes swinging from Kingsport to Tom, then downward to their notes. None of them wanted to hear the Olympian displeasure to follow. But they did. Everyone knew this meant expulsion. Tom had purchased the paper from a "research agency" maintained by one of the fraternities. Of course the paper bore no name, so Tom could not have guessed he was feeding his professor's own words back to him. As Jim and Frank later discovered, someone at the frat had stolen the paper from a locked section of the library containing not only recent faculty publications but also the professors' dissertations and graduate papers. Tom was not the only one booted, as he named names and took some of the "research" staffers down with him.

But that wasn't quite the end of the matter. Late one night, as Jim returned to his dorm room, he saw a clipping from the day's edition of *The Arkham Advertiser* taped to his door. It reported the discovery of Tom Anderson's bloated corpse in the reeds on the bank of the Miskatonic. There had been no announcement on campus. Jim was pretty sure this was part and parcel of the school's longstanding policy of hushing up campus crime, from cheating to rape, in order to protect the already dubious reputation the school suffered in some quarters. Jim hadn't been particularly close to Tom, but he had been an acquaintance through seminary thus far.

He felt the blow and stretched out on his bed to let the sadness have its way. He didn't want to shrug it off. That was the way to grow a hard heart. As he inventoried his best memories of Tom and tried to figure just how and why the promising young man had made a wrong turn, he could not help thinking of the monk Clithanus' Proof from Corruption. It certainly seemed to fit the case. So much so, that his recent study of it almost seemed to foreshadow Tom's fate. And this reminded Jim he'd better crack that book again. His own seminar paper would be coming up pretty soon now. So he sat up, reached for the book, and found the second proof, that from *degradation*.

> *The gospel telleth that no sparrow may fall dead from the branch except the heavenly Father allow it. But it forbeareth to say what agency doth cause it to fall, whether a beast or an ill wind. Even so, the parable avoweth that, though the seed of the Logos be sown, yet may another Power seize it and steal it away. And that Power all men call the Devil.*

He, uh, hadn't thought of *that*. For all the protestations of preachers, the chosen of God were often enough abandoned in their hour of need. Pious rhetoric equivocated. God had answered the prayer of the righteous, to be sure, but he had, ah, answered *no*. It usually boiled down to the cold comfort of Stoicism: the roof fell on your head, but you ought to be thankful. It was, after all, another opportunity to become indifferent to circumstances. Like mobster John Gotti said when he went to prison: "Mind over matter: if you don't mind, it don't matter." Yeah, great. So it seemed Clithanus was saying that the Christian God meant well but just could not be relied on. Someone else must be making mischief, and God just couldn't stop it. Sacrificing God's omnipotence seemed the only way to avoid sacrificing his goodness and love. And if he didn't have all the power, who had the rest of it? You guessed it.

Liz Logan was next up at the seminar. But she never showed up. At first Jim was not especially worried. It would be easy to find an alternate day for her presentation, since the small number of students made it easy to synchronize schedules. But where was she?

Jim recalled their last conversation, just two nights previous. Professor Kingsport had told her, she said, that the best way to grasp the import of the Witches' gospel would be to reconstruct, if possible to *witness*, its probable *Sitz-im-Leben*, its living context, first hand. But wouldn't that entail visiting a witch coven? The professor closed his eyes and gave a slight smile in amusement. What he had in mind was rather something of a "historical reenactment group" of Miskatonic alumni meeting nearby. They had been history majors at the University, most of them, though there were a couple from nearby Dunwich, and they had a special interest in the Arkham witch trials of old. That sounded fascinating to Liz. She was quite the feminist and as such had long been interested in the theory that European witchcraft was really the survival of a pre-Christian nature religion. She had heard of groups like this and was excited about going. Jim had a momentary mental image of a witches' sabbat with its altar a naked woman, and she was Liz. He thought it best to shake his head clear of the scene.

In lieu of Liz's presentation, the class asked their professor random questions about their own projects, eager for any suggestions. Jim didn't, thinking instead about Liz. He snapped out of his reverie when Professor Kingsport addressed *him* with a question.

"And *you*, Mr. Hart. How are you coming in your study of the mad Clithanus?"

"Huh? Oh, well enough, I suppose. The reading is full of new ideas, but I think I'm digesting them without too much stomach trouble. One thing I did want to ask, though, Professor. Was Clithanus out there on his own limb? Or did he represent any sect or heretical order? I mean, were these just his private theories? Or did he get them from some prior tradition?"

Kingsport paused a moment and answered, "Let St. Paul provide your answer, Mr. Hart. When you return to your room tonight, turn to Galatians chapter one, verse eleven."

So that is just what Jim did. He wiped the slight residue of Arkham House of Pizza from his fingers so as not to stain the pages of his Bible, then carefully turned the thin leaves till he found:

For I am letting you know, brothers, that the message preached by me is not human in origin, for it was not from human beings that I received it, nor was I instructed in it; on the contrary, it was revealed by Jesus Christ.

So Clithanus claimed it was a private revelation, just to him. But that didn't mean there wasn't some sort of sect. Maybe he had started one. After all, who would have recopied and passed down the *Confessions?* Well, that was not really the concern of his paper. It was the philosophy, if you could call it that.

Jim took out his phone and called Will, then Frank. Neither had seen or heard from Liz. Both were worried and promised to inform the others immediately as soon as they heard anything. As he hung up, Jim was on the point of deciding to go out and look for Liz. Perhaps something had happened to her at that sabbat reenactment Professor Kingsport had sent her to. Now where did she say it was being held?

There was a knock at his door, followed by the sound of receding footsteps. No one was evident when he got to the door and opened it. Then he looked back at the door and saw another news clipping. This one made him sick to his stomach.

Liz was horribly dead, her... remains discovered by a park attendant in some woods near the campus. She had been mutilated and sexually abused, apparently both before and after decease, by a number of men. They had left footprints, half-empty liquor bottles, and discarded food wrappers scattered all about the clearing. Her blood had been freely splashed about, ensanguining the inner ring of tree trunks. Certain "objects" (not further specified) had been found stuffed into all her bodily orifices, including empty eye sockets. Her hands and feet had been removed and could not be found. Almost as an afterthought, the article mentioned that what looked like mathematical or algebraic symbols had been chalked on the tree trunks.

While reading it, Jim had drifted back into his room and sat on the edge of the bed. His eyes welled with tears as his guts churned. On automatic pilot he stumbled into the bathroom to vomit, but then found himself back at the bed. All feeling had drained out of him, and he felt cold down to the finger tips. He sat there in a kind of waking coma for some hours, heeding only the dawn light filtering through his blinds.

Oblivious of their ringing, Jim later learned he had missed calls back from both Frank and Will, who had heard the same shocking news. All agreed the revolting detail of the news report seemed like an overcompensation for the self-serving silence of the campus authorities. But then this clipping came from the always more lurid tabloid, the *Aylesbury Monitor*. There would be no local funeral; rather Liz's closed casket would be displayed back in her home town in Denver. None of her Miskatonic friends and classmates would be able to afford such a trip, so they mourned her silently and alone. They mourned her spoiled beauty, her stilled eloquence, her extinguished future promise. And they cursed the degenerates who had destroyed her. It was only after some days had passed that Jim realized he had not thus far even thought of Liz as the victim of perpetrators, of murderers. It was somehow as if she had perished in an animal attack, so terrible was the ferocity of destruction. But who were the men? Jim couldn't help thinking there was a ready-made group of candidates in the "reenactment group" whose event poor Liz had sought out. Did it not occur to the authorities? Or, even more troubling, could it be that, if the men were in fact Miskatonic alumni of some status, the local police had looked the other way?

Bitterly, he thought momentarily how it seemed his old monk had a point: he did feel as if he were victim to a weird negative providence, a punching bag for someone whose attention he wished he had not attracted. Like Job.

To turn from the black hole of Liz's death to work again on his assignment seemed to Jim like half a betrayal, but he just had to do it. She would want him to do it. Life goes on. Death goes on, too.

He set to work on the third proof of Clithanus. It was succinct like the others.

> *The Savior decreeth that Capernaum and Bethsaida should not be exalted to heaven but instead should be cast down into hell. And so it is with every soul that is shaded by an infinite sadness without relief. All is dry desert, and the soul findeth no sustenance. When a*

man despaireth he can be cheered by no upturn of fortune. He is held in thrall. And every slave hath his master, even a cruel one. And this grim master do all men call the Devil.

Jim knew how that felt, though he was not normally depressive. No, the cause of his terrible grief was specific and plain. But he determined to work through it, confident that even these heavy clouds must one day part. Still, he felt guilty for even looking forward to that day. For the moment, he would not deny his pain. But his necessary work might distract him a bit.

Frank had decided to do his work on Anselm of Canterbury, he of the Ontological Argument and the Satisfaction theory of the atonement. But these two aspects of Anselm's work were spent: too much had been written about them for him to master in a single term paper, and by the same token, he should have little original to say. So he was concentrating on Anselm as Exhibit A as to the fatal separation of what Pascal later called the God of Abraham, Isaac, and Jacob and the God of the philosophers. Fatal because to define God in the static categories of essence and "pure act" required one to think of "him" as impersonal and timeless, incapable of being moved by human need, neither hating sin nor loving righteousness. Such a God by definition could not act, did not think, since acting implied he had been partly potential before acting, fully actualized afterward. Thinking meant he was not omniscient but had to follow a series of steps to reach a conclusion. He became the Unmoved Mover, the Form of the Good, but hardly the Living God of personal religion. Traditionally theologians just melded the God of the Bible with that of the philosophers by fiat, pretending that God might be both infinite and personal, as if personality (a discrete set of characteristics drawn from a large menu) did not require finitude. Anselm's attempt to solder the two God-concepts together was to say that, while God could not actually and literally "love" mankind, or anything else for that matter, his treatment of us is somehow analogous to love, as when we admire the fit of a garment and comment, "That dress loves you!" In short, the philosophical God must be an "it," not a "he."

Again at the House of Pizza, Frank was discussing the topic with

Jim. "The irony, Jim, is that while Anselm thought he was saving Christian theology by these moves, he was really *destroying* it! If you see through the ruse he fooled himself with, you see that even if he's right it means there is no God such as we always believed in. No Jehovah, no miracles, no providence, no Father who sent his son into the world to save us!"

"Frank, I think you've got a good thesis there."

"Yeah, that's not *all* I've got! I'm not one of these guys who can let challenges to the faith roll off my back! I can't assume all problems will evaporate in the sweet by and by! Once you take seriously the philosophical critique of the biblical God, you can't help seeing that Jehovah is just another Zeus. You can't take him seriously. *I* can't anyway. Sharing some lamb stew with Abraham around the fire one night, telling Moses to use otter hide instead of manatee hide for the drapes in the Tabernacle, or whatever. And on the other hand, try praying to the Ground of Being!

"I think I've looked too closely at my faith and found it wanting. I mean, every theology has to have some holes in it, I know that. But now it looks to be *all hole!* I don't see how I can go into the ministry like this. I mean, I'd given my life to this! And *now* what? I'm too used to thinking of a world without God as a big disappointment, a moonscape barren of meaning..." Frank's voice was beginning to shake. People at other tables were starting to steal poorly concealed glances at Frank and Jim. Neither man had eaten so much as a slice of their favorite pizza, which now cooled between them.

"Frank, I don't know what to say. I mean, I've had some of the same questions in the last year or so, but I've been pretty much parked in a holding pattern. I'm used to it. It's not so bad when you..."

But Frank had gathered his books and walked out into the cold night without a word. Jim knew better than to follow him. The man needed time alone. Jim resigned himself to seeing his friend, he hoped calmer and composed, when Frank gave his seminar presentation next day.

Jim had a premonitory chill invade his bones as he entered Professor Kingsport's office and headed over to the seminar table. He was on time, but Will and the professor were already sitting

187

there. He exchanged greetings, feeling uneasy that Frank was not there with his notes organized on the table in front of him. As soon as Jim pulled up his chair, Kingsport broke the silence.

"I suppose both of you have heard about Mr. Ford?"

But Jim needed to hear no more. Quietly he rose from the table, looking at neither of the other faces, and left the building. He only hoped he would not find yet another newspaper report of a suicide tacked to his door like Martin Luther's theses. Nor did he. He lay down, though his whole body felt charged with stinging electricity. Like he was going to blow. These last weeks had brought him way too much to absorb. But he dared not indulge in self-pity, as he was not the victim here. Three others were. He had to grieve for them, not for himself.

Fall reading week came and went, scarcely noticed as students labored beneath a Sisyphean load of books and papers. The way it was looking, Jim was thinking he would skip the trip home for Thanksgiving. He hoped his parents would understand. He had been procrastinating on assignments for his other courses, but most of it looked pretty easy, so he took the liberty of opening the *Confessions* again. After all, his presentation was coming up in only two weeks. He had puzzled over the mad monk's first three so-called proofs, making extensive notes of precedents for the arguments in ancient Gnosticism and Marcionism, even in Zoroastrianism. Naturally he was much interested in the inverted parallels with Aquinas' proofs for God in the *Summa Theologica*. It seemed impossible to believe that the greatest of Roman Catholic philosopher-theologians had cribbed from Clithanus, but the latter's *Confessions* was some centuries older. Anyway, on to the fourth proof.

> *The divine Apostle opposeth faith to knowledge but averreth that both shall pass away in the light of unmediated vision. Yet he who thinketh that he sees, let him take heed that he understand what he seeth. For what some deem deep darkness is verily the blinding of a superior light shining upon him. If he give up the old light, he shall awaken to the new. Wherefore doth the scripture say, If that light which is within you be darkness, how great is that darkness. And*

that darkness all men call the Devil.

Jim had to give the heretical monk credit: he certainly approached scripture with a hell of an imagination! Here he had come surprisingly near to the insight of some modern, or postmodern, scholars who distrusted the vaunted "self-evidence" of what one believed the truth. He even implied the notion that every paradigm carried its own criteria of plausibility and probability, and that therefore all supposed justification of propositions had to be completely subjective. Didn't various places in the Bible warn against "false prophecies" and "lying wonders" threatening to deceive the righteous? And yet one could only classify the miracle as false in the first place once you had committed to one side or the other. To one side a particular miracle would be true, to the other false. So the miracles only seemed to prove something depending on what side you had already chosen. This is the aspect of the fourth proof Jim decided to work on.

A few hours later, Jim was surprised to look up at his wall clock and to discover it was time to pick up Will for dinner. He was eager to compare notes with Will on their upcoming seminar presentations. They would be the first two and the last two. Jim fought back a momentary chill of superstitious dread and knocked on Will's dorm room door. He was excited over the progress he'd made as well as genuinely interested in Will's project. He had read Gershom Scholem's translation of the Hekhaloth texts, hoping it would help him get more out of the paper.

His knock went unanswered. Thinking his friend might be asleep inside, Jim knocked harder. At this, the door came open a few inches. Venturing a look inside to make sure Will was all right, Jim could see no one. He advanced a couple of steps into the room, calling Will's name, in case he might be out of sight, maybe in the bathroom, but still in earshot. Nothing. A quick look around revealed Will was simply nowhere about the place. Jim stuck his head back into the hall to see if anyone might be walking by. They might know where Will had gone. But there was no one at the moment. So he stepped back inside and did a slower, more careful sweep. This time he noticed a tape machine that must have run out and rewound, with the little red light still on.

He left Will a note and took the tape recorder back to his own room, skipping dinner without a further thought. He reclined on his unmade bed and clicked "play." Maybe it would be a message for Jim. But no, it was immediately clear this was a record of Will's visionary experiment. It seemed Will had hoped to enter a sort of lucid dreaming state in which he would have the presence of mind to describe what was happening to him. The machine was voice-activated and had begun to record when it first "heard" Will's voice. He must have silently meditated on Ezekiel's vision for some hours, something Jim knew he would never have had the patience to do. Hell, once he'd tried to repeat the Jesus Prayer the whole time he was walking around a single block, and it drove him nuts with its monotony. But Will had apparently gotten somewhere with his meditation. His voice was slow and dreamy, sometimes trailing off, but readily picking up again. First he said he was descending, falling toward the divine throne room. This was peculiar imagery, but that's the way the old Merkabah mystics put it, too: *down*. Then he said he saw a great light reflected as if on a vast ocean surface. He knew it was the Shekinah of God, his glory cloud that had appeared to Moses as the Pillar of Fire.

And then came the Merkabah itself, a wheel within a wheel, as the ancient prophet had struggled to describe. It was spinning as it arced across the blazing sky, coming to rest without impact or friction a few yards from Will's observing inner eye. There, upholding the disk, were the Cherubim, winged figures, each with four faces protruding from all sides of the skull. They, too, spun, albeit much more slowly, and Will peered intently. At first he thought he saw the same four visages Ezekiel had once described. (All the while, as he listened, Jim kept wondering what Carl Jung would have made of such a detailed, repeatable vision!) There were the beaked eagle, the horned bull, the fanged lion, and the godlike human face. But their spinning accelerated, slowing down again to reveal a different quartet of faces. Will said he could have sworn the faces were those of Tom, Liz, Frank, and—himself!

As for Him who sat on the throne amid a golden haze, Will stammered that his glory was very great, and that He was swathed all

190

in yellow silk, His face bulging oddly behind a snow-white veil, His eyes as a flame of fire. And the figure stretched forth His right hand toward Will, who noticed how the extended arm appeared to have one too many joints. But this was forgotten when a Voice sounded. "In My house are many lodgings. I will not leave you orphaned, but will take you to be with Myself."

And there the tape ended.

No one reported seeing Will Bell again. He certainly didn't show up to give his paper. Jim, the only student left, would have been surprised if he had. But just in case Will should ever return, Jim wanted to see him receive at least partial credit for the "research" he had done, so he brought the tape to class and played it for Professor Kingsport. The two of them sat there listening to it in silence. Now and then the professor nodded, occasionally smiling slightly but knowingly. Finally, "Thank you, Mr. Hart. That was quite considerate of you." No mention of Will's absence, not an iota of concern displayed. "And what of your own research? Will you be ready to present next week?"

With a sense of resigned foreboding, as if it were his turn to jump off the bridge, he said a simple "Yes sir." Jim left, unable to banish the mental image of the train of normalcy and sanity chugging down the tracks into the distance, leaving him and his suitcase far behind on the platform.

Robotically he began work on the last of the proofs.

> *The Savior saith, Seek and ye shall find. Knock and it shall be opened unto you. Ask and it shall be given you. For everyone who seeketh will find. Each who knocketh shall find an open door. And all who ask shall receive. If ye, being evil, know to give good things to your children when they ask, how much more will your heavenly father give good things to them who ask? But then whence come the bad things that in their ignorance men request? There must be a Giver of these things, too. And this Giver all men call the Devil.*

This one hit home. Jim had received far more than his share of bad things, though nothing compared to his friends and classmates. This could scarcely be mere chance. Had he in some way asked for such ill fortunes? Not consciously. Was it possible he had inadvertently attracted these blows of fate by studying these very proofs? In his seeking to understand them, had he asked someone for a demonstration? And would that someone be the one all men call the Devil?

On the appointed day, Jim made his way to the now familiar office of the venerable Professor Kingsport. He sat at one end of the table with the professor regarding him owlishly from the opposite end. The emptiness of the other chairs was conspicuous, as if it were all a set-up for a practical joke and any minute he should see the laughing figures of his vanished classmates parading out from off stage to tell him he was on a hidden camera program. But none came.

The intimacy between himself and the imposing old scholar was itself intimidating. This was a smaller audience than he should have had, and potentially a much less friendly one. Professor Kingsport was known to give encouragement to promising students, the ones he apparently regarded already as colleagues, albeit in larval form. At others he freely cast his thunderbolts, caring not for their effect. Well, now it was sink or swim, and the terrible semester would be over one way or another. Jim launched into his paper. Once or twice the professor interrupted with a reading suggestion or to ask for clarification. But so far, so good. The wrecking ball had not swung into action. In fact, to Jim's surprise, Kingsport broke the wake of post-paper silence: "Mr. Hart, you have exceeded my expectations, I must say. I hoped you would, and you have not disappointed me."

Jim heard this much, and he felt he had given a migraine the slip. But Professor Kingsport's words began to fade, as if Jim were losing his hearing. He was becoming confused.

He did not exactly see anything, mind you, but he suddenly felt as if he *remembered* something he had just glimpsed for a split second. He fancied that, momentarily, the vacant seats around the table were again occupied by his unfortunate classmates and friends. There were Tom, and Liz, and Frank, and Will. All looked in his direction, and from their empty eyes shone forth a withering glance of reproof. Jim flinched.

Then Jim began to doubt his sight for the second time that morning, for the interior of Kingsport's oak-paneled office suddenly glowed with a bright red light, then returned to normal. His puzzled eyes turned to the professor, whose snow-capped, shaded eyes were fixed intently upon him. He felt that a long contest was now ended and that he was about to hear the conclusion of the matter. Then a question formed in his mind and forced itself to his lips. "But where is the manifestation? It's called 'the Proof from Manifestation.' So where's the manifestation?"

The dry voice of his mentor sank into Jim's attentive ears.

"Have I been with you so long, Mr. Hart, and still you do not know me?"

The red halo still lingered about Kingsport's features, and Jim knew that his lessons were just beginning.

THIS IS THE DAWNING

Bud Williams had always been chuckled at, dismissed, and avoided by most folks. All they needed to know was that he took correspondence courses via newspaper advertisements for the Rosicrucians. Eventually, as is the fashion among eccentrics, Bud no longer sought or wished for common companions, deciding that most people were beneath him, unenlightened. To replace them, he associated himself with new friends, more like-minded, joining up with various occult groups. Some of these had overlapping memberships, which is how he learned of each new sect or circle: the Theosophical Society, The Mighty I AM Movement, various offshoots of the Golden Dawn and the O.T.O. There were a lot of them in and around Los Angeles.

He was soon a bit disappointed to learn that, instead of being genuine seekers, many of the "illuminati" attended the groups mainly for social reasons. Bud didn't stop to think that a great deal of his own interest had pretty much the same basis. But it was understandable that many of them were satisfied with the superficial, since, as he had to admit, many of the doctrines taught at the gatherings were somewhat abstruse, not easy to follow. No wonder most members gave up and just coasted. Of course, the confusion might be a device to keep the believers dependant on the group leadership who pretended to grasp all of the advanced secrets. It would not do for the average member to admit he or she did not understand those matters which everyone else seemed to understand, though they, too, were perhaps too embarrassed to let on that they didn't get it. The emperor's clothes, you know. Bud himself had trouble keeping straight the somewhat inconsistent tenets of the various circles he belonged to.

But after a while, Bud started to surprise himself. He often found himself mentally fidgeting with this or that bit of esoteric teaching, trying, and sometimes succeeding, in making real sense of some of these ideas, understanding for the first time that they *were* ideas and not just slogans designed to keep the average "initiate" bluffed and befogged. He began to comprehend the distinctions between Theosophy and Anthroposophy. And where the White Brotherhood of Alice Bailey differed from both. He stopped being a passive recipient at the meetings, spoon-fed dribs and drabs of the arcane. He started raising objections, asking for clarification, maintaining informed opinions of his own. He had even begun to read widely in the works of Steiner, Blavatsky, Godfre Ray King and the rest. He picked and chose the nuances of doctrine that appealed to him intuitively. And, not surprisingly, he finally dropped out of all his occult societies. He thought twice before making this decision, as he had half-entertained the hope of finding female companionship, long-term or short, among their ranks. But that had not panned out. Bud knew well enough that he was no catch. He was by no means handsome. Though slender, fairly fit, and wiry, he was, at forty, losing his stringy gray hair. And his face bore more than a passing resemblance to a seal's. And most "metaphysical" women ran short on the physical. Well, to hell with it.

If Bud had been more ambitious, less shy, he might have considered trying to start up an occult society of his own. But there were other goals, no less fateful, that he did resolve to pursue. He started laying plans for a trip up north to Mount Shasta. Godfre Ray King had famously claimed to have encountered, in a cavern under the mountain, a council of timeless, ageless survivors of sunken Lemuria. They were, he said, the ones who had instructed him in the lore that formed the basis of the Mighty I AM. To tell the truth, Bud had never really believed the story, though he found the sect's teachings interesting. But suppose it were true? Suppose King had actually encountered something or someone in the hidden recesses of Shasta? It was only a few years after the end of World War II, and there was an ongoing rash of sightings of Unidentified Flying Objects, flying saucers. There was a lot of interest in this phenomenon among Bud's former compatriots. Bud himself took the whole thing pretty seriously, and he thought Godfre Ray King might possibly have met space aliens. Might as well find out, even if it was likely to be a fool's errand. Besides, it would be a good break from L.A.

***

Bud had some vacation time coming to him. He bought a bus ticket and climbed aboard, shouldering his knapsack filled with sandwiches, socks, and underwear. He quickly got bored with the scenery along the Pacific Highway and briefly scrutinized those of his fellow passengers close enough to spy on. He could catch sufficient syllables to cringe at the cattle-brained stupidity of these fools. Was Bud really superior to the mundane travelers sitting around him? Or was it simply a matter of his devotion to a set of beliefs unknown and unsuspected by most people? No doubt Jehovah's Witnesses and Pentecostals felt the same way, hugging their dogmas to themselves and chuckling secretly. But, justified or not, he could feel his disdain for the common run of humanity climbing rapidly up the thermometer. He closed his eyes to shut out the buffoons around him and spent the rest of the ride slipping between meditation and sleep.

When the bus stopped to allow passengers to stretch their legs and line up outside a restaurant's restrooms, Bud picked up a few snacks. He had precious little cash, but his eye was snagged by the garish cover of a pulp magazine on the rack. Silly-looking scene with alien creatures menacing a scantily clad woman wearing a fishbowl helmet and little else in the way of protection. A saucer craft was hovering in a reddish sky. With a chuckle at both the picture and himself, given the fact that his own mission was not so far removed from this boyish fantasy, he flipped a dime onto the counter and left with his copy of *Astro-Adventures*.

Back on the bus, Bud paged from one story to another, some more extravagant than others, some unintentionally humorous. It was typical of the genre, one with which he had long been familiar. It was of course quite common for people like him to favor both scientifiction and metaphysical belief. Outsiders could not tell the difference, and there were moments when Bud wondered if there *was* much of a difference. In fact, he mused, his present pursuit was aimed at finding whether there was. Soon the rhythm of the bus sent him drifting off to sleep. Not a dreamless sleep, though.

***

Wow! This was, after all, the 1940s, and the special effects in the movies were pretty modest. Certainly Bud had never seen on the screen anything like what he was seeing in his dream. At least he figured it had to be a dream. He hoped it was, because it was fully as terrifying as it was dazzling. He found himself running like hell *through* hell. Explosions filled the sky. Bud had not served in the War, having been 4F'ed on account of a heart murmur. But this did look kind of like scenes from the European theatre he had seen on newsreels. There did not seem to be actual bombs bursting in the sky above; rather, he could swear it was the sky itself that was igniting, exploding. Where could you flee from *that*? People were in fact scattering in all directions in a blind panic. Women were being pursued by wild-eyed mobs of men. Stores were being looted. All at once, as the dream-Bud stood frozen in shock, a titanic shadow loomed over him, descending to shroud him in darkness. And at once his surging adrenalin subsided, replaced with the distancing suspension of curious contemplation: wasn't this scene very much like one of the stories he had read before dozing off? Only grimmer? And with that realization, Bud awoke.

***

Unlike his usual ones, these dreams remained pretty distinct, refusing to fade in the light of day. Maybe because it had been daylight when, sitting aboard the rolling bus, he had dreamed. But by the time he finally reached his object, it was mid-evening, and the sun was down. He couldn't afford a motel room, though there were plenty available, catering to the mountain-scaling tourist trade. He didn't know how long he might be here. He was prepared to camp out. So he found a cleft in the rocks at the base of the Southwest face of the mountain, unrolled his sleeping bag, and settled in. He planned to watch the stars for some hours, speculating about what or who might lurk up there, out there. He thought his long nap would make it hard to get to sleep for the night, but instead he fell deeply asleep almost at once, almost as if he had been given anesthesia.

The dream was even clearer this time. He found himself sprawled on a more or less even rock basin. It looked wet. He briefly thought he noticed blue-green cilia waving as if in flowing water. He glanced around to see fish swimming past! Yet he felt as if he was, as usual, surrounded by clear air. Was he immersed in invisible and intangible water? That made no sense, but then he remembered it was another dream. There was a free-standing monolith in front of him. Something was inscribed on it, letters. They seemed to waver slightly as if viewed through water currents or heat radiance. It was a foreign word or name: *L'MUR-KATHULOS*. It meant nothing to him at first, but something about it brought Godfre Ray King to mind. But then his attention went elsewhere.

Something, though nothing he could yet see, seemed to command his attention. There was the same looming shadow he had seen in his earlier dream. This time there was no raging chaos to obscure and confuse, yet neither could he see anything to cast the shadow. A voice began to speak with imperious thunder. But he could recognize at once that it was his own voice magnified.

You sought Me and found Me. Now serve Me. You who have grown to hate your fellow human vermin because you see the truth about them, will you not serve Me in destroying their bumbling dominion and restoring My own? For if you will, I shall reward you with a throne in My coming kingdom. In that day I will teach them that serve Me new ways to kill and to rampage and to exult in freedom.

Bud shook himself awake. He found himself in a cold sweat. But he knew two things for sure. For one, he understood what must have really happened to Godfre Ray King. He, too, must have experienced his transformative encounter in a dream. He had not physically entered a hidden cavern, but dreamed that he did. No mere fiction, but a revelation imparted by the oneiric medium. The message he had come away with was by no means the same as Bud's, granted, and probably not from the same source. But there must be something about Shasta that made it a contact point between sensitive minds and Outer entities. The medium of dreams
198

explained how the entity he had met seemed to speak in Bud's own voice. That would make even more sense if the being was so vastly alien that only a very rough gist could be communicated from it, broadly translated into Bud's own conceptuality and in his own accents.

Second, he was now convinced of the reality of the unseen realm, as well as of his role in opening the floodgates to release it into this one. It was a world that had no use for him. Well, he had no more use for it either. He did not yet know what specific steps he should have to take, but he felt absolutely sure his eventual course would become clear.

Bud was surprised to have achieved his trip's goal so quickly. His quest was over before it had begun! Not that he was complaining. He turned over, settled in to sleep the rest of the cold mountain night. He would make his way back to the bus stop in the morning.

***

Back home and back at work, Bud found it difficult to concentrate on his Sisyphean labors at the office and even harder to suppress his renewed contempt for the idiot drones he worked with. He grew impatient for some clue as to what steps to take next. And then he remembered a Buddhist story that shed some light on his situation. The Buddha had studied with a couple of prominent gurus and even joined a group of ascetic meditators before he became frustrated with all their ineffective methods. Then he got up and left his colleagues and went on strike. He staked out a shady spot under the Bodhi Tree, where he lowered his saintly posterior, refusing to move till true enlightenment should dawn. It did, in no time, whereupon he went back to his monastic buddies and shared his revelations. Their initial defensiveness melted as he explained what he had learned, and they became his first disciples. Yeah, that might be the very thing...

First, Bud dropped in at a meeting of the Theosophical Society. He was too tactful to say his piece during the meeting. When it was over and everyone headed out the door and to their cars, Bud lingered to talk to the host in whose house they met. He seemed willing to hear what Bud had to say, especially since Bud hadn't attended the meetings in some time.

"Let's sit down, Max. I've something I want to discuss with you." And he told him about the trip to Mount Shasta and the dreams. He half expected the Theosophist to show him the door without a word. He was surprised when Max heard him out in silence, his head dipped down, chin poised on knuckle. When Bud was done, the older man remained as he was for a few moments, still looking vacantly down at the pattern in the carpet. Finally he looked up, met Bud's eyes and spoke softly.

"You know, Bud, it's funny. I'm a Theosophist, so I say I believe, I *think* I believe, in some extravagant things, Ascended Masters, Children of the Fire Mist and so on. But when something strange actually comes my way, I'm flabbergasted. You see, you're not the only one who's been dreaming."

Something was up. Bud listened with new interest.

"In fact, about twenty years ago, a large number of our people all across the country had some pretty unusual dreams. They thought some great fulfillment was at hand and even dressed up in white sheets to wait on the hilltops. Nothing happened, and our movement nearly died from the embarrassment. But this new generation, at least in this neck of the woods, is dreaming again.

"You say you never saw a form or heard a name? And it was in your own voice? As if through a megaphone, would you say? Let me tell you *my* dream..."

* * *

Bud was excited. A few days later he stopped by a Rosicrucian gathering. The next week it was a Vedanta Society meeting. After that it was the Alice Bailey Lodge. To Bud's absolute astonishment, the same scene was replayed time after time. Then he arranged to revisit each group and to repeat his dream revelation to the whole membership. He had agreed with the leader of each meeting that they should not prepare the group for his visit other than announcing he would be the guest speaker. Bud didn't want anyone to be influenced by any talk before he told them himself. He wanted fresh, immediate reactions.

Most of the members in each small group (most of them fitting easily into a large living room or dining room) had in fact experienced very similar dreams. All seemed confused, speaking sheepishly, though the last few to address the group had gained a bit of confidence after hearing the first few. A couple had not experienced any dream, and two or three more wept. This was the scene, almost monotonously, in group after group. There were several individuals who, like Bud, attended more than one group and thus wound up repeating their stories two or three times. Bud couldn't help noticing how their stories tended to grow in the telling, memory embellished by imagination. The earlier versions tended to be more similar to one another than the later versions. But all were more or less like Bud's at Mount Shasta, the differences in detail likely attributable to the psychological filters of the individuals and their beliefs. None of them had learned the name or seen the form of whatever entity had communicated with them.

Bud was already personally acquainted with a number of these believers. He knew most of them were meek and gentle souls who would be repelled at any talk, such as he had heard, of a future orgy of license and violence. Few were confirmed misanthropes as he was. But when he pressed them for details, it seemed their unknown benefactor had spoken in terms more general and more appropriate to their hopes and dreams. Hearing this, Bud became confused—at least until further dreams reassured him he should inherit the power, glory, and freedom he relished.

Bud suggested to the several group leaders that they search their sects' respective scriptures and come back together to share results: did any neglected teachings or prophecies from their founders shed any light on the momentous events that loomed ahead?

***

"Well, Steiner said something that I think is relevant. See what you make of it. It's from an Easter lecture he gave at the Goetheanum the year before he died. 'In the latter days, Ahriman will descend from the Higher Etheric Worlds to plague mankind. Let those with

201

open eyes gaze into their deeper selves for the secrets they knew before this birth. Let them remember what Ahriman long ago caused them to forget.' Nobody's made much of this since it just sort of pops up out of context and off topic. Steiner's infamous for rambling, but this bit not only sticks out like a sore thumb, it doesn't really fit into the rest of his teaching. I'm thinking the entity we're seeing in our dreams is what or whom Rudolf Steiner called Ahriman."

That was Stuart, head of the local Anthroposophical Society. Next to speak was Swami Guptananda from the Vedanta Society. "As it happens, my brothers and sisters, I, too, have found something to share, among Sri Ramakrishna's parables. 'Once there was a poor slave who suffered naught but indignities at the hands of his wealthy master and his master's sons. Each night he was exhausted from his labors, but his hatreds and resentments preyed upon him and stole his sleep. He would have dreamed of a brighter dawn, but he sneered at such vain hopes, believing they could never come to pass. And all the time, had he but known it, deliverance was close by. In the hills there dwelt a mighty bandit who longed to invade and despoil the master's estate, but the compound was heavily fortified against him. He waited for the day when one of the servants might seek him out and pass him into the palace in the secrecy of darkness. Had the angry slave once thought of it, he might easily have sought out the bandit and conspired with him against his wicked lord.' Can it not be, dear friends, that we are dreaming of that bandit, a deliverer whose coming we delay and prevent simply by failing to seek for it?"

There were readings also from Blavatsky's *Secret Doctrine*, King's *Unveiled Mysteries*, and others. But all were ambiguous and equivocal, as might be expected. But there was one that spoke in a singular manner to Bud. It was a suppressed poem by Aleister Crowley, never officially published because the O.T.O. claimed it had been plagiarized by Crowley's inveterate enemy William Butler Yeats, and the Crowleyites lost the ensuing lawsuit.

Circling and circling in the gathering dusk,
The eagle spurns the voice of man.

Beneath him far below, his sharp eye sees:
The world of men lies helpless,
To become, as per his whim, his prey.
All sink beneath the bloody flood,
As he descends to pluck and rend.
Soft fools do whine and weep
As laws framed by the timid kings dissolve,
And ancient thrones fall down.
A revelation nears its hour,
The Beast from Inner Depths
With hydra heads and waving stalks,
Whose prophets render new the Law:
"Do what thou wilt without restraint,
With no reproach, in perfect joy."
Every man shall reign as king,
A bloody sword his scepter.
From the buried sea he shall arise
In glory and in fearful light
As islands rise and mountains plunge,
Till all are gods with all the world their feast."

The group of leaders departed with much to ponder, Bud included.

It was no surprise to him that his sleep was visited by another revelation. It was almost a replay of what he had seen in the cold night of Mount Shasta, though this time he had the frustrated feeling that he should be able to behold the outlines of the one who addressed him, almost thought he could for a moment. There was a bit more to it, though: he heard a string of seeming gibberish: *Ph'nglui mglw'nafh Cthulhu R'lyeh wgah'nagl fhtagn.*

Amazingly, when he awoke suddenly he had no trouble remembering the weird combination of syllables. Indeed, he appeared incapable of forgetting them. The utterance, the formula, was etched as deeply into his brain as his own name. Through the dawning day, as he went to work and tried to converse with others, even to order lunch in a coffee shop, he found himself distracted, forgetting his train of thought as the phrase reverberated unbidden in his mind, almost audibly. A few days later, he was shocked to hear the words spill out of his mouth when he opened it simply to give a passerby the time of day. The man whose watch had stopped went blank, but no more so than Bud's own face. It took him real effort to get his mouth shut, and he fled down the street, holding his jaws closed with his hands. Puzzled stares followed him all the way back to his apartment.

When he dared to relax his jaws again, nothing happened. He was afraid to try to say anything now, but at least he could keep silent. That night, sleeping proved easier than he'd dreaded, but a couple of hours into it, he woke up jabbering. Talking in his sleep, he guessed. Or maybe just talking to someone in a dream. Didn't matter. He suspected someone was trying to tell him something.

***

He stayed home, not daring even to call in sick. He couldn't even answer the phone when someone, probably his office, called. Suddenly it dawned upon him that he could write a note and hand-deliver it to the office, claiming to have severe laryngitis. So he hunted up pencil and paper. Guess what he wrote? He crumpled up the paper and dropped it to the floor. He began to sob. He flopped onto his bed.

Then something else came to him. For some reason he thought he ought to get up, go over to his bookcase and remove his copy of Rodwell's translation of the Koran. He flipped it open and glanced at the page. His eye rested on a passage in which the Prophet Muhammad recounted his first visit from the angel Gabriel. The archangel knelt on the prone chest of the soon-to-be prophet and barked out an order: "Recite thou, in the name of thy Lord, who created! Created man from clots of blood! Recite thou! For thy Lord is the most Beneficent, who hath taught the use of the pen! Hath taught man that which he knoweth not." Henceforth Muhammad was the faithful spokesman for mighty Allah. Hmmm...

Bud began to do what he had not thought to do before: he began to utter the unutterable syllables voluntarily. He felt a definite sense of relief, and he began to repeat the phrase. After a few more rehearsals, he paused and, with a lump in his throat, tried to say something, something in English. "Uh... soon it'll be 1950." It worked.

He sat down and did his best to figure out the implications of his experiment. Finally Bud concluded that it was a trade-off. His hidden patron must want him to give some time each day to chanting the formula (whether aloud or mentally, he would have to determine by trial and error), and as long as he did, he should be able to indulge in normal speech the rest of the time.

The purpose of the chant now seemed clear to him. It might function as a meditation mantra, a spiritual exercise. But whether or not it did, it must somehow be a tool for hastening the new era. And in that case, Bud guessed, he would no longer have to reckon with involuntary repetition. And to test out his recovered freedom of speech, he began making phone calls to Max, Stuart, the Swami, and the others. He told them what had happened to him. One or two of them sounded frightened, especially when Bud explained that he wanted all of them to start chanting the formula, too. None of them had received Bud's recent dream, so his pronunciation of the chant over the phone was the first time they'd heard it. He set up another meeting of the heads of the Theosophists, Thelemites, Anthroposophists, etc., to coach them in the foreign phrase so they could pass it on to their flocks. None of these groups was very large, but that made it all the more important that they all join in, if they planned to get somewhere.

He had to chuckle when he thought about the absurd improbability of the thing: this bunch of would-be mystics and Gnostics fancying themselves delvers into the lost secrets of the ages—they were going to chant a whole world into existence! But Jesus, Muhammad, Hitler had all started small the same way. Even a huge oak grows up from a tiny acorn. But he didn't really doubt. After all, he had experienced some pretty strange things since all this began, and even if it did turn out to be crazy, it was a grand dream. If the world were not finally turned upside down, granting him revenge against the scum he so hated, he was getting pretty good satisfaction even now, just relishing the prospect.

***

Bud and his compatriots had planted the seed as best they could and continued to water it by chanting their mouth-twisting mantra both individually in private and together in larger and smaller groups. But life went on in its maddeningly mundane, patience-fraying manner. Over the years, the group dwindled in size. Eventually the devotion of the members of the local societies to an unsanctioned deity and prophecy led to their national parent organizations cutting them off. Ironically, these ostensibly freethinking sects did consider some things heresy. It was natural for the excommunicated members to merge their cliques. Their small membership already overlapped to some degree anyway. And their new apocalyptic faith tended to push their various original concerns into the background. Rarely, new members joined and learned the chant, but the older ladies, whose like always formed a significant portion of these metaphysical groups, died, one after the other, and membership steadily petered out. Meetings became less and less frequent until, as far as he knew, Bud was pretty much on his own again.

He wondered if he were now the only one chanting anymore. If he were, would that lessen the chances for the great change to transpire? His zeal never flagged; still, for the whole of the decade of the Fifties, he had to make some kind of truce with normalcy, and he went on waiting, waiting and chanting. And looking for signs. For instance, he thought it potentially quite significant when 1954 saw a record number of giant squid sightings. That had to presage something, did it not?

***

His never well defined heart ailment gradually turned into something more serious over the next several years, and Bud, approaching retirement age anyway, was largely confined to his apartment. He did have to take occasional cab rides to the doctor's office. He was startled one day when the taxi driver said he was sorry but he'd have to turn back. Bud recoiled at the sight of bricks and rocks flying across the windshield, and the driver had to dodge bodies rushing into the street in front of him. They had driven into the advancing edge of an urban riot.

Back home, Bud ascended the stairs to his door and went straight to the television set. Sure enough, the coverage of the ongoing disturbance dominated the news all that day and the next. Bud felt disturbed at first, fearful for his safety and that of his shabby neighborhood. But in the back of his mind he had a vague sense of a silver lining. As rioting spread across many urban centers and college campuses that summer, Bud experienced an odd sense of rekindled hope.

One evening, as he sat at a local bar watching the tube with some of the other neighborhood regulars, he suddenly noticed he was garnering some dirty looks from nearby patrons. Why? With a flush of embarrassment, he knew, then rose and exited. You see, there had been a string of news items about new disturbances around the country, and Bud, blithely oblivious of his reactions, was smiling, almost cheering as if he and the others had been watching a football game. Nobody seemed to appreciate this. Come to think of it, it *was* a pretty odd reaction, he mused. What had he been thinking?

The Sixties were proving to be quite turbulent. The dull Fifties were now seen to be the calm before the storm. Commentators as well as people you met in the bar or ran into in grocery stores bemoaned the developments, increasingly worried about the oncoming future. The Cuban missile crisis had conjured up a pall of tangible fear of annihilating nuclear devastation. Unlike everyone else, old Bud couldn't feel too bad about it, though he pretended to. You had to, right?

Nor was that all. Poor JFK was assassinated, then his buck-toothed brother, then that civil rights leader. Marches turning into riots. But not just violence. The youth exploded. Bud found it hard to keep track, like a sports fan who couldn't keep the game schedule straight. Ready access to birth control ignited the sexual revolution. Promiscuity was nothing new, but now it was out in the open, everywhere, and the young people were proud of it.

Hallucinogenic drugs erupted from a cultural volcano. Timothy Leary and his buddies pied-pipered a whole generation on a vision quest into vast new worlds. Bud thought of his own revelatory dreams of some years before. Hell, it was like Pentecost! Young people were flocking to a whole new crop of unfamiliar religions, even to publicly acknowledged Satanism! Many more were exploring general occultism and witchcraft. All this made the fading world of Vedanta, Thelema, and Theosophy seem like the PTA and the Rotary Club by comparison.

Woodstock appeared to be one massive orgy of license and chaos. Motorcycle thugs killed people at another concert, the one at Altamont. But the greatest of these was the massacre inspired by a Beatles album, when Charles Manson received messages though the lyrics that instructed him to butcher "political piggies" in hopes of igniting a racial Armageddon.

When Bud found himself in the Intensive Care Unit the following month and got the bad news of very numbered days, he didn't much mind that he would be just missing the big rewards he had long counted on. He could die with equanimity. The world he had so despised was already falling. He had lived long enough to see his hopes coming true. Though he had not actually seen his gods, probably wouldn't be around to see them, they had finally arrived. The proof was on the news every night: they were teaching men new ways to shout and kill and revel and enjoy themselves, and soon all the earth would flame with a holocaust of ecstasy and freedom.

Made in the USA
Coppell, TX
18 March 2020

17119944R00115